PRAISE FOR SUS~~~~ ~~~~ ~~~~

The Rancher's Legacy by Susan Page Davis is a beautiful tale of hope, loss, and redemption. Rachel's grit and determination to continue her father's legacy amid such devastating grief, and Matt's vulnerability, paired with his strength and kindness, had me cheering them through each chapter. A lovely story that asks the question, how far will love go to protect family? This is a book to be treasured!

— TARA JOHNSON - AUTHOR OF ENGRAVED ON THE HEART, 2019 FINALIST IN THE CAROL AND CHRISTY AWARDS

I thoroughly enjoyed reading *The Rancher's Legacy*. It was filled with excitement, a heart-tugging mystery, and a sweet romance. A wealth of interesting secondary characters added to this wonderful story. Can wait to read the next in the series.

— VICKIE MCDONOUGH, BEST-SELLING AUTHOR OF 50 CHRISTIAN NOVELS AND NOVELLAS

Published by Scrivenings Press LLC
15 Lucky Lane
Morrilton, Arkansas 72110
https://ScriveningsPress.com

Printed in the United States of America

Paperback ISBN 978-1-64917-094-1

eBook ISBN 978-1-64917-095-8

Library of Congress Control Number: 9781649170941

Cover by www.bookmarketinggraphics.com.

All scriptures are taken from the KING JAMES VERSION (KJV): KING JAMES VERSION, public domain.

All characters are fictional, and any resemblance to real people, either factional or historical, is purely coincidental.

Homeward Trails  Book One

THE
RANCHER'S
Legacy

Susan Page Davis

Scrivenings
PRESS
Quench your thirst for story.
www.ScriveningsPress.com

Fort Lyon, Colorado
Tuesday, May 5, 1863

Matt Anderson spotted Rachel in the doorway of the stagecoach. She hesitated before stepping down and glanced about the street in front of the Fort Lyon station. Matt sucked in a breath. She was lovely—much prettier than he'd expected. But this striking young woman with the splendid chestnut hair showing beneath her broad, feathered bonnet couldn't be anyone else.

Her dress looked different from the ones Vida, the housekeeper, wore around the ranch house, much fuller and fancier. When his mother was alive, she hadn't dressed nearly as fine as Rachel Maxwell. The bodice molded to her figure, and the way the skirt belled out around her made it questionable whether she could get it through the coach's doorway. She begged to be stared at. After all, most of the ladies in these parts wore simple calico dresses.

He stepped from under the station's eaves, breathing faster than the short walk to the stagecoach accounted for, and placed himself in her path. Apparently, the skirt wasn't the problem he'd anticipated, because the station agent had handed her down onto solid ground by the time Matt reached her. She thanked him and turned toward the station.

"Miss Maxwell?" Matt snatched his gray felt hat from his head.

Her brown eyes widened as she turned her gaze on him. "Yes, I'm Rachel Maxwell." She waited, offering nothing further.

"I'm Matt. Your father asked me to meet you and drive you to the ranch."

She frowned slightly, her arched eyebrows dipping just a bit. "I'm not sure I understand. Is my father ill?"

"Oh, no, ma'am. I was coming into town anyway to pick up a keg of horseshoes and some lye. It's a busy time of year for ranchers. Your father said it would save him some time if I'd bring you, and ..."

Her shoulders sagged, which didn't bode well.

"So, you are in my father's employ?"

"I ... uh ... I work on the ranch, ma'am." He swallowed hard. Matt didn't like deception, but their two fathers had come up with this plan and talked him into executing it. He didn't have to say *which* ranch he worked on.

"I see." Her tone was distant. Hurt.

Matt felt lower than the creek bottom. "I've got a wagon yonder." He pointed toward where he'd tied up the team. Why was he talking like a hick, anyway? He cleared his throat and looked at the bags she carried—a soft leather handbag and a tapestry valise. "Do you have a trunk, ma'am?"

"Yes, and a portmanteau."

He nodded. Those huge skirts must take up a lot of luggage space. "I can see about them now, or I can take you to the wagon first."

"I'll stay with you and make sure—" She looked away for a

moment and then said, more gently, "and make sure they don't make a mistake."

Ha. She was afraid he'd mess up a simple task like retrieving her baggage. This gal may have grown up on a ranch, but she'd developed an uppity attitude somewhere along the way. Probably that fancy eastern school.

"Yes, ma'am." Wondering whether to act servile or to take charge of the situation as he normally would, he took her valise and ambled to the rear of the stagecoach. The sooner this ruse was ended, the better.

Two tenders were wrestling a large camel-back trunk with brass fittings from the boot. Most of the passengers had claimed their bags and walked away by the time the men had the unwieldy chest on the ground.

One of the men straightened and looked at Matt. "Help you, sir?"

"Yes, we'd like Miss Maxwell's luggage, please."

"Right here." The man pointed to the trunk and the leather portmanteau beside it.

"If I drive over here, can you help me load those?" Matt asked.

"Sure can."

Rachel opened her purse and held out a quarter. "Thank you."

The man eyed the coin for a moment. "You don't need to pay me, ma'am."

"No insult intended," Rachel said. "I guess I've been in the East too long."

"That could be." He turned back to his work.

Matt suppressed a smile. "We'll be right over with my rig."

Ten minutes later, he was driving out of town. Rachel sat demurely beside him on the wagon seat, the pheasant feathers on her hat nodding and her back as straight as the buggy whip sticking up from its bracket.

"So, you've never seen your father's ranch?" he asked in as affable a tone as he could muster.

"No, we were living in north Texas when I left home three years ago. But I'm anxious to see it. Papa was quite excited when he found this property for sale."

"It's quite a choice spread," Matt said. "And your pa seems to know what he's doing."

"Indeed." Her voice went frosty.

Matt gritted his teeth. He'd have to be more careful what the "ranch hand" said to the owner's daughter. He cast about his mind for what he knew about Bob Maxwell's operation. "He's got some fine cattle. The ones he bought last month are going to help him build a first-rate herd."

They managed a restrained conversation for the next twenty minutes, but Rachel didn't let down her guard for an instant. Matt supposed a well-behaved ranch hand would keep quiet and not try to carry on a conversation, but that was the main reason her father had wanted him to come and fetch her—so they could get to know each other. Why on earth he couldn't have just introduced himself properly as the neighbor's son, he couldn't understand.

Oh, sure, the two fathers had thought it was a great idea. Let them get acquainted without Rachel realizing this was the man her father had earmarked to marry her. Apparently, she'd taken umbrage at the suggestion, and in her last letter had told her father to forget that notion. What did they expect to come from her spending an hour with him without knowing who he was? That she'd fall head over heels for a cowboy?

"When we top that rise, we'll be able to see your pa's place." He nodded toward the hill ahead. The team slowed for the grade and leaned into their collars.

Rachel looked about. "It's very hilly here."

"Different from Texas, I guess."

"Well, the part of Texas where we lived, anyway."

Matt nodded. He and his father had moved to this valley a scant four years ago, after his mother's death. Miners were flocking to the goldfields then, nearer Denver and Golden City, and it hadn't taken long for homesteaders to see the potential for farms and ranches in this part of the territory.

They were two-thirds of the way up the hill when he noticed a plume of dark smoke billowing up from beyond its crest.

"What on earth?" He frowned.

Rachel looked at him sharply. "What is it?"

"That smoke. It's big. Something's not right."

She studied the sky before them as Matt urged the horses onward. Their sluggish pace irked him to no end. This was the steepest hill on the road home. He could climb it faster himself than the horses could pull the loaded wagon.

"Can you drive?" he asked.

"Yes, but—"

He thrust the reins into her hands, jumped down, hit the ground running, and charged up the last hundred yards. When he reached the top, he was panting, and sweat rolled down his back and off his brow. He lifted his hat and swiped his cuff across his forehead, staring at the scene below.

A huge, black cloud rose from the comfortable ranch house Bob Maxwell had just finished building in anticipation of his daughter's arrival. The acrid smell filled Matt's nostrils, but even worse, amid the faint shouts and shrill screams of horses that reached him came a steady stream of pops that could only be gunfire.

The Maxwell ranch was under attack.

RACHEL SHOOK the reins and clucked her tongue. "Come on, boys," she called softly to the horses. "You can do it." How would anyone get up this steep grade in winter, when the road was icy?

She looked beyond the team to the young man at the top of the hill. Matt seemed nice enough, and he had the rugged look of a man who worked outside every day. He was handsome, too. She hadn't seen so fine-looking a specimen for quite some time. But he was too cheeky. You'd almost think he owned the ranch. He ought to know better than to address her with such familiarity. Oh, well, that was the West for you. People out here had forgotten common courtesy.

Rachel wished he hadn't worn that pistol. In the East, gentlemen didn't go about with guns strapped to their hips. She'd almost forgotten about that. The ranch hands in Texas always had a six-shooter handy for rattlesnakes and such. Did they really need them these days, so often that they carried them about like spare change? She supposed there were rattlesnakes in Colorado, too.

At the crest of the hill, Matt stood with his back to her, gazing at whatever lay beyond. To her dismay, the plume of smoke had increased to an ominous cloud hanging in the sky directly beyond the hill. Was it a prairie fire? Surely not, in this hilly country.

She slapped the reins against the horses' hindquarters. Only a few yards to go. The cowboy didn't turn to look at them. Finally, the team reached the summit and heaved onto an almost flat stretch of road. They walked a few more steps until the wagon was also on the level, then they stopped without her bidding.

In the distance below, a building burned furiously, and the smoke billowed up, higher and higher. She could see the angry flames, and animals milling about in fenced enclosures. The sounds that the wind brought her seemed too small—whinnies from the troubled horses, shouts, and banging. A dark dread seized her.

"What is that place?" She turned and stared at the cowboy.

Slowly he looked over at her. "I'm sorry, Miss Maxwell. That's your daddy's ranch."

In speaking, he seemed to gain purpose and strength, while Rachel's stomach tightened and she found it hard to breathe.

He strode to the side of the wagon but did not climb up. "You see that road that branches off down there?" He pointed down the slope to the right. A byway branched off and was soon lost to view in a stand of pine trees.

"I see it."

"That goes to the Anderson ranch—your nearest neighbors. Take the wagon and drive there. Tell Mr. Anderson your father's being attacked and needs his help."

She gathered the reins. "What about you?"

"I'll run down the hill and help your father if I can." He reached into the back of the wagon and took out a rifle. He took a moment to rummage about in a sack and brought out a small pasteboard box. Ammunition.

Rachel shivered. The wagon was a rolling arsenal, and she hadn't realized it.

"Go," he said. "Hurry!"

She looked once more toward the fire below them. The roof of the ranch house was alight. Her father had written her just a few weeks ago about the cozy home he had prepared and described the comfortable rooms and furnishings. Rachel wouldn't allow herself to think about that. She grabbed the whip and popped it.

"Get up!" She barely had time to gather the reins. The team took off at a canter, but she managed to pull them in so that they headed down the incline at a safer pace. Her stomach clenched as they swung around a curve, but the horses kept their footing.

Was the Anderson ranch so far away they couldn't hear the clamor from her father's place? What if she couldn't find it, or it was too late for the neighbors to help her father and his men?

And who was attacking her home? She should have asked Matt. Somehow, she didn't think it was Indians. Why that was, she couldn't be sure. She hadn't heard wild war whoops—was that it? They'd been too far away to tell much about the tiny figures she'd seen moving about near the barn and the burning house.

The house was already lost. What about the people? Her father had written that he and the foreman had hired ten hands. How many of them would survive this day?

Gulping in deep breaths, she tried to concentrate on her driving. The road leveled out, and they barreled along the valley floor. So long as she could keep the team in the middle of the road, she would let them go as fast as they wanted.

They must have come two miles or more. How far was it to the Andersons'? Again, Matt hadn't said. He'd done enough talking on the way out from town. Why couldn't he have told her something useful, instead of asking about school and telling her how beautiful the sunsets were here?

A structure loomed off to her left, and she traced the ridgepole of a barn. She watched for a lane leading off toward it and pulled the horses in. They snorted and high-stepped, but their passion was spent, and they jogged on, still nervous from the excitement of their headlong rush.

She realized she was on the ranch lane. The road she'd followed down from the hills led only to this place. The yard opened out around her, with the barn and a couple of sheds, a corral, and a vegetable garden surrounding the ranch house. Beyond was open rangeland.

"Whoa!" She hauled back on the reins.

A man came out of the barn, and another ducked between the rails of the corral fence. Both walked toward her.

"Ma'am," the older one said, touching his hat brim. The second man was a little younger and followed suit.

Her heart still pounded, but she tried to calm her voice. "Mr. Anderson?"

"No," the first man said. "I'm Pard Henry, and I work for Mr. Anderson." He eyed the wagon and team of panting horses. "Are you Miss Maxwell?"

"I am. And my father desperately needs help. His ranch is being attacked."

The older man's eyes whipped to hers. "By whom?"

"I don't know. We saw from the hilltop that the house was burning, and we heard gunfire. One of my father's ranch hands was driving me, and he told me to come get you."

He turned to the man beside him. "Pete, the boss and Jimmy went up to clean the spring. Ride up and get him. I'll get the rest of the men. We'll go across the range. Make sure everyone's armed." He held up his hands to Rachel. "Let me help you down, Miss Maxwell. You can wait here with Vida."

A woman of about forty had come to the door of the house, and now she stepped out onto the stoop, wiping her hands on an apron.

"What's happening, Pard?" she asked.

"Maxwell's place is under fire. This is Miss Maxwell, and I expect she just came in on the stage. Give her something to eat and make her comfortable." While he spoke, the ranch hand guided Rachel past the woman, into the house. In a spacious room that seemed part parlor, part dining room, and part office, he hurried to a rack on the wall where several rifles stood, took one down, opened the breach, and checked the load.

Another cowboy, who looked to be barely out of his teens, came to the door. "I've got my gun." He patted the revolver strapped to his hip.

"There's three more rifles here. Take one." Pard gestured toward the gun rack.

Within moments, both men were gone. Rachel heard someone giving orders in the yard and then hoofbeats drumming as they rode away together. Her heart pounded faster than the horses' hooves.

"Well, then," the woman said dourly. "Take a load off your feet, missy. Would you like some bread and butter? I've got coffee hot."

"I couldn't think of it," Rachel said, wringing her gloved hands together. "My father—"

"Now, now, fretting won't help him one whit. You'd best sit down and eat something. We'll know more in a bit, and you might need your strength then."

Rachel could see the sense of this, though she wished she had insisted on going with Mr. Anderson's men. But that would have required them to saddle a horse for her. Time was of the essence.

"Are you Mrs. Anderson?" she asked hesitantly.

The woman barked a short laugh. "Me? No. I'm Vida Henry. My husband's Pard, the man you just met. I just keep house for the Andersons."

"I see." Rachel tried to recall what little her father had told her about the Anderson household. Wasn't Mr. Anderson a widower? He had a grown son. That was the main thing she'd gathered. Her father thought she and the son might make a match of it. That hint incensed Rachel so violently that she'd sent her father a scathing reply, saying she would pick out her own husband, thank you, and he wouldn't be a saddle bum.

She supposed she'd gone a bit overboard. A ranch owner's son wasn't exactly a saddle bum—especially one who was heir to a spread that was obviously prosperous. This house sprawled comfortably large, and the furnishings, while not fine quality, were certainly better than the pioneer bits and pieces her own parents had used in north Texas.

"Come on in the kitchen," Vida said.

Rachel followed her meekly. The kitchen was warm, but not oppressively so. She noted an open window, probably offsetting the cookstove's output. A long counter lined one wall, with cupboards below and above. Several pans, a large pottery bowl, and a two-gallon crock sat on the counter. Nearby sat a pie safe and an oak cabinet that appeared to be a crude icebox. Across the room was a square oak table with three chairs pulled up to it.

"Coffee?"

"Oh, thank you." Rachel sat down and removed her gloves. She looked around for a place to lay her hat but didn't see a suitable spot. Near the back door, a peg rack hung on the wall with a couple of frayed coats and a battered man's hat on the pegs, but her elegant bonnet was not to be hung up for storage. She'd just have to keep it on.

Vida brought a thick crockery mug and set it on the table before her.

"Sweetenin'?"

"No, thank you," Rachel said. "But have you any cream?"

Vida's eyebrows lowered. "Yup." She walked to the icebox and opened it.

Rachel felt a bit petty, asking for cream when her father was in mortal danger. Still, one couldn't be expected to drink coffee that had perhaps been simmering for hours black—and tea had not been offered.

Vida brought a small pitcher to the table and set it down with a thunk. "Anythin' else I can get you?"

"No, thank you. This is fine."

The housekeeper turned away, and Rachel lifted the pitcher. She'd gotten on someone's bad side, that was certain. After pouring a generous dollop of cream into her cup, she realized she didn't have a spoon. She glanced at Vida's stiff back. The woman had gone to the counter and begun to cut up something with quick chopping motions. Her knife whacked the cutting board repeatedly.

Best not to ask for a spoon, Rachel decided. She raised the

cup to her lips and took an experimental sip. It was all she could do not to spit the bitter liquid back into the cup. Even with the cream, it tasted so awful she wouldn't have called it coffee. She made herself swallow and then sat gazing dolefully down at the cup that was still nine-tenths full. Maybe she should have accepted the offer of sugar. She saw nothing of the bread and butter Vida had mentioned earlier.

"How far is it to my father's ranch?" she asked.

"About three miles, across the range. Five by road."

"Oh. I wonder why they didn't hear the gunshots."

Vida chopped faster. How could the woman be so calm when people's lives were in danger? After half a minute, she paused her chopping. "They's a ridge between hither and yon."

"I see." Rachel stood and picked up her gloves. "I think I'll stroll out into the yard and see if I can make out anything."

"Suit yourself."

2

Portland, Maine

Abigail Benson clung to the railing of the widow's walk atop her grandmother's three-story home and looked out across Casco Bay. The sharp wind told her that Maine, as usual, would let go of winter grudgingly. No doubt they'd see more snow before nightfall.

How many times over her fifty years of marriage had Grandmother climbed up here to the rooftop? Probably she'd stayed up here for hours at a time when she was younger, watching the horizon for a speck that might be her husband's ship. Now, he and the ship were gone from this world.

Abby had a different watch to keep. She gazed down into the front garden, but no one stirred there. She looked farther afield, down the hill toward Fore Street and the harbor. Ships' masts studded the waterfront, dozens of them. At least five large vessels were docked, and countless smaller ones.

The bustle of the waterfront fascinated her. She raised her grandfather's spyglass to her eye and turned it toward the observatory tower on Munjoy Hill. Captain Moody was flying two pennants just now—more ships were on their way to the wharves. Turning seaward, she made out a vessel just rounding the cape, scudding before the fresh breeze. The sight of it thrilled her. She had never ventured outside Maine. It must be splendid to travel to far-off places.

After a couple of minutes, Abby lowered the brass telescope with a sigh and flicked another glance downward. She caught her breath. Striding up the carriage drive was a man in a black overcoat and a beaver hat. He carried himself jauntily, and he didn't use a walking stick. A young man.

She whirled about and hurried through the slender door that led to the stairs. This flight was narrower than the ones between floors of the house, and each tread was only about four inches wide. Abby grasped the railing tightly. She respected the twelve treacherous stairs, having tumbled down them once as a youngster. Only last summer, she'd prevented her grandmother from having a nasty fall down them. That was the last time the old woman had climbed to the widow's walk.

When she reached the hall on the third floor, she dashed along to the landing and followed the broader staircase down to the second story. Her grandmother now lived in rooms on the ground floor, and Abby took the final flight—carpeted stairs that curved gracefully down into the front hall—at an unladylike gallop.

The thud of the brass knocker, wielded by the young man's gloved hand, no doubt, resounded throughout Rosemont as she gained the main hall. Patsy, the maid who came in days, strode from the kitchen at the back of the house. She glanced at Abby and headed for the door. Abby waved and hurried on toward the elderly woman's sitting room.

Grandmother was seated in her comfortably upholstered Louis XV chair. In her black taffeta dress and periwinkle shawl, she looked like a small, bright-eyed grackle.

"What is it, dear? You mustn't dash about so."

"He's here."

"Who is here?" Grandmother peered up at her through her spectacles, though only one possible *who* had been discussed that morning.

"The young man from the lawyer's. At least, I assume it is he. Who else could it be?"

"Ah. Collect yourself." Her grandmother held out a painted fan from the liberal supply Grandfather had brought from the Orient. "Sit, child. You mustn't receive our guest all gasping and red-faced. Has Patsy let him in?"

"She was going to the door when I came down the stairs."

"Then calm yourself while we await him."

Abby tried to breathe slowly and fluttered the fan with what she hoped was a graceful turn of the wrist. Grandmother had spent a great deal of time instructing her on how to properly fan oneself and in the intricacies of the language of the fan, but all Abby could think of now was that the meager breeze her motion provided would be inadequate for the task. Her cheeks were certainly scarlet.

A moment later, Patsy appeared in the doorway, sober-faced in her gray dress and white apron. Poor Patsy. They really should keep a footman, and Grandmother sometimes spoke of replacing Will Tardiff, who'd gone off to fight the South. Until she did, Patsy must answer the door as well as keep up the fires and tend to several other chores Will used to do.

"Mr. Atkins," Patsy said. She dropped a slight curtsy and stepped back against the white six-paneled door, allowing the visitor to enter. Abby stood, as young people should when elders entered, but Grandmother remained seated.

The man, it turned out, was not much older than Abby. Without his heavy coat and brimmed hat, he looked quite slender and fit, and really quite handsome, if a bit wind-whipped.

"How do you do, madam." He stepped forward as he

addressed Grandmother, who held out a hand sheathed in black crocheted gloves.

"How do you do. I am Edith Rose, and this is my granddaughter, Abigail Benson."

Atkins took the old woman's hand for a moment and dipped his head. He then turned to Abby. She extended her hand and met his gaze.

"Hello, Miss Benson." He smiled as though he'd encountered an unexpected treat. "It's a pleasure to meet you."

Abby's cheeks would have turned crimson had they not already been flushed. She made herself break their gaze. "How do you do, sir."

"I am Ryland Atkins, from Mr. Turner's office." He turned to include her grandmother as he spoke.

"Thank you for coming," Grandmother said, waving a hand toward a wing chair.

Abby resumed her seat on the settee, smoothing her lavender skirt. Grandmother stuck with her mourning dresses, but she allowed Abby to wear colors now—not too bright. Two years had passed since Captain Rose's death, and even Grandmother used a few colorful accessories now. She looked so much prettier with the soft periwinkle shawl about her shoulders than she had in unrelieved black.

"You are Mr. Turner's detective, then?" The eagerness and longing showed in Grandmother's eyes as she studied the young man.

"I'm an investigator. Mr. Turner hires me occasionally to find people for him."

"Ah, yes. I believe that's what's needed. You see, I've sent letters and telegrams and done all within my power to find my dear grandchildren, but to no avail. I've appealed to Governor Cony and Mr. Blaine, hoping they could exert some political influence for me, but alas!"

"The result was not favorable, I take it?"

She shook her head. "They both counsel me to wait until this war is over. But I can't wait, Mr. Atkins. The war has dragged on for more than two years now. My health is not good. If I wait, it may be too late."

"I understand." Atkins reached inside his jacket and brought out a small notepad. Glancing at it, he said, "Mr. Turner showed me the documents you had accumulated concerning your grandchildren—your correspondence with the authorities in New York and the copies of their birth certificates." .

"And the letters from the director of the orphanage in White Plains?"

"Yes. Mrs. Rose, it's my hope that we'll be able to find them. Could you please tell me a little more about the children? Anything at all that you remember?"

Abby's heart sped up. Her cousins were the objects of discussion. She barely remembered the oldest, and she'd never met the youngest, but all her life, she'd heard about these phantom cousins of hers. Poor Aunt Catherine's lost children. Grandmother had grieved over them for nearly twenty years.

With Mr. Turner's help, Grandmother had written a will, bequeathing a share of her estate equal to Abby's to any of her missing grandchildren who came to visit her before her death. The possibility that they would be reunited seemed like an incredible dream. But Mr. Atkins sounded confident. Could this dashing young man really find them?

Patsy entered with the tea tray and set it before Grandmother. Once they were all settled with a steaming cup, and the maid had withdrawn, Grandmother cleared her throat.

"The eldest is named Zephaniah, after my husband, the captain. Of course, I realize his name may have been changed. But he would be six-and-twenty now, and he had his mother's fair hair ..."

3

Colorado

Matt pulled up within the tree line a hundred yards from Maxwell's bunkhouse and took stock of the situation. The fire roared, engulfing the house, and black smoke billowed skyward. The outbuildings and haystacks were far enough from it that, with luck and the grace of God, they might not catch fire. But the men couldn't do anything to prevent it. They were pinned down near the barn and the bunkhouse.

A tremor ran through him. This was too much like Glorieta Pass, where he'd received his leg wound last year. His hands tightened on his rifle stock. He had no captain to order him forward this time, but he couldn't let Maxwell and his men down.

Gunfire issued from several points outside the yard, and Matt observed carefully for a couple of minutes, trying to determine how many attackers there were. Three on horseback circled the yard, turning back when they approached Maxwell's corral fences near the road. They were able to go behind the burning house in a wide arc and get behind the bunkhouse as well. He concluded they were hoping to take some of Maxwell's horses from the corral.

A couple of outlaws were on foot, and Matt focused on learning exactly where they concealed themselves. Those he could see were white men, which was a relief in a way. He had feared a large party of Cheyenne might have decided to raid the settlers in these parts. They'd raised havoc in the goldfields, but so far, the ranchers in this valley hadn't been targeted.

Maxwell's strategy seemed to be holding fire until the outlaws showed themselves and then letting loose with a wild volley. That might hold the bandits off for a while, but it would also likely run the rancher and his men out of ammunition soon.

Sweat broke out on Matt's brow, though a cool breeze fluttered through the cottonwoods. He'd have to go out in the open to get to a position where he could help his neighbor. The outlaws couldn't ride behind the barn because of the fences. That might be his best chance.

He waited for another round of gunfire, and while it was at its height, he slipped through the trees to the corral fence behind the barn. Ducking between the rails, he hauled in a deep breath, and then he sprinted across the corral, hunched over. The back door of the barn, where they hauled out manure in winter, was closed. It creaked when he pulled it open, the counterweight rising on a rope. When he let go, the weight would plunge downward, and the door would close.

"Maxwell," he yelled into the barn. "It's Matt Anderson."

One of Maxwell's cowhands rose from near the big front door and whirled toward him, pointing his rifle straight at Matt. For an instant, Matt thought he was a dead man. No doubt the shooters' ears were ringing, and the cowboy hadn't heard him identify himself.

"Hey!" He held up one hand. "Don't shoot me! I'm here to help."

"Matt? Thank God."

Matt recognized Bud Lassen, Maxwell's foreman, in the dimness of the barn. Hurrying across the barn floor, Matt joined him near the front entrance.

"Who is it?" he asked.

"We don't know. Raiders. There's about ten of them."

Matt frowned. "I counted five, or maybe six."

"That's all? Seems like more. I know one of 'em's down."

"How are you doing?"

"Lost one man, and the boss is hit bad."

"Mr. Maxwell's shot?"

"'Fraid so. Hank and Dusty have got him in the bunkhouse. We've got a man in the hayloft door upstairs, and four more scattered around, if they haven't been hit. Is your father coming?"

"I sent Miss Maxwell to tell him. He'll be here, but it might take a while."

Shooting erupted again. Bud turned his attention to a crack at the edge of the big, rolling door and stuck the barrel of his rifle through it. Matt squeezed in below him and peered out. The riders had dismounted and left their horses out of sight. Now all of them hid behind trees, bushes, building corners— whatever would give them cover.

Bud squeezed off three shots, during which Matt focused on a copse of pines several yards beyond the well. He'd seen gunfire emanate from those trees earlier, and he waited for it now. Sure enough, he saw a puff of smoke right where he'd calculated one of the outlaws hid. He trained his sights on the spot and waited, trying to ignore the cracks and pops of other weapons. The man he watched for leaned out from behind a tree to take another shot, and Matt squeezed his trigger.

He couldn't tell whether or not his bullet found its mark, but overhead came a loud grunt, followed by a thud.

The shooting quieted, and Bud looked at him then up at the ceiling.

"Charlie?" he yelled.

"Yeah," came the reply. "I'm hit."

"Stay down. We'll get you later. Matt Anderson's here, and help's coming." There was no reply, but Bud eyed Matt soberly. "You've had experience in the militia. What do you think?"

"How many cartridges you got?"

"A few more rounds. The men in the bunkhouse probably have more. We keep our stash in there. But the outlaws got what was in the house."

"How'd that happen?"

"They were in there when the boss and a couple more men discovered them, ransackin' the place. He drove 'em out and made a stand. Me and the rest of the boys were out working on a holding pen half a mile from here, but we heard the gunfire and rode back. By then, they'd set fire to the house."

"Everyone get out?" Matt asked.

"Yeah, but that's when they shot Mr. Maxwell. I got caught out here. Lucky to have my rifle. All Charlie has is his Colt."

"How do you know about Mr. Maxwell?"

"One of the men hollered up to Charlie."

Matt nodded. "We probably can't wait for my pa. They're picking your men off one by one."

"What do they want?" Bud peered through the crack at the edge of the door.

"Money. Guns. Horses." Matt shrugged.

The outlaws had likely rifled the house for valuables before they were caught and chased out. Apparently, they hadn't found enough and wanted more. The ranch's stock of firearms would be attractive to the gang, as would the horses in the corrals.

Matt thought of Vida in his family home. In the kitchen most of the day, she would be vulnerable in an attack like this.

"Here we go," Bud said as the shooting resumed. He stuck his rifle barrel out the door and fired off several rounds, then withdrew to reload. Matt took his place and fired once at a spot where he knew one of the outlaws was concealed. Movement on the far side of the yard drew his attention. Were they heading for their mounts?

"We'd best not wait," he said. "They could get around back and throw a torch into the bunkhouse."

"Listen." Bud held a hand out, and Matt cocked his head to one side.

He could hear more shooting, but from farther away. "That's my father and his men. Come on!" Matt shoved the door open a few more inches and sent several quick shots toward the stand of pines. No gunfire was returned.

Yelling and hoofbeats were punctuated by more shots, and several horses pounded into the dooryard. Matt saw Pard and two more of his father's men flash by, and close behind them came his father and two more men, riding hard. Matt ran out into the yard and looked all around. In the distance, a half dozen horsemen streaked it for the hills.

"There they go!" Matt pointed.

His father wheeled his bay horse and tore after them, with his men right behind him. Matt wanted to mount and go with them, but he'd arrived on foot.

Three of Maxwell's men ran from their hiding places. "Saddle up," one of them yelled.

"No. Wait." Bud stepped out into the middle of the yard and held up his hands. "By the time you all reload and saddle your horses, it'll be too late. Let Mr. Anderson and his men handle it now. We've got to see to the boss and Charlie."

"Charlie's hit?" One of the other men strode toward them, his leathery face etched with dismay.

"He's up in the loft, and he needs help. I don't know how bad it is. You and Telly bring him down to the bunkhouse."

Matt looked off the way his father had gone. "What if my pa needs help, the way you did?"

Bud sighed. "All right. Joe, you boys go. Take horses from the corral. They're pretty jumpy now, but—"

"Bud, one of the horses is shot."

Bud swore and strode toward the corral fence.

The cowboy they called Dusty appeared in the doorway of the bunkhouse.

"Matt Anderson," he called.

Matt jerked his chin upward, signifying he'd heard.

"Mr. Maxwell wants to see you."

Matt limped toward him. His injured leg was tired from the exertion he'd given it in his run down the hill. Most of the time, he could walk almost normally, but when fatigue caught up with him, the old wound made his leg throb, and he favored it.

He reached the bunkhouse steps. "What does he want? I'm surprised he even knows I'm here."

"We told him you'd come to help us, and when the shooting stopped, he said he wanted to talk to you. I expect he wants to know if Miss Rachel is safe."

Matt sucked in a deep breath. He'd almost forgotten Rachel's existence, but his father's arrival laid proof she'd completed the task he'd given her. He mounted the steps.

As he passed Dusty, the cowboy caught his arm. "They're bringing Charlie. Looks like they winged him."

Three men came from the barn. Charlie was on his feet, supported by Telly, whom Matt knew slightly. The other man walked on Charlie's other side, one hand in midair, as though he expected Charlie to pitch forward any second.

"He'll make it," Dusty murmured.

"Looks like." Matt went on into the bunkhouse.

A teenager named Hank, one of Maxwell's newer employees, sat on a stool beside the bunk where they'd laid the boss. He rose and nodded. "We're sure glad you came, Matt. Think your pa will catch those no-goods?"

"I don't know. I hope so." Matt sat on the stool and let his eyes adjust to the dimness.

Mr. Maxwell's eyes turned toward him, and his mouth twitched in his stark face. "Matthew."

"Yes, sir," Matt said.

"Thank you, boy."

"Don't know as I helped much. Wish I could have got here sooner."

"Rachel?" Mr. Maxwell gasped as he said his daughter's name and grimaced.

"She's all right, sir. I sent her to my pa's house, and she told him what happened."

"Your father ran off the outlaws?"

"Yes, sir. He's chasing them now."

"Good." Mr. Maxwell's mouth pressed into a thin line.

Where was his wound? The wool blanket covering the rancher hid the damage.

Dusty rushed in and strode to a bunk to clear it off. The other men came through the door with Charlie leaning on them.

"We'd best send for the doctor," Matt called to Dusty, Hank, and the world at large.

Dusty looked over at him, a box of cartridges in one hand and several items of clothing in the other. "Sam went."

Maxwell's eyes were closed, and his face contorted. Matt touched his shoulder. "You hear that, sir? Sam's gone to fetch Doc Nolan."

The older man's eyelids flickered. "I don't know as I can hold on, boy."

Matt's stomach plunged. "You can, sir. Doc will help you."

Maxwell groaned then looked up at him for a moment, his eyes wide. "You ... take care of my Rachel."

RACHEL HAD STAYED out near the corral, not wanting to miss any signs, but all she could tell was that the smoke continued to rise from her father's ranch for the better part of an hour, then dissipated until she couldn't tell where it had been.

She stroked the team's noses and considered unhitching the wagon. She could do it—she'd learned that as a girl. But she wanted to be ready when word came that she could go to her home. After a while, she compromised by removing the horses' bridles and letting them browse around the edges of the yard.

The sun was lowering before she picked up the sound of hoofbeats. Far across the grassy valley, two horsemen came into view. She climbed up to sit on the corral fence and watched them grow larger. When they were within two hundred yards, a bittersweet pang ran through her as she identified the men. Matt, the one who had driven her here, and Pard, the hand who'd met her in the dooryard when she arrived. Their faces were smudged, but she recognized Matt's bearing and both the men's clothing.

She hopped down from the fence as they gained the dooryard. Matt swung down from his horse, doffing his hat at the same time. He moved as gracefully as a gentleman at a ball. She almost forgot for a moment that he was one of her father's employees. Any of the girls back at her school would be thrilled to dance with a man of his pleasing appearance and carriage. Of course, if he were at a ball, his face wouldn't be smeared with soot and dirt.

As he walked toward her, she noticed for the first time that he limped slightly, further marring the impression.

"What's happened?" She stepped toward Matt, her extended hands trembling. She drew them back and hugged herself, knowing she would hear bad news.

Matt stopped a pace away, looking into her eyes.

"Tell me," Rachel said.

"I'm sorry."

Her stomach plummeted. She looked past him to the other man, Pard, but he had dismounted and was undoing the cinch of his saddle, his back toward her.

She reached out again. "Please! Is my father all right?"

"I'm afraid not," Matt said.

Her knees gave way, and her head spun.

"Let me help you, ma'am." Matt grabbed her arm, then called sharply, "Pard!"

Things went gray for Rachel, all hazy and swirling, like a funnel cloud without sound.

4

Matt gulped down a cup of coffee while anxiously watching Vida dab at Rachel's forehead with a damp cloth. She looked so pale!

"Why isn't she awake yet?"

Vida frowned at him. "No idea. Probably exhausted from traveling."

He set his cup on a side table and got up from his chair. He strode over to the sofa where Rachel lay. "Should we try to wake her up?"

Rachel's eyelashes—long and dark against her stark white skin—fluttered. He caught his breath and waited. Vida paused in her ministrations.

When Rachel opened her eyes, she stared straight at Matt with those soft brown eyes that had nearly melted him at the stage station.

"What—where ..."

"You're in my family's house, on the sofa. You swooned, so Pard and I lugged you in here. How are you feeling?"

Rachel's brow furrowed, and she shut her eyes. "Terrible."

Her eyelids flew up again. "Your family? I don't understand." She struggled to sit up.

"Now, take it easy," Vida said, grasping Rachel's arm.

Matt sighed. He hadn't meant to break it to her this way. She had enough other shocks to bear.

"Ma'am, I apologize. The important thing right now is your father and what happened over to his place."

"Yes." Rachel put a hand to her forehead for a moment, then looked up at him. "Tell me—is Papa alive?"

Matt sat down again so she wouldn't have to crane her neck to see him, and to give him more time to prepare his words.

"I'm sorry to have to tell you, but your father and one of his ranch hands were killed in the fight. They got two of the outlaws, but ... well, I'd never call that an even trade."

Rachel's face froze and then crumpled as he spoke. She sucked in a breath. Tears filled her eyes and ran freely down her pale cheeks.

"It can't be."

"I'm sorry, but it is." Matt gulped and blinked back tears of his own.

"And ... and you said ..." She glanced around at the leather-covered chairs and sofa, the fireplace, his father's desk, the gun rack, and the beaded Cheyenne parfleche hanging between the front windows. "This is your family home?"

The lump in Matt's throat got bigger. "That's right."

"But how ..." She swung around and fixed him with a penetrating stare. "You don't work for my father, do you?"

"No, ma'am. I didn't want to deceive you, but your pa—and mine too—they wanted me to get you from the station so you could ..." This wasn't the time to talk about their crazy matchmaking scheme. Matt shook his head. "Look, we can talk that over later. There's more urgent things to tend to now."

"Yes." She stood slowly, wobbling a bit as she straightened.

Vida and Matt jumped up, and Vida put a hand under Rachel's elbow.

"Easy there."

"Thank you. I'm fine." Rachel gazed at Matt again. "Where is your father now?"

"He and half a dozen men went after the outlaws. Most of your pa's men are still at the ranch. A couple of 'em's wounded."

"Take me there."

Determination glinted in her eyes. He wagered she could be almost as stubborn as her father had been.

"Yes, ma'am. We'll take the wagon."

"Horseback would be faster."

He flicked a glance at her fancy, poufed skirt and hastily looked back at her face. "That might be a problem. We don't have a sidesaddle, and I don't believe you're dressed to ride astride, begging your pardon, ma'am."

Her face flushed, and she looked beautiful again, now that the deathly pallor had fled.

"You're right. We'll have to take the wagon. By the shortest way, of course."

"Of course." Matt turned toward the door.

"I unbridled the team so they could graze," Rachel called after him.

Matt hurried out to where the team was placidly cropping grass outside the corral fence. A couple of horses inside had come over to see what they were up to. The harness bridles hung on one of the posts, and it took him only a couple of minutes to put them on the horses. He looked to the house, surprised that Rachel had not followed him out immediately.

The door opened, and she pushed through it, compressing the ridiculous skirt until it slid past the jamb on each side, and she carried a large basket. Vida came right behind her with a covered platter and another basket.

"What's all this?" Matt asked.

Vida jerked her head for him to come and help her place the items in the back of the wagon. "You said Maxwell's house burned flat. Well, I figure their hands will need something to eat tonight. I started baking soon as our men headed out for their place."

"That was very thoughtful of you." Matt settled the platter and baskets in the wagon bed and turned to help Rachel up onto the seat. "I expect some of our men will be back soon," he told Vida.

"I'll go start another batch of biscuits and see if I can stretch the stew, so's we can share with the bunkhouse tonight."

"Good." Matt jogged around the wagon and bounded up to the seat beside Rachel. He turned the team and wagon in a wide arc and headed up the road. It would take them nearly an hour to get over to the devastated ranch. Meanwhile, the sun had begun its descent. He judged it to be a good four hours past noon.

"Did you eat dinner?" he asked.

"Just coffee."

Rachel was silent for several minutes as the team labored up the first hill. Vida should have fed her in the midst of all that cooking she'd done. He would have to make sure she ate something later.

"Are you sure the outlaws are gone?" she asked.

"Yes'm. My father and the rest of the men chased them into the hills."

Rachel frowned and rode without speaking for a few minutes, while Matt guided the team back along the road. At the base of the final hill—where they'd seen the fire from the crest—a cutoff branched more directly toward Maxwell's ranch, saving them a half mile and one steep climb. Matt turned the team into it.

"Are you sure about the rest of it?" Rachel asked.

He looked over at her, not comprehending her meaning.

"About my father, I mean." Her features were drawn, and she looked pale again. Her knuckles had gone white, where she clutched the edge of the wagon seat.

So. It had begun to sink in. He wished he had a word of encouragement for her, but he had none. She would find no solace in the fact that most of the men had lived through the attack, or that the barn and bunkhouse still stood and the herds of cattle and working horses were intact.

"I'm afraid so. He spoke to me before he died. You were his main concern. I was glad I could tell him you were safe."

Before she looked away, he saw tears glistening in her eyes.

"I'm sorry," Matt said gently. He wanted to tell her she'd done a good job, but he doubted that would help either. She must have been terrified when he left her and told her to go to his father's ranch. If he'd taken longer to think it through, maybe he would have gone with her instead of sending her off alone.

Later, she might realize how much courage she'd shown in driving off into unknown territory with vicious outlaws on the loose, to bring aid to those in danger. But not now. Now she could only see that the last member of her family was dead, and she hadn't been there to comfort him.

They rode for a while with both wrapped in thought. Then holding her chin high, she turned to him. "How did it happen?"

"He was already wounded when I got there. The foreman told me afterward that the outlaws came from the hills to the south. Surprised them while they were all either near the corrals or out working a ways from the house."

She nodded, her brown eyes huge.

"The ones farther away heard the commotion and rode in to help the men near the house," Matt went on. "One of them was shot first thing. Your father and some of the others drove them out of the house and barricaded themselves in there, but the outlaws set the place on fire, and they had to get out. Your father was shot while they tried to escape and get over to the bunkhouse."

He shook his head. The whole business was senseless. Those outlaws could have ridden in with their guns leveled and demanded whatever they wanted. There was no need to kill people and burn the house down, but he couldn't say that.

"I wish I'd known who you were when you came to get me at the stage depot," she said.

"I'm sorry." It seemed like he had to keep saying that, but it did no good. He could tell her again that their fathers had cooked up that scheme, but what was the use? No sense making her pa look bad, now that he was dead.

Rachel drew in a deep, ragged breath and faced forward.

THEY CAME DOWN OUT of the trees, and the ranch buildings lay beyond them. The remains of the house still smoldered. Rachel stared at the ruins, but quickly shifted her attention to the clusters of men about the yard.

The barn was larger than the one they'd had in Texas, probably out of deference to the harsher winters here. They'd need to store more hay. At least a dozen men milled in the yard before it. To the left lay what must be the bunkhouse—a stout log building that looked large enough to house a full crew. Her father's foreman was talking to a distinguished-looking man with graying hair, and Rachel's pulse fluttered in recognition.

"There's Bud Lassen."

"You know him?" Matt asked.

"He was with us in north Texas. Pa brought him along when he bought the place." At least she had one person who had known her before this catastrophe.

Bud turned as Matt pulled up the team and nodded to her. He and the other man walked toward the wagon.

"Miss Rachel." Bud held out his hands to her. "This is a poor welcome home for you. I'm sorry it turned out this way."

The crying lump swelled in Rachel's throat, and tears pooled in her eyes. She placed her hands in his. "Bud, you're a sight for sore eyes. They tell me Papa's gone." Her voice broke.

Bud's whole face drooped. "Yes, ma'am, I'm sorry to say it's true. The boys and me—we'll do everything we can to help you."

"Thank you. I want to see him."

"He's in the bunkhouse." Bud helped her down from the wagon. "This here's Mr. Anderson, Matthew's father."

She tried but failed to see a family resemblance. His hair had been medium brown but was now streaked with gray. His eyes were also brown—not like Matt's blue ones.

"Pleased to meet you."

"I'm glad you arrived safely," Mr. Anderson said, clasping her hand for a moment. "And I'm very sorry about your father."

"Thank you."

Bud guided her toward the log building. "It's kind of a mess inside—some of the boys were in there during the shooting, and we haven't had a chance to clean anything up."

"That doesn't matter."

They entered the dim, low-ceilinged room, and she paused to let her eyes adjust. Six sets of double bunks dominated the furnishings, three on each side. Closer to her were two tables, several chairs, a small woodstove, and two tiers of cupboards. Another, smaller room opened off the main one, and she could see the corner of a cookstove out there.

"He's right over here," Bud said.

Rachel let him lead her to one of the lower bunks.

"Careful." He guided her around a spray of shattered glass on the floor near the front window. Articles of clothing and spent cartridge casings were strewn about, but she ignored them.

Her father lay in shadow, covered with a dark wool blanket up to his chest. His face was an unnatural white against the pillow ticking, and he seemed to have more wrinkles than she remembered. His eyes were closed, and his lips slightly parted.

She reached down and touched his cheek. Its pallor startled her, and she drew back her hand. If only she'd had the chance to see him before he died. A minute was all she'd have needed to tell him how much she loved him. She cleared her throat.

"Where is his wound?"

"Stomach," Bud said quietly. "He was one of the first ones shot. He got into the house, but when the outlaws set the fire, he didn't quite make it from there to the bunkhouse. Dusty and Hank reached out and hauled him in. He'd emptied his six-shooter and was helpless against 'em." Bud sniffed.

A low groan came from a bunk across the aisle, and Rachel realized another man lay there.

"Some of the cowhands were shot as well?" she asked.

Bud nodded. "One man was killed outright—Billy Snow. He'd only been with us a year. Don't think you knew him."

Rachel shook her head.

"Well, Charlie was wounded, but it's not too bad. And that's Ran Crowder over yonder. He's not so good. We're waiting on the doc for him and Charlie." Bud grimaced. "Sent a man to get him for your pa, but he didn't last."

"Thank you for that, Bud." Rachel squeezed his forearm. "What will we do now?"

"Well …" Bud pushed his hat back and thought for a moment. "You can't stay here, miss. There's no place for you now. I expect Mr. Anderson would take you in. He's got a woman living in the house over there, Vida Henry."

"I met her," Rachel said.

"There's no one else closer'n ten miles."

Rachel glanced down at her father's body. "And Papa?"

"The boys will make a box for him. Anything else you want us to do?"

"Is there a graveyard?" she asked.

"We buried an old fella up on the hill behind the house last spring—behind what was the house, that is."

"All right. It will do. I can't see taking him back to Texas, where Mama's buried."

"No, ma'am."

Rachel turned toward the doorway, anxious to get out into the sunlight again. "Let the doctor look at him, won't you?"

"I surely will."

She nodded and walked down the steps.

Matt Anderson had been in conversation with his father and a couple of other men nearby, but they stopped and watched her as she approached.

"Miss Maxwell," Mr. Anderson said. "I'd like to offer you our hospitality until you decide what you want to do. If there's anything at all we can do to help, please say so."

"Thank you. What happened to the raiders?"

"We chased them for about five miles, but we lost them in the foothills. I figured it wouldn't pay to follow them into an ambush or to get caught out there after dark, so we left off and came back."

Rachel wasn't entirely satisfied with that, but she would have to take his word for it. She looked toward the charred pile of timbers. "Papa was so anxious for me to see the house. He told me about some of the things he'd done to it, but he said he had a lot of surprises waiting for me."

Her eyes filled with fresh tears, and she pulled her crumpled handkerchief from her sleeve. Where was her luggage now? She could do with one of the dozen clean ones in her portmanteau. She looked around vaguely and spotted the wagon, but she couldn't remember if her things were still in the bed or not. Maybe Matthew had set them out at his house, to lighten the load for the horses.

"He was eager to see you, and I know he went to a lot of

trouble, trying to make things homey for you," Mr. Anderson said.

Behind her, Bud cleared his throat. "There's one surprise that didn't get burned, Miss Rachel."

She turned toward him, mildly curious.

Bud gave her a wan smile. "Your pa picked out a nice little paint gelding for you to ride, and he sent to Denver for a sidesaddle. It's out in the barn, I'm glad to say. Anytime you want to ride, you just tell me or one of the boys, and we'll fix you up. That is—" He eyed her warily. "—if you decide to keep us on, ma'am."

Rachel arched her eyebrows. He was nervous about his job. "I'm sorry, Bud. I haven't had time to think about the ranch yet, and what I'll do."

"Of course not. Sorry." He looked down at the ground and shifted his weight from one foot to the other.

"I'll rely on you and—and Mr. Anderson for some advice, I expect."

"I'd be happy to help in any way I can," Mr. Anderson said.

Bud nodded. "Same here."

Rachel drew in a deep breath and surveyed the yard, buildings, and fenced areas. She was now mistress of a three-thousand-acre ranch. Her father had sold eight hundred cattle in the spring and had about two thousand left, according to his last letter, mostly breeding and young stock. She also had about a dozen employees to think of.

"It looks like I'll be staying the night at least with the Andersons." She looked Bud in the eye. "May I return tomorrow and discuss business with you?"

"Of course. Or I can ride to their place if it's easier for you."

She considered that. "No, I think I'll want to come here and tour the ranch. You can show me what we have to work with."

"Sure, as long as you feel up to it."

She nodded. "Perhaps we can settle the ..." She swallowed

hard against a suddenly tight throat. "... the funeral arrangements then."

A man rode in at a canter and reined in his horse.

"Doctor's coming," he called to Bud.

"Thanks, Sam," Bud replied. He turned back to Rachel for a moment. "I'll take the doc in to see Ran and Charlie."

"I expect he'll need to write the death certificate," Rachel said as calmly as she could, but her voice quavered anyway.

"We can have him bring it over to our place when he's done," Mr. Anderson offered. "You don't have to stay here any longer."

She heard hoofbeats and the creak of harness as the doctor's rig approached.

"Could I take the horse to the Andersons' now? Then I could ride over tomorrow without taking their team."

"Surely," Bud said. "I'll have one of the boys fetch him."

"I'll help." Matt followed the man Bud assigned into the barn.

His father walked toward the lane to meet the doctor.

"You come back tomorrow, after you've rested, Miss Rachel," Bud said. "We'll have your pa fixed nice by then. And maybe the ashes will be cool enough for the boys and me to poke around a little. You might be surprised what we could find in that heap."

She looked at the smoldering timbers and tried to imagine the cowboys finding a single thing of value in the mess. "I doubt there's much, but thank you for thinking of it. It would be a dirty job."

"Well ..." Bud hesitated. "We'll need to clean it up at some point, anyway. Lug it all off or bury it. I s'pose it depends on if you want to rebuild. But you got time to think about that."

Rebuild. Without her father? What would be the point? But she couldn't continue to run the ranch from the neighbors' house, either.

"I'll mull it over, Bud." She squeezed his hand and walked over to the wagon. When she reached it, she turned just in time to see Matt Anderson lead a bright reddish-brown-and-white horse from the barn. Its full mane lay dark against its linen-white neck. She couldn't help but stare.

The compact horse looked well fed, its deep chest and well-muscled legs reflecting glints of sunlight as Matt led the gelding toward her. On its back sat a handsomely tooled sidesaddle of dark leather, almost the same color as its gleaming coat's darker splotches.

Rachel and the animal gazed at each other for a long moment, then the horse stretched his neck and sniffed her. She reached up and patted its satiny muzzle. "He's beautiful."

Matt smiled. "Your pa was so looking forward to this moment. He did most of the training himself."

"Then I know this horse will be well behaved." Rachel ran her hand up the gelding's nose and let her fingers slip under his luxuriant forelock. She scratched, and the horse leaned into it with a snuffle.

Her heart surged as she imagined Papa working with this horse in the corral, schooling it to change its gaits smoothly or to stand still while being saddled. How had he taught it about skirts, if there was no woman on the place? She imagined him sacking out the animal with one of her old dresses.

Her father's loving presence was so real that, for a moment, she almost believed he was still alive and would join her in the barnyard at any moment. If she didn't look toward where the house had stood a scant three hours ago or inhale the sharp, smoky air too deeply, she might keep herself fooled for a minute or two.

The onslaught of grief was so sudden she couldn't prepare for it, couldn't brace against the tears or hold back the sobs that burst from her throat. She took a step and wrapped an arm beneath the horse's neck, burying her face in his warm hair, and wept. He stood patiently with only a quiver rippling through his forequarters, so solid and strong.

Rachel knew in that moment that he was her horse. He

belonged to her and no one else. They would spend many hours together, and, she hoped, many years. The ranch may be her father's legacy, but this was his gift.

A strong but gentle hand patted her shoulder.

"Miss Maxwell? Are you all right, ma'am?"

She straightened and sniffed. What she wouldn't give for a fresh handkerchief. She wiped her cheeks carefully with her sleeve and turned to face Matt Anderson.

"Yes, thank you." She quelled the last little sob and inhaled deeply. "Did my father name this horse?"

Matt looked over his shoulder at Bud, who stepped closer, hat in hand. "He always called him Herald."

The unexpectedness of it made her frown. "Harold? Where did that come from?"

Bud smiled sadly. "He said you'd be like a princess in the old days, when a herald went before them and blew a horn, announcing who they were. He said this horse would be your herald. Everyone would know from a mile away that it was you coming because of his markings. Sort of a joke, you see."

She saw. She wanted to laugh, but the tears won out again.

Matt grabbed her elbow, as though he wanted to do something, anything, to help her, but wasn't quite sure what.

Calmly, Bud removed his bandanna from around his neck and held it out. "If you can use it, miss."

She took it and wiped her nose and eyes. As sweaty and smoky as the bandanna was, it was a help, though she probably now had soot streaks on her face.

"I'd like to go now," she said to Matt.

"Yes, ma'am. I'll tie the horse behind the wagon."

Bud walked with her to the side, where the small iron step was bolted to the wagon box, and helped her climb up. When she was settled on the seat, he looked up at her gravely.

"I'll look for you tomorrow, Miss Rachel."

MATT KEPT silent on the way home. Rachel sat beside him, her back stiff, occasionally dabbing at her face with Bud's grimy bandanna. She would likely swoon when she caught a glimpse of herself in a mirror and realized how filthy she'd gotten. Not that her smudged face could be compared to the blackened clothing and skin he and the other men now sported.

His father and the men would beat them home. They would ride across the range, while Matt and Rachel made the longer, slower drive by road. Probably Pa would have Vida prepare a bath for Rachel.

Matt would join the men in the creek. Their favorite swimming place was down in a dip in the pasture—out of sight of the house. Thank heaven the creek was high, and they wouldn't have to haul and heat water for all the men. The creek would still be icy from the snowmelt in the mountains, but Matt couldn't wait to plunge into the clear, cold water and cleanse the smell of smoke from his nostrils.

Rachel swiveled on the wagon seat and looked behind them. Matt turned too. The paint gelding jogged placidly along, keeping his tether slack.

"He's a good horse."

Rachel dipped her chin a fraction of an inch, the barest acknowledgment of his comment, then twisted around to face forward.

Matt thought about the Maxwell ranch. Bud Lassen could run things for a while, until Rachel got her feet under her, but probably the smartest thing would be for her to sell out and go back East. For some reason, he hoped she wouldn't do that.

He didn't know her well, but he'd seen strength in her when she'd gazed down at her father's body. She'd grown up in the West and knew the hardships ranchers encountered. She might have the makings of a fine ranch wife. Or a rancher, if she chose not to marry. Right now, his chances were not looking very good.

Five minutes later, she broke his reverie.

"It was very thoughtful of Papa, training that horse for me."

Matt glanced over at her. She held her head erect and didn't look at him. Was she really so in control of her feelings now? He couldn't maintain that poise if his father had just been cut down by outlaws. Maybe she had determined not to break down until she was by herself. The specter of her aloneness tugged at his heart.

"I think you were mostly what he thought about these last few months. Getting you home."

"You talked to him a lot?" she asked.

Matt shifted uneasily. "Your pa's men and ours go back and forth a lot. We help each other out. We share three miles of boundary, and we're mostly a friendly lot."

Her eyes narrowed to slits. "You're the one."

"The one?" he asked, but he knew what she meant.

"Papa wanted to see me settled, as he put it. He didn't just pick out a horse for me, did he?"

"I ... don't follow," Matt said.

"Sure you do. You're the man he chose for my husband. Well, I'll tell you now what I told him, in case you've got any notions. I don't intend to marry you, Matthew Anderson."

5

The hot bathwater soothed Rachel's aching muscles. The hours spent in the wagon had taken a toll, and, coming hard on the heels of a five-day journey by railroad and stagecoach, had sapped her last reserves. She was ready to fall into bed when she'd dried off, but Vida tapped on her door and announced that supper was ready. Rachel realized she was famished and quickly got dressed.

Her traveling clothes had grown stains and smelled horrifically of smoke. She wadded them up in a bundle. Tomorrow she'd see what she could do about them. Perhaps Vida also did laundry for the family. If not, Rachel would wash them herself. She put on a serviceable blue dimity dress that she had often worn in the classroom. Back in Boston, it was considered a plain, utilitarian garment, but out here it would probably stand up well against many a ranch woman's best.

When Rachel descended to the large main room, Matt and his father, scrubbed, combed, and wearing clean clothes, rose from their chairs in the sitting area.

"Good evening, Miss Maxwell," Mr. Anderson said. "We're ready to sit down if you are."

"Yes, thank you."

She let him usher her to the dining table, which was set with three places on a white twill tablecloth. Mr. Anderson seated her and then took the chair at the head of the table, facing the front door of the house, his back to the kitchen wall. Matthew sat down on his left, across from Rachel. Vida set several dishes on the table and paused to address the boss.

"Everything all right?"

"Yes, Vida. Thank you. Take your dinner and go on home."

"I'll come back and redd up the kitchen after Pard and I eat."

Mr. Anderson nodded, and Vida retreated into the kitchen. A moment later, Rachel heard the back door shut.

"Shall we pray?" Mr. Anderson said with a weary smile.

Rachel bowed her head.

Her host's voice was hoarse, but his words soothed her. "Dear Lord, we thank You for the bounty of this meal and for the hands that have prepared it. Father, we ask that You would comfort Miss Maxwell tonight and give her wisdom and peace of heart in this trying time."

A moment later, she joined her amen with the others and opened her eyes. Mr. Maxwell seemed almost jovial as he passed her each dish and urged her to take larger helpings. Matthew filled his own plate in silence. His blue eyes, a little bloodshot from the time he'd spent near the fire, seemed to avoid her gaze.

"I hope your journey wasn't too uncomfortable," Mr. Anderson said.

"Oh, no. Thank you." Her trip seemed weeks past, and compared to what had awaited her here, the delays and discomforts seemed trivial.

"Were there troops on the trains?" Matt asked.

She nodded. "Yes, as far as St. Louis." She had found it disconcerting, as up to that time the war had seemed more distant, something Miss Edgerly read about in the papers and discussed with the advanced students in their conversation times. The conflict had struck closer when one of her classmates learned her brother had been killed in battle. But the young woman left them to go home and mourn with her family, and the war had once more become a worrisome but distant fact of life.

Rachel pondered this as she ate. Vida's stew wasn't the most savory dish she'd ever tasted. It teemed with chunks of beef so large she had to cut them up before she could chew them. Swimming among them in the broth, she recognized a meager scattering of potatoes, turnips, and carrots. No doubt they were near the end of last fall's harvest and awaiting fresh vegetables from their spring garden.

Mr. Anderson and Matt used the saltshaker liberally, and when Matt offered it to her, she took it with a murmur of thanks. After she added a generous amount to her bowl, the stew went down a little easier, but it still came nowhere near the standard her mother used to meet regularly. Perhaps Vida had no herbs to add flavoring to her cooking. A little basil would have worked wonders here, and a thicker broth.

"... and it might be wise for you to consider your father's wishes so far as the ranch is concerned."

Rachel whipped around to stare at Mr. Anderson. "I'm sorry —what did you say?"

Clearing his throat, he glanced at his son and started again. "You must know that your father and I talked about the possibility of you and Matthew ... well ... consolidating your assets, so to speak."

Rachel's heart began to pound. Her cheeks heated as if she stood next to a roaring stove. "I'm not ready to think about that, sir. I've only just arrived, and I have other things on my mind this evening. Burying my father, for one."

"Of course. Forgive me. We won't speak of it again until ... "

She waited, expecting him to say, "until you are ready to discuss it."

Instead, he came out with "… until after the funeral service."

The ironstone dish before her was still half full, but she didn't care to eat any more. She ought to shove back her chair and rise, giving the man a royal set-down. Oughtn't she?

Matt was watching her. Was that how he viewed her? The holder of valuable assets that he would benefit from annexing?

"Pa, Miss Maxwell isn't looking to get married right away," he said gently, his vibrant blue eyes holding her gaze all the while.

"Oh." Mr. Anderson gave a little cough and took a drink from his coffee mug. When he set it down, he smiled. "Of course. Forgive me for pressing the issue so soon. It just seemed so … sensible. With things the way they are, I mean. You wouldn't have to worry about rebuilding the house quickly, or how you …" He shook his head apologetically. "There I go again. I'm sorry. I'll try to keep quiet."

By this time, Rachel's cheeks burned so fiercely she knew they had gone scarlet. "I'd appreciate that," she managed.

Matt gave her a tight smile and a nod that seemed to say, *There, you told him.* He picked up his knife and sliced open a biscuit.

Rachel hadn't had a proper lunch, and her meager breakfast on the train was so long past that it was only a hazy memory. Not eating now would be foolish. She made herself take another spoonful of the stew.

She declined a second helping, though Mr. Anderson went to the kitchen and returned with the kettle and a ladle. He and Matt both took extra portions of the stew and claimed several biscuits apiece. Vida had been a bit heavy-handed with the saleratus on those, but Rachel got a whole one down, telling herself that if she didn't fill her stomach now she would regret it later.

At last the meal was over. Mr. Anderson offered no sweets, nor an apology for the lack of them. Rachel didn't mind—the school she had so recently left served them only occasionally, instead presenting cheese or fruit as a dessert course.

However, her memories of her former ranch life included lots of cookies, cakes, and doughnuts, which her father's men had devoured in great quantities. Mother used to say they needed the extra nourishment because of the hard work they did. But the Anderson men seemed content with another cup of coffee and an extra biscuit.

China rattled in the kitchen.

"It sounds like Vida has returned. Perhaps I can help her."

Rachel rose, and the two men jumped up.

"There's no need," Mr. Anderson said. "You should rest."

"I don't mind." Rachel picked up her own dishes and the empty biscuit plate. As she turned away, she noticed that Matt was picking up another load of dirty crockery.

She pushed open the kitchen door. Vida was pouring hot water from a teakettle over the biscuit pan.

"Where would you like these?" Rachel asked.

Vida frowned at her. "Anyplace."

Rachel set the dishes down on the worktable. "May I help you clean up? If you have another apron ..."

"I work just fine on my own."

Rachel forced a smile. "I'm sure you do, but I'd like to help. I must have made extra work for you."

"Not really." Vida dipped water from a bucket on the floor to refill the teakettle and walked over to the stove. She set the kettle down with a thump.

The door opened, and Matt came in carrying his dishes and the stewpot, with the ladle's handle sticking precariously over the edge and nearly snagging on the doorjamb.

"I don't mind, really," Rachel said.

"I work better alone." Vida's tone was far from friendly.

Matt stopped in his tracks and looked from her to Rachel

and back. "Miss Maxwell only wants to help you, Vida. Get you out of here quicker."

"I said no." Vida turned and looked sullenly at Rachel from slits of eyes. "But thank you. Ma'am."

Rachel could feel embarrassment radiating from Matt. Before he could speak, she nodded at Vida. "Well, then, I'll retire. But thank you very much for the meal."

Vida only grunted.

Matt set down his burden and grimaced behind Vida's back. "Is there anything I can do for you before you go upstairs, Miss Maxwell?"

"No, thank you." This was where she ought to tell him to call her Rachel. They would be neighbors, after all, even if nothing more than that. But she wanted to maintain the distance between them, and she certainly didn't want Vida to think she was dangling after the boss's son.

"Well, good night then," Matt said.

"Good night."

Rachel went out through the big room, where Mr. Anderson sat near the gun rack, cleaning one of the rifles they'd used that day.

"Good night, Mr. Anderson."

He smiled as though he hadn't a care in the world. "Good night, Miss Rachel."

She kept her neck and shoulders as straight as a yardstick while mounting the stairs. Miss Edgerly, at the Ladies' Seminary in Boston, would have been proud.

But when she reached the privacy of the small room they'd given her, she slumped down on the bed. Her pride had reared up tonight, and she didn't like it. This wasn't the way she normally behaved.

What was it about Matt Anderson that antagonized her? He wasn't homely—far from it, with that thick, sandy hair and eyes as blue as the Texas bluebonnets. He wasn't rude, or mean, or thoughtless. So, what was wrong with him? She couldn't think of a single thing or a single reason why she shouldn't be friendly to him.

It would be the easy way out to fulfill Papa's wishes—to take Matt Anderson as her husband and give him title to the Maxwell ranch. To have a man who would take care of her and make all the difficult decisions. She had the impression he would gladly step up and do that. He could ease the heartache of the days ahead, if she would let him.

But that would be the wrong reason to marry him.

"GUESS I OVER SPOKE." Matt's father plunked down in his chair at the table, frowning, and picked up his coffee mug.

"She does seem a bit touchy on the subject of marriage," Matt said. "Apparently her pa wrote to her about his hopes for her, and she kicked over the traces. Wants to make up her own mind."

"Hmm. Bob hinted she wasn't keen on the idea, but I hoped, since she'd met you, that she might see the sense of it. Especially now that her father's gone. There's no place for her over there now—no house. Just a crew of rough men. She can't stay over there, even if they rebuild the house for her. She'd do much better to marry you now and stay here with us. Let her foreman run the ranch."

Matt sat down slowly, thinking that over. "Well, it does seem like that would be best. To us, anyway. But, Pa, we don't always know everything, do we?"

Sighing, his father sat back in the chair. "Meaning God might not want you two married?"

Matt hesitated. He loved his father dearly, and he appreciated all John Anderson and his wife had done for him.

Disagreeing with his pa went against the grain. Ever since he'd come to them as a little boy, he'd wanted to please them.

Finally, he met his father's gaze. "Right now, I feel like I don't know a thing—especially not where women are concerned. But God does, right?"

"Yes, son. You've got your head on straight."

"Yeah, well, she rejected me before I even suggested I might ask her." It still stung, and he couldn't see any sense in pushing the issue.

"We'll take Rachel over to Maxwell's tomorrow and help her tend to things, if she'll let us. And we'll give her all the time she needs to think on her situation."

"Thanks, Pa."

The kitchen door opened, and Vida came in. She stopped beside the table, her face as homely as a lump of biscuit dough.

"You done with them cups?"

"Yes, Vida. Thank you." Pa placed his coffee mug in her hand, and Matt stretched across the table to give her his.

"Pard told me all about the fire and all. Is that girl staying here a spell?"

Matt was mildly surprised she hadn't called Rachel a woman. She was obviously grown up. Vida's sour attitude and expression made him uneasy. Was she emphasizing Rachel's youth on purpose?

"Probably so," his father said. "I don't know how long."

Vida harrumphed and strode into the kitchen with their mugs.

"Vida's got a burr under her saddle," Matt said quietly.

"How come?"

Matt shrugged. "Not sure. But she doesn't like Rachel much."

"I've never known her to be rude to a guest before," his father said.

"No? Well, you didn't hear what went on in the kitchen."

Pa sighed. "I'll make sure she knows to treat Rachel with respect."

"Too late, I'm afraid. But a word in her ear couldn't hurt."

His father's frown deepened into a scowl. "Miss Maxwell could end up being Mrs. Anderson. Vida had better bury whatever perceived injury she's nursing."

"I'd go easy on it, Pa, at least until we know Rachel's plans. Pard's a good worker, and there aren't many women looking for housekeeping jobs in this territory. If we get on the wrong side of those two, we could be left high and dry."

6

May 6, 1863
Anderson Ranch, Colorado

W hen Rachel went down to breakfast wearing her green Valencia riding habit, she was surprised to find Matt alone at the table. As she reached the bottom of the stairs, he poured himself a cup of coffee from the blue enameled coffeepot.

"Good morning." He smiled as his gaze swept over her.

She dropped the handfuls of skirt she'd been holding up slightly as she negotiated the stairs. Perhaps the ranch men would think she was putting on airs with this habit, but the comfortable older clothes she used to ride in had probably burned with her father's house. By all rights, she ought to be wearing black, but she was determined to get to the ranch on horseback this morning, and she couldn't ride in a mourning dress. She wouldn't apologize for that—Papa would say it was all nonsense and she should dress as she pleased.

"Well, hello. I slept late, and I thought you'd be out on the range." She approached the table.

Matt set the coffeepot down and stood. "Pa's out with the men, but I stayed behind to ride over to your place with you."

"I can find my way there."

"I'm sure you could, but we didn't think it would be safe. Not until we hear the sheriff's caught that band of outlaws."

She hadn't considered that the thugs might still be out there and ready to strike again.

"You don't think they'd attack here, do you?"

Matt shrugged, gritting his teeth. "You never know. They might, since they didn't get everything they wanted at your father's place."

"What do you mean?" she asked.

"Bud said they'd ransacked the house, so they probably got a few guns, but your father didn't keep many extras about the house. They maybe got some money of your pa's, too, but they stayed around to fight after they set the house afire, so we think they must have wanted some remounts."

"The horses."

"Either that or the beef herd. That seems less likely, but they may have planned to run off most of the cattle. Still, I think they'd have come in the night, if that was their plan. Instead, they picked a time when everyone was out of the house. Seems to me the guns and ammunition were probably important to them—and any valuables they picked up in there."

Rachel hated the idea of those vile men handling her family's things. What had they taken, and what had they left to burn? Either way, her mother's miniature portrait was lost to her, as well as the china, furniture, and clothing. She looked into Matt's sober blue eyes. "Maybe they planned to kill all of Papa's men and get their guns and horses and ... and everything. Are the men safe over there now? And will they be able to protect the horses and cattle?"

"We can't be sure, but I know Bud's a good man. He and the

others will be extra careful from now on. They'll keep the horses close at night, too, and mount a guard around the clock."

"I didn't realize the men were risking so much to protect my property."

Matt let that pass. "Why don't you have something to eat, and we'll ride on over and see how they're doing."

"All right. What is your usual routine for breakfast?"

He smiled. "I'll let Vida know you're down, and she'll bring you a plate. Flapjacks and eggs this morning. Is that all right?"

"Of course."

"Coffee?"

"Thank you." She would really prefer tea, but between Vida's prickliness and her own knowledge of range life, Rachel thought it would be more polite not to ask for anything her hosts didn't offer.

Because Matt fetched her meal for her from the kitchen, Rachel didn't have to face Vida that morning, for which she was grateful. She couldn't decide whether this was thoughtfulness on the young man's part, or if he simply hoped to hurry her along. He returned and placed her plate and coffee cup before her.

"Is this the first time there's been an attack of this nature in the valley?" she asked.

"I wish I could tell you it was. A stage stop down the line was hit a couple of months ago, and all of the livestock was taken. The sheriff didn't think it was Indians, but no one was sure. Now we're all wondering if it was this gang." He put on his hat. "If you'll pardon me, I'll go out to the barn and get the horses ready. Come out when you're through."

Rachel ate quickly. She rose after downing two flapjacks and a mound of scrambled eggs, leaving half her coffee in the cup. Perhaps Matt wanted to put his duty behind him and get back to work on his own ranch.

He smiled as she crossed the yard toward him, and in that

gesture, she took some comfort. It didn't seem a scheming smile. She wanted to believe he was genuinely pleased to see her. Of course, that might mean he was glad she hadn't dawdled —or that he approved of her riding habit. It could mean anything, really. And did she honestly care what he thought?

Yes, she did. That realization was a little unsettling. Her pride again? Part of her wanted not to care what Matt Anderson or any other man thought. The other part wanted friendship.

He'd put the tooled sidesaddle on Herald, and the pinto looked magnificent. Matt's broom-tailed bay, beside the paint, impressed her as common with his short-coupled body, squarish face, and plain stock saddle. She supposed Matt had chosen a useful mount for himself from their working remuda.

As they rode across the valley, they passed clusters of cattle grazing.

"These are ours," Matt said once, nodding toward a herd of about a hundred. "Once we cross the stream up ahead, most of the beeves you see will be your own."

"Do they cross over?" Rachel asked.

"Sometimes. We don't worry about it much until roundup."

She wished she could forget for an hour their grim errand. Cantering in the sunshine on a horse that moved more smoothly than a rocking chair brought her pleasure she hadn't had in a long time. She'd missed this—the outdoors, the animals, the freedom.

Around her, the fresh, emerald-green prairie grass spread out in a deep carpet for miles on any side. And here in the foothills of Colorado, they didn't seem to have the oppressive heat she remembered in Texas. But maybe that would come later, in high summer.

They topped a ridge, and her father's place came into sight. The barn was the biggest, most impressive structure. She tried to imagine what it had looked like with the house standing.

When they loped into the barnyard, Bud and two other men

were poking about in the ruins of the house. A pile of charred timbers was stacked to one side, and the men prodded the debris with tools, apparently trying to salvage bits and pieces for her. The scent of smoke lingered.

Bud walked over to where they dismounted, took off his gloves, and shoved his hat back.

"Mornin', Miss Rachel. I hope you slept well."

"Fair enough," she said. "Was it quiet here last night?"

"Yes, ma'am. I've got the boys out checking the herd this morning. We don't want them outlaws coming back and rustling the cattle while we work on things here." Bud glanced toward Matt and back to her. "The boys finished the coffin, and one for Billy. We've got your pa laid out in the barn, if you'd like to see him."

Rachel caught her breath. For some reason, she hadn't expected that, and she felt unprepared.

"I—Yes, I suppose so." She shot a glance at Matt.

He stepped forward, removing his hat and inclining his head solicitously. "Would you like me to go in with you, Miss Maxwell?"

Having him and Bud beside her would make it easier. She nodded. "Thank you. Both of you."

They entered through the big door, which was already rolled halfway open. Inside, her eyes adjusted to the dimness. The coffin, set up on two sawhorses on the barn floor, looked stark white because of the brightness of the new wood.

Rachel walked toward it slowly, with Bud on her left and Matt on her right. Neither of them touched her, but she felt their solid presence. High rafters and haymows stretched overhead. The air smelled of hay and leather, manure and wood shavings. If not for the trace of smoke, even in here, she would have felt at home, though she'd never been in this barn before.

"Do you keep a lot of hay indoors for winter?" she asked Bud.

"Quite a bit, yes. We get some deep snow here—not like Texas, where it's gone the next day. The horses need it, and in the worst of it, we have to take some out to the cattle, too."

She couldn't stall forever. She reached out and touched the top of the closed box with her gloved hand.

"Let me open it," Bud said. "We shut it up because I didn't know when you'd come, and I didn't want …" He stopped and cleared his throat. "It just seemed best."

He was keeping out the vermin, Rachel surmised. She shuddered.

Bud stepped to one end of the coffin and Matt to the other, and together they raised the lid. Rachel gazed down at her father's pale face. How many times had she imagined their reunion? In all of those reveries, his face had been vibrant with pleasure, his joy in seeing her again spilling over into his features. Now his expression was a blank. He didn't look like Papa. Whether happy, angry, worried, or amused, his face was always animated, not this flat, unresponsive mask.

"Are you all right, Miss Rachel?" Bud touched her elbow, and she stirred.

"Yes, thank you. You may close it."

Carefully the two men lowered the lid.

"Have you thought about when you want the service?" Bud asked. "The minister says he can ride out this afternoon or tomorrow, if we just send him word."

She looked to Matt for guidance. "There's no sense putting it off, is there?"

"None I can think of," Matt said. "If you want to do it later today, we can come back after dinner. Pa and I would like to be there."

She hadn't thought of all the trouble it would cause the ranchers to go back and forth. The Anderson men had already lost most of a day's work because of her troubles, and her father's men needed to get on with whatever work she decided to have them do.

"All right. Bud, if you can take me around this morning and show me what you think it would be wisest to do—what's urgent, that is—and tell me what Papa had planned for this summer, I'll be better equipped to make plans. Meanwhile, you could send word to the minister and tell him this afternoon is fine."

"I'll send one of the punchers into town now." Bud hurried out of the barn.

"Are you sure you feel up to doing ranch business today?" Matt asked. "It could wait until tomorrow."

"The men need leadership. They have Bud, but even he needs to know how to proceed. I could see his uncertainty. He needs to know things."

"If you'll stay on, for one."

She jerked her chin up. "Why do you say that?"

He wriggled a little and looked away. "I just didn't know … Pa thought maybe you'd go back East, since your father's gone. You don't know anyone here. Well, except Bud and maybe a couple of your pa's older hands. Anyway, we weren't sure you'd want to take on ranch life."

"Oh, I'm staying," Rachel said firmly. "There's no question about that."

"Right." Matt turned toward the door, and they walked across the barn floor together. "We'd best get on with it, then, so you know what you're up against."

BUD LASSEN TOOK a good hour to escort Rachel around the nearer parts of her father's ranch. Matt rode along with them in silence. She laughed at the antics of the calves that frolicked on the range near their mothers. Seeing her smile gave Matt hope that Bob's death hadn't totally crushed her spirit.

Bud led them to a couple of high points, so Rachel could look out over her father's holdings and, in some cases, see to the boundaries. He explained to her what the water rights were, and the arrangements Maxwell had made with a couple of the neighbors for access and rights of way.

Matt knew most of it already, and he focused on Rachel more than on Bud's words. She remained attentive and asked some insightful questions about the operation. At one spot, while they sat on their horses in the shade, talking, Matt dismounted and stretched his legs. Long hours in the saddle brought on the ache in his leg, but a few minutes of walking on solid ground usually helped.

When he walked back to the horses and scooped up Buster's reins, Bud was saying, "Of course, all the paperwork burned. You'll need to get a copy of the deed from the county courthouse, but that shouldn't be a problem."

"Were you able to salvage anything?" Matt asked.

Bud sighed. "A few things."

Matt glanced at Rachel. "Pardon my asking, but did the boss have a safe?" His own father kept his important papers and cash for the monthly payroll in a safe that was reputed to be fireproof.

"He had a metal cashbox, but it looked like they'd forced it open before the fire. Everything inside it was gone or destroyed. Apparently his desk was in the hottest part of the fire. But I'm pretty sure he didn't have much cash in the house. Payday was last week, and the money from the cattle we sold last month is in the bank in town." Bud looked at Rachel. "The boys and I saved a few bits out of the kitchen and some hardware. Oh, and there's one thing that I guess was in his bedroom. I put it aside for you, Miss Rachel."

"What's that?" she asked.

"His knife, that he had made from his saber."

She closed her eyes briefly. "Papa set a great deal of store by that knife."

Matt had seen it before, several times. Rachel's father had served in the Cavalry during the Mexican-American War, and afterward, he'd had the blade of his saber retooled into an eight-inch bowie knife.

"It's back at the bunkhouse," Bud said. "I thought you'd want to keep it."

"Thank you."

He sniffed and nodded. "Found your mama's teapot, too, and the sugar bowl, though the lid to that's missing. All the cups broke, though, when the cupboard burnt."

"I'm glad you found something of Mama's."

"We have your father's watch, too. He had it on him yesterday. That and his revolver."

When they got back to the bunkhouse, Bud went inside and came out with a small wooden box. He balanced it on the hitching rail and handed Matt Mr. Maxwell's gun belt.

"Hold that, would you?" He reached into the box and picked out several coins, which he held out to Rachel. "Those were in his pockets."

Bud handed her the pocket watch and bowie knife in turn. She examined each piece and nodded, her eyes misty.

"Thank you, Bud. I'll treasure these."

Bud hesitated and took a faded bandanna from the bottom of the box. "He was wearing this when he was shot."

Her tears broke loose then. She held the bandanna up to her face for a moment, smelling it, then crumpled it in her hand. After a moment, she drew in a deep breath and squared her shoulders. "I'm ready to go, Mr. Anderson."

7

R achel lay down after the mid-day meal, certain she couldn't sleep. Matt and his father, however, had insisted she take a nap before they drove to her father's ranch for the funeral.

Not Papa's ranch. She stared up at the knotty pine boards of the ceiling. *My ranch. I have to think of it that way now. I'm the boss lady, and I need to decide what to do with the place.*

Options Bud had mentioned, along with a few more Matt had come up with on the way home, swirled through her mind. Her father had bought more cattle, and Bud expected them to be delivered soon. She could keep the new herd or turn around and sell them, keeping the operation on a fairly small scale while she got used to things. Or she could sell them all, old and new, and go away, but that seemed all wrong to her.

One thing she knew she wanted to do, and that was to rebuild the house. Oh, not as large as the one that had burned, but she needed to be able to live on her own land and be close by for the foreman to consult. The men needed the owner's presence. After things settled down and they established a routine, Bud could oversee the construction of a small cabin for her, with an eye toward expanding it later.

To her surprise, she woke some time later to knocking on the door of her chamber. She sat up.

"Yes?"

"It's one-thirty. Thought you'd want to get ready."

"Oh, thank you." Trust Matt Anderson to keep her on schedule. She picked up her father's pocket watch and opened the case. One-thirty on the dot. The minister had sent word that he'd arrive at her ranch around three.

She rose and put on her black byzantine dress. The wool and silk blend shouldn't be too hot this afternoon, and it was the only good black dress she owned now. She'd counted on being reunited with her everyday clothes when she reached home, and her father had written that he'd also brought the trunk containing some of her mother's best things when he moved from Texas. They'd saved them over the years, and Rachel had made up her mind to go through them and choose the best to alter for herself and get rid of the rest. But that was before the fire.

A small looking glass hung inside the wardrobe door, and she gazed into it as she arranged her hair. Papa had always said she looked like her mother. She hoped so. The sober hue of the dress made her look older, and her eyes looked darker than usual in her pale face. Miss Edgerly would be glad if she could see Rachel—the teacher advocated avoiding the sun whenever possible, and a pale complexion was the mark of a refined woman.

Something inside Rachel had rebelled at that, though. Her first year at the seminary, she'd been reprimanded several times for escaping the building whenever possible. Eventually, she'd submitted to the school's restraints, and her tan had faded. Now she had the ivory skin many of her classmates had envied.

With a sigh, she pulled a lacy shawl from her trunk. It

seemed a bit decorative for a funeral, but it was the only black one she owned and, for today at least, she must shun color. She wouldn't keep the Eastern conventions of mourning, however. She intended to ride every day, and not wearing black.

Her small black purse would do. She tucked a handkerchief and a couple of dollar bills into it. She would have to ask Bud about that bank account of her father's—the cash she had carried on her journey was nearly exhausted, but she must pay the minister for his effort. The doctor probably needed payment as well.

When she went downstairs, Matt and his father waited for her in the sitting room. The wagon stood outside, and both Anderson men climbed aboard with her. Rachel was touched when two of their cowboys fell in behind on horseback.

"Most of our men didn't know your father well," Mr. Anderson said, "but Josh and Pete asked if they could come along today, out of respect for him."

"That's thoughtful of them."

"I expect Bud and the boys will have coffee brewing in the bunkhouse, and Vida's packed a cake and a basket of sandwiches."

It wasn't much for a funeral feast, but Rachel hadn't expected anything. "How kind," she murmured. Vida seemed to avoid Rachel whenever possible and spoke shortly to her when necessary. The woman was able to cook quantities of food, even if some of it seemed flavorless, and it appeared she kept the Anderson house tolerably clean singlehanded. Rachel supposed efficiency counted more than personality out here.

On the way over, Mr. Anderson talked about the local ranching community near Fort Lyon, the nearest town.

"Matthew said the outlaws who attacked my father's ranch might be the same men who raided a stagecoach station a short time ago," Rachel said. "Do you know anything about them?"

"No, ma'am," Mr. Anderson said.

On her other side, Matt drove in silence to that point.

She glanced at him. "Two were killed in the gun battle, were they not?"

Matt nodded, frowning. "Bud and his men buried the outlaws after the sheriff looked at them. They didn't have any papers on them, and nobody knew who they were."

"But they were white men."

"Yes, all of them."

Mr. Anderson cleared his throat. "It's the first time a gang has besieged a ranch."

"Well, that we know of," Matt said.

"True. But it does seem odd. Most ranchers don't keep much cash on hand."

"Except after they sell off some cattle," Rachel said.

"Yes, but most men do those transactions in town and put the money right in the bank. We get cash out for our payroll every month, but that would be at the end of the month." Mr. Anderson shook his head. "It just doesn't make sense to me that they attacked your father's place at the time they did."

She glanced at Matt. "There was speculation they wanted horses."

"Then why didn't they take them and light out? There were several in Bob's corral when they rode up. But they went into the house first."

"Too good an opportunity to miss, I guess," Matt said. "And Bob and his men discovered them before they could get out and ride off with the extra horses."

"Yes," his father mused, "but they still stayed and fought it out. Were the horses that important to them? They all seemed to have mounts."

"Can you think of another explanation?" Rachel asked.

"Not yet, but I'm thinking on it. A gang robbed a bank in Colorado Springs late last summer. It could be the same bunch, but no one knows for sure."

"That must have been while I was away," Matt said.

Where had he gone last year? She wouldn't ask.

"Well, if it's the same bunch, they waited a long time to start thieving again, and an isolated ranch is a far cry from a bank," his father said. "The sheriff seemed to think this wasn't the same ones. Or that stage robbing bunch either. It's just not like any other attack in the area."

They drove into the Maxwell ranch's barnyard, made desolate by the charred ruin of the house. To Rachel's surprise, several wagons and saddle horses were tied up, and about twenty men and women stood about talking in small groups.

A tall, gangly man in a black suit walked over to them as Mr. Anderson helped Rachel down, and the rancher nodded to him.

"Miss Maxwell, this is our minister, Mr. Bixly."

Rachel extended her hand. "How do you do?"

"Pleased to meet you, Miss Maxwell, though I wish the circumstances were happier."

Rachel nodded, dismayed that this oblique mention of her father's death caused her throat to tighten and her eyes to fill with tears. How would she ever make it through this day?

"Thank you," she choked out.

Mr. Anderson placed a hand beneath her elbow. "Shall we walk up the hill? Is that the plan?"

The preacher nodded. "We buried the ranch hand, Billy Snow, earlier. Mr. Lassen and his men took Mr. Maxwell's coffin up there on a wagon. They've prepared the grave. If you're ready, I'll tell folks it's time."

He turned away, but Rachel stood still, trying to get a full breath into her constricted lungs.

"Are you all right?" Mr. Anderson asked.

Matt, who'd tied up the team, came up on her other side. "We could drive up there if you're not up to walking."

"No, I'll be fine. Thank you." Rachel blinked hard against the tears, glad she'd slid a fresh handkerchief into each sleeve, as well as the one in her diminutive handbag.

"At least take my arm," Mr. Anderson said.

She did so, and with one sturdy Anderson on each side, set out to trudge up the hill in the wake of the neighbors and cowboys. The walk was less than a quarter mile, and the grass wasn't long yet. Those ahead of them would have routed out any lurking snakes, and Rachel didn't bother to watch the ground closely.

At the top of the rise, a buckboard stood to one side, and the austere pine coffin rested on the ground beside the gaping hole. The dirt had been heaped on the far side, and the onlookers had formed a horseshoe around the perimeter. They parted as Rachel and the Andersons approached. She took her place near the minister, still flanked by Matt and his father. She looked around at the somber faces, but they all blurred together into one mask of grim sympathy.

All of it put her in mind of her mother's funeral, when the neighbors had gathered for the ritual. Death was one of the few things that would tear these hardy people away from their work. That day, they'd congregated in the house after the burial, plying Rachel and her father with cake and telling all the little kindnesses Mama had done for them. It had seemed almost like a birthday party, except the guest of honor was missing and would never return.

Mr. Bixly led them all in singing a hymn and then read from Scripture—the Twenty-third Psalm, as she had expected. He then spoke for a few minutes about her father.

"Bob Maxwell was a hard worker and a good rancher. He knew how to use the land God gave him. He was a godly man. He rarely missed Sunday services, and he encouraged his men to attend as well." The minister smiled. "I've spent several evenings in the house that stood down there not so long ago. Bob enjoyed wrangling over doctrine now and then, but he also liked to tell a good story, and I derived a great deal of pleasure from his company."

Rachel relaxed a little. Her father had found friends here and was well liked in the community.

"He was also a good father," Mr. Bixly said. "We all heard about his daughter, and we knew how hard Bob worked to provide for Rachel and how he anticipated seeing her again. He delighted in preparing a home for her."

Everyone seemed to focus on Rachel.

"Well, that home has been destroyed," the minister continued, "but her father's love will always be there. And it was Bob who went home to the mansion his loving heavenly Father prepared for him. He's up there now, waiting for the day when Rachel will join him, in a home far more splendid than what he could prepare here on earth."

The tears were back. Rachel whipped out the first handkerchief as Mr. Bixly began to quote from the fourteenth chapter of John. Several of the other women sniffed and applied their hankies as well.

"In my father's house are many mansions; if it were not so, I would have told you. I go to prepare a place for you."

She sobbed, unable to hold it back. Everyone stared at her—she knew without seeing them. She felt exposed, even though these people were here out of kindness and empathy. They were Papa's friends, not hers. She was all alone, and she couldn't stop weeping.

A strong arm encircled her waist and held her firmly. For a moment, it was as though Papa had reached down to give her the loving support she needed.

Mr. Bixly began to pray, and Rachel tried to control her sobbing. She turned her head and hid her face with her handkerchief. As the minister's prayer continued, she realized Matt was the one holding her, and she was leaning against his chest, weeping onto his broadcloth shirt. She wanted to pull away, but he continued to hold her with one firm arm, and his other hand came up to pat her shoulder gently.

She allowed herself to enjoy his warm comfort for only a few seconds. How many people were peeking as the preacher continued to pray?

"... and we beg Your mercy on his daughter, Lord, who is now an orphan, alone in this cold world. Show her Your care and compassion, dear Father. Use us to show her Your love, and to help her through this difficult time."

By the time Mr. Bixly had wound down to the amen, Rachel had pulled away from Matt, though he kept one hand at the small of her back. She wiped her face with her second handkerchief and squared her trembling shoulders. Surely they wouldn't read any impropriety into her momentary weakness. She sneaked a glance around the circle of mourners. Many of them stared at her, as she had suspected, and she felt a blush creeping up her neck.

Bud and three other men stepped up to the coffin. The rest of them watched as her father's men lowered the casket into the grave.

The minister nodded to her. Rachel gathered her skirt and moved around to the pile of earth. She removed one black glove, stooped, took a handful of dirt, and tossed it into the hole. It plunked onto the coffin lid, and she caught a sharp breath. Matt, beside her, also threw in a handful of dirt, and the other mourners came over to do the same. Rachel stepped back and watched.

When all seemed to have finished and milled about uncertainly, Mr. Anderson raised an arm and shouted, "Folks, Miss Maxwell's got no house to welcome you into, but it's a fair day. We'll gather in the yard down below, in front of the bunkhouse. Vida sent along some eats, and I know some of you other ladies brought food, too. Let's have at it."

The neighbors set off down the hill, but Rachel lingered.

When nearly everyone had left, she and Matt remained with two of the cowboys, who stood by with shovels.

"Did you want to see him again?" Matt asked.

"No, I … I'm sorry. It's hard to leave him. If I'd had a chance to say good-bye, it might have been easier."

"I understand. Take as long as you want."

They stood for another minute. Rachel wished she had some flowers. Anything to make this ritual seem more normal. The breeze was cold on her cheeks, where her tears had left wet streaks. She took out her third handkerchief and carefully blotted her face, though she knew it was hopeless. Her ivory complexion was now undoubtedly blotched with crimson, and her tears would return, time and again.

"I'm ready." It came out with a little croak.

"Are you certain?"

She nodded, wishing she hadn't let him see her so vulnerable. Matt and his father must think her very weak and not strong enough to run a ranch. They would press her again to sell it to them, or marry and let her husband run it for her. She would have to delve deep into her soul to find the stamina she needed. Straightening her shoulders, she determined to prove to the Andersons and all of the people gathered today that she didn't need Matt, or any man, to run a successful ranch.

8

White Plains, New York
May 7, 1863

Ryland Atkins paid off the hackney driver who'd brought him to the orphanage in White Plains. He would probably be inside for some time, and he could walk to a cabstand at the corner when he was ready to move on.

The air still held a nip, but spring had progressed much farther here than in Maine. Flowers lining the walkway to the front door exploded with color. The orphanage building loomed before him, a rambling clapboard house. It seemed in good repair, but austere. Ryland took the flowerbeds as a good sign. Someone in charge cared to make a good impression.

A middle-aged woman in a black dress and apron opened the door to his knock.

Ryland took off his hat and held out a calling card. "Hello. My name is Atkins, and I am here to see the director."

She looked up at him for a few seconds, and then took the card and stepped back to allow him entrance. "I'll tell him you're here, sir."

When she left him standing in the hall, Ryland sat down on a wooden bench at one side. He laid his hat and the ebony walking stick that Mr. Turner had given him on the seat beside him.

The building seemed very quiet for one that housed dozens of active children. A minute later, as the maid was returning, a bell tolled brightly overhead, and doors opened in several parts of the house. Feet pattered across bare wooden floors, and a stream of boys catapulted down the stairs. A man stood on the landing above, watching them.

"Walk, boys. Walk."

His sack coat appeared to be a little threadbare and somewhat rumpled, but otherwise, he looked quite ordinary for a schoolmaster. Ryland supposed he must look quite the dandy himself, in his neat black suit.

Each boy slowed momentarily as he passed the supervisor but picked up his pace again as he reached the stairs. They scurried to the lower hall and toward the back of the house.

They were gone as quickly as they'd appeared. The man attending them came sedately down in their wake, nodded at Ryland in passing, and followed the boys. Ryland heard hushed voices and footsteps as other people moved about in the house. By the time the maid reached him, all was still again, except for the distant cry of a baby.

"Mr. Woods will see you now," the woman said.

"Thank you." Ryland followed her around a corner and down a narrow corridor. She stopped before a white-painted door and gestured toward it. Ryland nodded and went in.

"Mr. ...Atkins?" The superintendent looked to be about thirty-five or forty, with short, crisp brown hair and alert eyes behind gold-rimmed spectacles.

"Yes." Ryland advanced and shook his hand.

"I'm Frank Woods, the superintendent here. How may I assist you?"

"I'm here on behalf of some children who were in the care of this institution about eighteen years ago. Their name was Cooper, and I believe they were adopted from this house."

Mr. Woods sighed and glanced at the mantel clock. "Won't you sit down, Mr. Atkins? I can give you half an hour, and then I must address the boys' deportment class."

Ryland settled into the chair he indicated, and Mr. Woods sat behind the desk.

"Now, give me all the details you can. Of course, I was only a boy then, and I had nothing to do with the orphanage at the time. There are old records, but searching through them will take time and may be tedious. I'll need as much information as you can give me."

"Of course—and thank you." Ryland opened his jacket and took his small notebook from an inside pocket. Briefly, he told Woods the story of the Cooper children and their grandmother in Maine. "Mrs. Rose is elderly and quite fragile now. Her dearest wish is to see her grandchildren before she dies."

"And when exactly were they under the orphanage's care?"

"In 1845. We believe they were here a few months at the most."

"And how old were they?" Woods began to take notes of his own.

"The oldest was seven years old when their mother died. The other boy was five, and the girl was an infant. These young people would now be 26, 24, and the baby, Jane, would be 19."

Woods frowned. "I'll do what I can for you. Can you come back this afternoon? Say, about three?"

"Yes, of course." Ryland was disappointed, but he could take a stroll and find a place to eat a late dinner. He'd hoped to have something in hand by now and spend a productive afternoon. Instead, he took his leave and ambled outside.

He paused near a construction site a block away. His stomach rumbled as he watched the workers putting blocks of sandstone in place for a new building. After observing for a few minutes, he strolled on down the street, bypassed a tavern, and turned in at the first eating place he came to.

While he waited for his meatloaf plate, he rehearsed in his mind what he would put in his report to Mrs. Rose today. They had agreed he would write to her weekly during his travels, detailing his progress. If he found something promising, he would send a telegram.

So far, he'd endured crowded train rides, subject to frequent delays. Of course, priority was given to military men, and yesterday he'd been stalled in Boston for hours before he'd been able to secure a seat on a passenger train out of the city. Unless something more exciting happened, Mrs. Rose's report would be dull indeed. If nothing else, he could tell her about his meeting with Mr. Woods.

At last the time had passed, and he returned to the orphanage. Mr. Woods greeted him with a somber face.

"I have found some information about the children you're seeking. I'm not sure how much good it will do you, but I'll share what we have. First, Mr. Atkins, let me assure you that this institution always does what is deemed best for the children." He paused, as if expecting Ryland to agree. When his guest said nothing, Mr. Woods cleared his throat and went on. "Sometimes it is necessary to separate children. Now, today we make every effort we can not to do that. It's one of my policies. But twenty years ago ... "

Ryland's heart sank. "Tell me. They went to different homes, is that it?"

"Yes. It's unfortunate, but you see, the orphanage was going through a low period financially at the time, and the house was overflowing. When those three children were brought in, I'm afraid Mr. Cresswick—the superintendent at the time—tried to move them out as quickly as possible. Of course, that can be good for the children. Although we make every effort to educate and nurture them, the institution's resources can stretch only so far."

Ryland's throat tightened, but he tried not to show his concern. The orphanage seemed well run at the moment. He wouldn't assume it hadn't been two decades ago.

"What can you tell me about their arrival here? Did their father bring them in himself?"

"No, I'm afraid not. Apparently Benjamin Cooper stayed in town a scant fortnight after his wife's death."

"A fortnight? He abandoned his children that quickly?"

"So it seems. The widower asked a neighbor woman to watch the children for a day and never returned to claim them. After three days of waiting, the woman reached the end of her patience and called in the constable. He went to her house and bundled up the three Cooper children and delivered them here."

"How long were they together here?"

Woods's cheeks colored slightly. "Less than two months."

"But the grandparents wrote as soon as they knew. They wanted to take the children to their home in Maine. They had family, Mr. Woods. The grandmother would gladly have reared them."

"I'm sorry, sir. I suppose when the grandparents first learned of Mrs. Cooper's death, they were not told that the children came here."

"No," Ryland admitted. "Their father sent a letter saying Catherine Cooper, the mother, had died. Mrs. Cooper's father was at sea when the letter arrived. Her mother wrote back to Cooper, offering to take the children for the summer, but she received no reply. Mrs. Rose continued to write, and after a few weeks, in her frustration, she sent a telegram to their address. She thought surely Cooper would pay attention to that. She was told it was undeliverable. Cooper was gone."

"How did they learn the children were here?" Woods asked.

"When Captain Rose—that is, their grandfather—returned

home, he made further inquiries. After some months, they established that the children had been here at the orphanage, but they were already adopted to other families. By then, nearly a year had passed. The superintendent told the grandparents the records were confidential and refused to give them any further information, except that they'd gone to respectable families."

"I'm so sorry."

"Do you have names?" Ryland asked. "Of the families?"

Woods frowned as he looked down at the papers before him. "Mr. Cresswick was correct—we are not supposed to give out this type of information. But since the children are all adults now, and since such a tragic misunderstanding took place back then, I am willing to share what little I have with you."

Ryland held his breath.

The superintendent picked up the top sheet of paper. "The little girl went first. It's often the case. Childless couples come in hoping for an infant. You can understand it—they want to have the child from its earliest, most impressionable days."

"Where is she?" Ryland ran a finger around the inside of his collar. His necktie seemed about to strangle him.

"The couple was from Brooklyn. I have an address, which I've written out for you."

The kink in Ryland's neck relaxed a little. Brooklyn was fairly close by. "And the boys?"

Woods cocked his head to one side. "Their records say they protested—violently, I imagine, or Cresswick wouldn't have noted it. They cried and screamed when they learned their sister was gone, and they refused to eat for several days. I suppose Cresswick entered it into his records in case he had to call a doctor for them. He'd need to show that the boys were not abused but had refused food on their own account."

"What happened to them?" Ryland asked, a slow fury building in his chest.

"After a week, they tried to run away. Mr. Cresswick felt at that point, the best course would be to adopt them out as quickly as possible." Woods's voice became more businesslike. "Within a couple of months, the older boy went to a family from Tarrytown. That's a short distance up the Hudson."

"And the younger lad, Elijah?"

"He was here about nine months all told."

"I take it he ate during that time?" Ryland regretted letting acid tinge his voice. After all, it wasn't Woods's fault.

"I saw no notes to the contrary. He was examined by a physician prior to his exit, as is customary, and was pronounced in good health, though thin and a bit undersized."

Ryland gazed at him for a long moment. That could mean the boy was malnourished. But perhaps not. Ryland himself was always slim and wiry. "He went to a good family?"

"So far as I can tell, yes. You see, a group of children was sent that fall to Albany. I believe this institution had an arrangement with another orphan society up there. The idea was to get able-bodied orphans out of the city and place them with rural families. I assure you, they all went to families who were able to give them adequate provision."

Ryland didn't trust Woods's smile completely, though he felt the man's heart was good.

"Unfortunately," the superintendent went on, "I don't have an address for that one."

"How is that possible?"

"I assure you, Mr. Atkins, it's very possible. Some of the old records were damaged by floods or other events. And some are … just more complete than others. I cannot answer for those who compiled them."

"Of course. What do you have?"

"Well, it seems the boy Elijah Cooper was sent with eight other boys from this house. Most of them were older than Elijah, but all had been here for at least several months. The families who adopted them from the Albany institution were mostly farmers. Elijah was taken by a man named Miller."

"Just a man? Not a couple?"

Woods shook his head. "All I have is 'Mr. C. Miller of Pennsylvania.' No doubt he was married, but it's not noted in the record book."

Ryland almost groaned. With a name that common, the family would be hard to trace. "That's it? Not even a town?"

"I'm sorry. You might check with the orphanage in Albany—although they have moved from the building they had then to a new location. I can give you the address if you'd like."

Ryland talked to him for a few more minutes, hoping to discover more details, but he left Woods's office with only the barest information. Since he was fairly close to two of the families' addresses, he decided to stay overnight at his hotel and head for Brooklyn in the morning. He hoped he could find the girl first. Then he'd strike out for Tarrytown. Perhaps he'd find two of the children on this foray and be able to take them back to Maine with him within a few days. The thought excited him. Mrs. Rose would be so happy!

Pennsylvania, where the middle child had gone, was far too large to tackle without some further direction. He hoped somehow he could pick up a trace of young Elijah as he inquired about the other two. If not, he might have to travel to Albany.

In his hotel that evening, he penned a letter to Mrs. Rose. Nothing worthy of a telegram yet—but at least he had something. He hoped Abigail Benson would read it to her and cast a hopeful light on today's developments. Miss Benson would be eager to finally meet her cousins.

In his letter, Ryland wrote that the oldest boy, Zephaniah, went with a family named Anderson to Tarrytown, and he would look into that soon. Elijah had gone with Mr. Miller to

Pennsylvania, and little Jane with the Weaver family of Brooklyn.

Sparing the grandmother the details of the children's enforced separation, he described the orphanage in White Plains as being clean and well maintained, with ongoing classes and activities for the children. While he couldn't vouch for its condition eighteen years ago, it seemed more comfortable than some of the dismal places he'd read about, and he hoped Mrs. Rose would take courage from that.

He closed by saying he sincerely hoped he could soon send her more news of a positive nature. He'd go to Brooklyn in the morning and, the Lord willing, seek out her youngest grandchild.

Brooklyn, New York
May 8, 1863

IT TOOK Ryland a full day to locate the house where the Weaver family had lived in the 1840s, but they'd long ago departed. He slept in a nearby hotel and wished he'd taken the time and borne the expense to hunt for a better one. The place smelled, and the sheets were rumpled and gray.

He tossed and turned all night, waiting for dawn and wondering about little Jane Cooper. Had the Weaver family kept her all these years and raised her as their daughter? What kind of life had she led? Was she well taken care of?

The neighborhood they'd lived in was made up of small, poorly constructed single-family homes, crowded close together. He didn't like to think of Mrs. Rose's granddaughter—Abigail's cousin—growing up in such a place.

If only Captain Rose had succeeded in retrieving the children between his voyages! Then little Jane and the boys could have lived in the big house in Portland, with plenty of space and fresh air. Their grandmother would have seen that they were well nourished and had suitable clothing and a good education. What had become of the three waifs?

In the morning, he went to the nearest post office. The postmaster had been at the job only seven years. The Weavers were not in the area at the time he took the position. Ryland pressed the issue, and the man at last asked an older mail carrier.

"They been gone ten years or more," the old man said, stroking his short beard. "They were on my route. Didn't get much mail, but I remember the little girl. Pretty little mite. And they had a dog."

That was all Ryland could get from him. The postmaster checked again at his insistence, but he found no record of a forwarding address.

Discouraged but not defeated, Ryland began canvassing the neighborhood where the Weavers had lived when they took Jane from the orphanage. If God blessed him, he might find a neighbor to whom Mrs. Weaver had given an address.

The cramped, dingy houses lining the streets made him want to wash his hands. He kept reminding himself that nearly twenty years had passed since Jane was adopted. The area might not have looked so tired and rundown then. The small house where they'd lived would have been newer—not new, but, he hoped, in better repair.

Young men lingered on street corners in the afternoon, eyeing him sullenly as he passed them. Ryland kept his stout ebony cane handy.

"I recall Mrs. Weaver," one of the neighbors on the block told him. "Her husband worked at the mill. Don't know where they went to. They was just gone one day."

Most of the residents had moved into the area more recently. He pumped those who remembered the family for information but gained very little beyond what he already knew.

The next day, he decided to give it one more try. If he didn't get a clue to the family's whereabouts, he would go on to Tarrytown and look for the older boy.

A grandmotherly woman on the street behind the Weavers' gave him a small reward. She remembered Mr. and Mrs. Weaver—and their little girl. She had attended the same church they did. The fact that the couple were regular churchgoers encouraged Ryland. Surely they were good people. Mrs. Deeks even recalled the day the Weavers brought Jane home.

"They doted on her," she said, her eyes dreamy. "Such a pretty child, with flaxen hair and blue eyes."

Although Jane Cooper's name had been changed to Molly Weaver, Ryland was sure he was on the right track. But none of the neighbors, not even Mrs. Deeks, knew where the family had gone. The best he could find were vague memories that the Weavers "went West." Time for him to move on. He would ponder the question of how to find Jane later.

He went back to the hotel, paid his bill, and collected his bag. The owner told him a train heading upstate would leave in an hour. The train station was less than a half mile away, and Ryland set out on foot.

Once he was settled in the passenger car, he could review the notes he'd taken during his conversations with the Weavers' acquaintances and perhaps pen a short note to Mrs. Rose. He hoped the train would have a dining car, or perhaps he'd have time to stop at a café near the station. He'd gotten a meal there on his arrival, and it might be wise to get something now, as it was nearly two o'clock and he hadn't eaten dinner.

A block from the depot, a bearded man in tatters stepped out from an alley between two buildings. Ryland hesitated.

"Gimme yer wallet," the man snarled.

Ryland's heart leaped into his throat. He glanced at his

assailant's hands. The man had a knife—a small clasp knife with a blade of only about three inches.

"I said give it!"

Ryland set down his suitcase and reached slowly inside his jacket. The man looked about fifty years old, and alcohol fumes wafted off him. Without thinking too hard about it, Ryland swung his cane up and, with both hands, raised it over his head.

"Hey!" The man lunged toward him, and Ryland brought the cane down hard on his head. The ebony stick cracked, but the robber sank to the ground with a moan.

With a quick glance over his shoulder, Ryland seized his suitcase and ran for the depot.

9

May 10, 1863
Fort Lyon, Colorado

On Rachel's first Sunday in Colorado, she readily accepted Matt's invitation to go with them to church, which pleased Matt. After the service, he introduced her to several people who hadn't attended Bob Maxwell's funeral. Most of the women who'd been there made a point of speaking to Rachel. She responded graciously, and Matt was proud to be at her side.

Her dress outshone most of the other women's, although the wives of a couple of businessmen who attended the church also wore hoop skirts. It seemed the fashion had come to their humble village. The banker's wife, Mrs. Leigh, looked quite smart in a rose-colored dress. Even though it was cut less lavishly than the hoop skirts, its ruffles and silver buttons gave Matt the impression her husband's business prospered.

Mrs. Leigh approached Rachel with Mrs. Dexter, who ran the mercantile with her husband.

Matt introduced the ladies, and Rachel responded, "Oh, I

believe I met Mrs. Dexter when I came into town with Bud Lassen."

Soon the three were chatting amiably, until Mrs. Leigh asked, "And what are you going to do with all of those cattle?"

"Why, raise them to beef, of course," Rachel said.

"Oh. My husband seemed to think you would sell them off soon."

Rachel smiled. "I have five hundred head of new breeding stock coming in this week. If I sell them off, I'll be selling my father's dream."

She seemed quite positive about her decision. Matt hoped she would succeed and not see that dream crumble. Another raid by the outlaws, or even something as simple as a dry summer, could wipe out all the gains her father had made in the last three years.

A few minutes later, as they walked toward the wagon, he smiled at Rachel. "I'm glad you've decided to stay here."

"I suppose I sounded very confident."

He couldn't see her eyes, which were shaded by the brim of her hat.

"Pa thought you might pack up and go back East."

"He's mentioned that. I expect it's what he wants me to do."

"What? Of course not!" Matt bent his head to see her face.

"Perhaps I should have said it's what he thinks I *should* do."

"Not at all. You should do whatever you want."

She stopped walking and looked fully into his eyes. "Do you mean that?"

"Of course. If you decide to keep the ranch and run it yourself, it will be hard work. But you could do it. You've got some good men on your outfit."

"We're short a couple right now." She glanced about uneasily. Pa was still talking to Ed Hustings, another rancher. Rachel glanced up at Matt again. "Bud thinks I should hire a couple more men if I'm going to see this through. He said he'd ask about in town for me."

Matt nodded. "Probably best, with those new cattle. You'll need to do a lot of work this summer."

He helped her into the wagon, and his father came over to join them. On the ride home, Pa remarked on how warm the weather had gotten and then launched into a list of all the summer work ahead.

Rachel was quiet, and Matt let his father go on. When Pa advised her to divide her herd in order to take best advantage of the water available, Rachel told him calmly that she was relying on Bud to help her with ranch business. After that, Pa was quieter, pointing out a few interesting things they passed on the way.

Once they reached home, Matt helped Rachel down, and she headed for the house. One of the men came out of the bunkhouse to take the team.

"Well, son, what do you think?" his father asked.

Matt hesitated. "I don't know, Pa. Mostly, I think Miss Rachel is mighty independent."

AFTER BREAKFAST ON TUESDAY, Matt and his father headed out to work with their men, and Rachel stayed behind. The entire Anderson outfit would be tending to chores on the ranch today, but Mr. Anderson had promised to assign a man to accompany Rachel to her own property after dinner, if she wanted to go.

The thought of not going had never occurred to Rachel. She had ridden to the Maxwell ranch the day after her father's funeral and every day since except Sunday. She'd intended to go again today. Mr. Anderson seemed to think she might want to stay at his house, but what she would do there, Rachel couldn't fathom. But she understood that riding across the range alone would be foolhardy, so she stayed, but the restriction made her fret. Her work was at the Box M.

Her father had named the ranch, he'd written to her, for a deep box canyon in one far corner. That, and the fact that an *M* with a square around it made a pretty good brand. Rachel had brought the letters she had saved with her in her trunk. During the past two evenings, while Matt and his father read or played checkers or talked laconically about the ranch work, she had gone through them all and made notes about the things her father had planned to do with his property.

Every day she pumped Bud Lassen for information. He agreed with everything her father had written and was able to expand on some of his plans. Rachel now felt she had enough knowledge of the operation to plan her work for the summer.

The Anderson men wouldn't be back for at least four hours, and she felt at loose ends. She thought of hitching up the wagon —she was almost certain she could manage it alone—and driving into town. But Mr. Anderson would probably think that was as dangerous as riding to her ranch without an escort. Until the raiders were caught, she would probably be wise to avoid going off alone.

She wandered about the sitting room, examining the furnishings. Two scant shelves of books hung on one wall, and she scanned the titles. Sermons, agriculture reports, a dictionary, a couple of histories, and a handful of novels. The lone book of poetry surprised her, but maybe that had belonged to Mrs. Anderson.

She blew a thin layer of dust off the top edge of *Martin Chuzzlewit*, one of Dickens's novels she had yet to read. Maybe she should make herself useful and dust for Vida, instead of whiling away the morning with a book. She stuck the volume on edge between the balusters of the staircase, where she could retrieve it easily on her way up, and headed for the kitchen.

"Good morning," she said brightly as she passed the threshold.

Vida was hanging up her dishpan. She glanced over her shoulder with an expression so sour Rachel could only interpret it as a scowl.

"I wondered if you have a rag I can use. I thought I could do some dusting for you this morning."

"No need." Vida walked over to the white-painted cupboard and opened a door on the top tier.

Rachel decided not to contradict her assessment. "Is there something else I could help you with?"

"Don't need any help."

"All right." Rachel hesitated near the door. She had been dismissed, but it didn't feel right. "Vida, I'd be happy to share in the chores while I'm here. I always helped with the cooking and cleaning when I was at home, and—"

Vida slammed a tin of cream of tartar on the worktable. "I said I don't need help."

Rachel gulped. "All right. I'm sorry—I only—" She exhaled in a puff. "Excuse me." She backed out of the room and swung the door shut.

For a moment, she stood still, a hollow forming in her stomach. Had she somehow offended Vida? She pulled in a slow breath, trying to steady her shaking knees. If her labor wasn't wanted in this house, she would find something else to occupy her until she could get to her own property. The book still lay on the stairs, but she doubted she could concentrate on it now.

Her green habit was becoming stained and bedraggled, and she didn't have the proper supplies to clean it. She didn't like to ask Vida. Besides, she really needed something more suitable for riding the range, something less formal. Maybe she could work over one of her classroom dresses into a riding skirt that would be more practical than the elegant habit she'd worn while trotting about the park in Boston.

She hurried up the stairs, snatching the book on her way. In her room, she opened her trunk and the door of the wardrobe. Methodically, she laid out each of her "everyday" dresses on the bed. She had six.

Suddenly her abundance seemed recklessly extravagant. Vida probably owned two calico dresses. Rachel could only be certain she'd seen one, a faded and threadbare gray. The housekeeper probably wore the same garment all week and had a nicer dress for Sunday. Rachel had six plain dresses appropriate for wear around the house, three nicer ones for calling, church, and shopping, and two more elegant gowns suitable for evening events.

And all of those had been part of her school wardrobe. She had left behind in Texas several other dresses she had deemed too worn or outdated to take with her to Boston. Her father had brought them to Colorado, but they'd no doubt been consumed in the fire. Still, Vida and the Andersons must think her a pampered, wasteful creature. She'd worn a different dress nearly every day since her arrival. Was this contributing to Vida's disdain for her?

While Matt and Mr. Anderson had shown her utmost courtesy and gone out of their way to accommodate her, she had to wonder if they, too, thought her spoiled and lazy. Maybe they were simply too polite to show it, while Vida had no such scruples.

She pushed aside one of the full skirts and sat down on the edge of the bed, surrounded by her opulence. Did she have something to prove in this community? Would the ranchers around her ever see her as a hardworking, savvy businesswoman? Or would she be viewed as the upstart girl who thought she could do a man's job?

Maybe she should go back East. She could probably find a teaching post without much trouble. So many male teachers had joined the army that some schools had trouble filling all the positions.

She considered the idea for a few minutes. With her education and a recommendation from Miss Edgerly, it would be easy to get a job and take her place in some quiet town, among the genteel society there. Vida would love to be rid of her, she was sure.

Rachel raised her chin. Was that what the Andersons wanted her to do, if she wouldn't marry Matt? Since she'd refused to let him court her, they probably saw her leaving as the next best thing. If she sold them her ranch, Mr. Anderson would have what he really wanted. Matt could marry whomever he pleased, and the combined ranches would form the largest spread in the county.

She picked up the plainest of her school dresses, a dark blue gabardine. This would do for a riding dress, if she let out every possible bit of hem. She opened her trunk and took out her sewing kit, determined to accomplish something useful this morning.

As she picked at the stitches, she thought back to the day she had arrived and set Matt straight on her thoughts about marrying him. They hadn't mentioned it again, but then Mr. Anderson began his broad hints as to her father's wishes. Papa had suggested it months ago, of course, in a letter, and she'd dismissed the idea. He'd pressed the issue in his next letter, citing reasons why it "made sense" for her to marry the neighbor's boy.

At the time, Rachel had formed an unfavorable impression of Matt. Her father made him sound in his first missive like a raw-boned teenager. But when she'd objected, he'd given her a fuller description, making Matt out to be a paragon of physical attributes, mental acuity, and ranching skill. Now that she knew Matt, she wondered how he'd react if he read her father's litany.

He'd probably blush to the roots of his hair and never meet her eyes again.

She threaded her needle, but she couldn't shake off her thoughts of Matthew. When it came right down to it, he was a handsome young man. She could admit that without straying into admiration. But that first day, with the discomfort of being met at the depot by a stranger, the horror of the attack on her home, and her father's murder, her mind hadn't focused on such trivial things.

That day, she'd wondered as she waited several stressful hours if it was possible the Andersons were involved in the raid. But how could that be? Matt and his father were nowhere near the Maxwell ranch when the outlaws attacked. Were they? She hadn't seen his father until later. Vida's husband, Pard, had told her the boss was off somewhere on the Anderson ranch when she arrived. How did she know where he really was?

Pard had sent someone to fetch him, she remembered, and later she'd been told all of the Anderson outfit had gone to aid her father's men. Still, Matt had told her himself that when they'd run the raiders off, John Anderson and his cowboys had pursued them only a short way. They had let them escape into the hills. Had they deliberately let the outlaws get away?

She shook off the dark train of thought. All the evidence showed the Andersons to be honest, good-hearted men and friends of her father's. John wanted to see the two ranches united, but that was incidental. Wasn't it?

After an hour's work, she held up the skirt she'd altered. She hoped it would cover her limbs modestly when she used the sidesaddle. Women did wear their skirts shorter out here than in the East.

She tried it on, and though it hung fairly long when she stood on the floor, she kept it on. That way, she wouldn't have to change again when the time came to go to the Box M.

Her doubts about her future returned. Perhaps she should

write to Miss Edgerly, just to keep the lines of communication open. If she found the ranch life too hard without her father, she might be glad of another option.

She put away her sewing kit and took out paper and pen. As she began to write, telling Miss Edgerly of her father's death, her tears flowed, but she was glad she had someone she could open up to.

In the end, she confessed that underneath the confidence she exhibited to the men around her, she wasn't certain she wanted to undertake a life of ranching on her own. She asked humbly if her dear teacher had any advice for her. In her final paragraph, she told Miss Edgerly how beautiful the valley was and expressed her longing to bring her father's vision to fruition.

You see, I am of two minds, she wrote. *I am sure, once the newness of it all and the sharp grief I feel just now pass, I shall know what to do. Meanwhile, when you think of me, lift up a prayer for your devoted student and friend, Rachel Maxwell.*

She reread her letter, wondering if it was too personal, or if she had lapsed too much into melancholia. No, she and Miss Edgerly had become quite close in Rachel's final year at seminary. For a woman who had just lost her parent, sharing her grief with her friend was appropriate. She sealed and addressed the letter.

Hoofbeats sounded outside. Her room was on the front of the house, and she ran to the window. Bud was dismounting in the front yard.

She lifted her skirt and dashed down the stairs. Vida had gone to the door and opened it.

"Bud! I hope nothing's wrong," Rachel called to him as she descended the last few steps.

"No, ma'am. I just wasn't sure you were coming today, and I wanted you to know—a rider came in from the new herd of cattle. They'll arrive tomorrow."

"Wonderful! But I need to go to the bank for the money to pay them with."

"That's right. I thought maybe you'd want to go now. I'll go with you."

"Thank you. None of Mr. Anderson's men will be available until after dinner. But our men won't need you?"

"Naw," Bud said. "We're ready for those cattle. Some of the boys'll ride out in the morning to meet 'em. They plan to camp about five miles below your south boundary tonight. I look for 'em by midday."

Rachel smiled. "I'd like to be there to see them brought in. Shall we head for town now?"

"Do you want to take Anderson's wagon?" Bud asked.

"No, I can ride. If you think this outfit is presentable at the bank, I'm ready. Or if you think my habit is more suitable—"

"You look fine, miss."

Vida, who had stood by listening to every word, sniffed and whirled toward the kitchen.

"Please tell Mr. Anderson where I've gone, Vida," Rachel called after her. The housekeeper didn't reply. Rachel looked at Bud and shrugged. "I'll get my purse and be right with you."

In her room, she put her letter into her handbag and then hurried back downstairs. When she reached the barn a couple of minutes later, she found him saddling Herald for her. In no time, they were on their way.

In the small town that had sprung up near the fort, Rachel was able to mail her letter before they went to the bank. The banker came out into the lobby to meet them, and Rachel recognized him as one of those who had come out to the ranch for the funeral.

"How are you doing, Miss Maxwell?" he asked, clasping her gloved hand for a moment.

"I am well, thank you, Mr. Leigh."

"Have you decided whether to keep the ranch or sell it?"

Rachel glanced at Bud, who had accompanied her inside. "I believe I'm here to stay. I have a competent crew, and Bud and I have discussed having the men build me a small house this summer. It won't be as fine as the one that stood there, I'm sure, but it will be adequate for my needs."

He frowned, and she wondered if he was thinking of the money she'd need for that project. Instead, he said, "Will you have a housekeeper, Miss Maxwell? You can't stay on the ranch alone with a bunch of men."

Rachel's cheeks warmed. She hadn't discussed her plans with Matt or his father yet, but she'd wondered if this objection would be raised.

"I'm not sure yet," she said. "Under the circumstances, I may have to make do for a while. But I can't go on running the ranch from a distance. I hope to move over there next month, if the men have time to do the work that quickly."

Mr. Leigh turned away with a frown and went to get her the cash she needed for the cattle. Rachel shuddered at the thought of having a companion like Vida at the Box M, but would the whole town censure her if she moved out there without another female who could serve as a chaperon?

"Here you go." Mr. Leigh counted the bills into her hand. "I expect you'll be in at the end of the month for your payroll money. Or sometimes your father sent Mr. Lassen for it. You'll want to have two or three men to guard it on the way back, though, with these outlaws on the loose."

"Do you think they'd attack someone on the road?" Rachel asked.

"I don't know why not. And they probably know most ranches pay at the end of the month. Pretty easy pickings, if you ask me."

"Yes. Well, thank you, Mr. Leigh."

Rachel put the money in her purse, and they stepped out into the sunlight.

"Hey, Lassen!" A man ran toward them across the rutted street while Rachel was tucking the purse into a saddlebag.

"Oh, hi, Sheriff." Bud turned to Rachel. "Miss Maxwell, this is Sheriff Smith. And this here's Bob Maxwell's daughter."

The sheriff halted three feet from Rachel and looked her up and down. She hoped her made-over riding dress passed muster. Smith whipped off his hat. He wasn't bad looking, in a fortyish, ride-the-plains-all-day way.

"I'm sorry about your father."

"Thank you," Rachel said.

"I'm also sorry that I wasn't on hand the day your ranch was attacked." Smith glanced at Bud and back to Rachel.

"You have news about the outlaws?" Bud asked.

"That's what I wanted to talk to you about. They've struck again."

10

Matt and his father walked out into the yard when they heard horses arriving. Rachel and Bud dismounted and joined them on the front porch. Rachel wasn't wearing the fancy green riding outfit—she had on a plain dark blue dress instead. Her hair was braided and pinned up under a straw bonnet Matt had seen her wear before, and a few tendrils escaped and fluttered around her neck. Her cheeks were tinged with pink, and her eyes shone bright. He thought she looked fine.

"Have a nice ride into town?" Pa asked.

"Yes," Rachel said. "Bud was kind enough to take me to the bank. My new cattle will be here tomorrow—at the Box M, that is."

"Well, that's fine," Pa said.

"They's something you should know," Bud told him. "The sheriff stopped us as we was leaving the bank."

"Has something happened?" Matt asked.

Bud grimaced. "Them outlaws. They hit a ranch on the other side of the valley. All the men was off working. They let his wife and children get out of the house, and then they took what they had for cash savings, a couple of guns, and three extra horses. And some stockpiled food."

"No fire?" Pa asked.

"No, thank the good Lord."

"It's less than a week since they attacked Maxwell's." Pa shook his head. "They're getting greedy."

"I guess it takes a lot to feed all those men. The woman told the sheriff there was eight or ten of 'em. And they weren't Cheyenne. All whites, she said."

"Just like at Maxwell's."

"The sheriff's almost certain it's the same gang," Bud said.

Matt glanced at Rachel. She kept her mouth closed and let Bud talk, her lips pressed in a thin line.

"Sounds like more men than they had at Maxwell's," his father noted.

"So, either they weren't all there last week, or they've added a couple of men," Bud said.

Matt scrunched up his face. "It could be the lady overestimated. When you're looking down a gun barrel, things sometimes get exaggerated."

"Well, that's the truth. But the sheriff wonders if they ain't got someone local working with them." Bud lifted his hat and set it down again, farther back on his head. "Well, maybe not with them exactly, but giving them information."

"Why would he think that?" Matt asked.

"They seem to know the ranch routines. This fella was helping his brother a few miles away when they attacked. The Ensley brothers—you know 'em?"

"I've met them," Pa said. "They're good men."

Bud nodded. "Seemed to the sheriff they knew when all the menfolk would be over to Frank Ensley's, so they could attack Tim's place without any opposition."

That didn't seem right to Matt. "But the day they attacked Maxwell's, several men were still near the ranch house. The rest of you were close enough to hear the gunfire. Doesn't seem to me they knew what they were up against."

"I don't say it's true," Bud said. "Just telling you what the sheriff said. And besides—I been thinking on it while we rode out here from town."

"And?" Pa asked.

"Well, Mr. Maxwell had heard the new cattle would be delivered a week ago, and he asked them to hold off. We'd just got back from driving our beeves to the railhead, and he wanted time to get ready for Miss Rachel. They wasn't coming far, so they waited. We heard this morning they're on the way in now."

"And the sheriff thinks the outlaws knew about the new herd?" Pa frowned, as though he'd eaten something that didn't agree with him.

"It doesn't add up," Matt said. "None of your men would tell a bunch of outlaws when to attack. That's stupid. You saw what they did."

Pa didn't seem to reject the notion as quickly. "Who knew about the delay?"

"I dunno. Mr. Maxwell didn't make a secret of it, but it might not have got around. And if the outlaws thought the cattle were coming in the day they attacked, and that Mr. Maxwell had the cash to pay for them out at the ranch ..."

"I think it's a lot more likely they're just sneaking about and choosing a target that looks vulnerable," Matt said.

Bud shook his head, frowning. "I don't know, but the sheriff's got a few men and was heading out again this afternoon. Said he'd followed their tracks from Tim Ensley's into rough country yesterday, and he was going out again to see if he could pick up their trail. Well, I'd best get back to work." He turned toward his horse.

"I could ride over with you now," Rachel said. "It would save having one of the Anderson men bring me later."

"But you haven't eaten," Pa said. "Dinner's on the table."

Rachel hesitated. Matt figured she knew by now how Vida would take it if Rachel rode off without eating a bite of her cooking. He was about to assure her that it would be no trouble for him to take her to the Box M later, when Pa spoke up.

"You could eat with us, Bud. I'm sure there's plenty."

"Oh, I don't want to make Miz Henry no trouble."

"Nonsense." Pa clapped him on the shoulder. "Tie up your horse—or turn him into the corral if you want—and come on in."

"I'll get Rachel's horse," Matt said and took the porch steps. As he removed Herald's saddle, he realized he was a little disappointed. While his work schedule would have suffered, he'd been looking forward to the ride with Rachel.

Quickly he stripped off the saddle and bridle. He and Bud turned out the two horses, and Matt closed the gate. Rachel was keeping her distance from him since she'd refused to marry him. Not that he'd proposed, but it seemed she didn't need to wait on him for that. She knew her mind without him speaking up. Now she'd begun making arrangements to avoid riding with him. He'd actually enjoyed their few times together, but apparently she'd rather ride with her fatherly foreman than with him.

Could he blame her? Matt told himself he might as well bury the idea of ever marrying her. The trouble was, the more unlikely an alliance with Rachel seemed, the more he wanted it.

OVER THEIR MIDDAY MEAL, the men hashed over all they knew about the outlaw gang and the various crimes they'd committed. As Vida cleared away their plates, Mr. Anderson turned to Rachel.

"You really mustn't plan to move back to your father's ranch now. It just isn't safe. I know Bud and his men would do everything they could to protect you, but I must insist you stay here until those outlaws have been caught."

"Surely I'd be as safe there as I am here." Rachel looked to Bud for support. He seemed to be the only one who sympathized with her and was willing to see her installed at the Box M.

Bud took a sip of his coffee and set the mug down deliberately. "Miss Rachel, I'm afraid he's right. If those men came back again while we was working, I don't know how we'd protect you. We couldn't protect your pa, though we tried."

"I'm not blaming you for what happened," Rachel shot back. "I'm only saying that it could happen here, too. And it's inconvenient for Mr. Anderson and his men to escort me back and forth, but I want to be involved in my own ranch business. I don't want to be shut up here all summer while we wait for the county sheriff to take action."

"You're welcome here as long as you need a haven," Mr. Anderson said.

"And we really don't mind seeing you back and forth," Matt added with a smile.

Vida emitted a small *hmpf* as she headed for the kitchen door.

"I'll feel guilty as long as I impose on your hospitality." Rachel looked at Matt and his father. "I want to be independent. Please let me try."

After a moment's silence, Mr. Anderson said, "When it's safe."

Rachel's hopes plummeted. They would never let her leave here if those bandits weren't apprehended—unless it was to get on a stagecoach heading east.

On the ride to the ranch beside Bud, she had time to think about it some more. While Matt and his father seemed willing to house her indefinitely, she didn't feel exactly welcome in their home. They were, of necessity, gone much of the day, and

Vida had made it clear that she didn't appreciate Rachel's company and wouldn't accept her help. Rachel hadn't felt so ostracized and so utterly alone since her father had put her on the train in Illinois three years ago, bound for Boston.

By the time they'd reached her ranch, she knew one thing for sure: no matter what the Andersons thought, she needed to make a decision, and soon.

The men had finished their dinner and dispersed, except for Charlie Lagrande. Charlie had taken it easy since he was wounded, but his arm was healing. Today he'd helped Dusty prepare the men's meal, and he came from the bunkhouse as Bud and Rachel rode up.

"Everything quiet?" Bud asked him.

"Dull as dishwater around here—and I mean that. I got volunteered to clean up the dishes while ever'body else rode off to work. Nobody here but me. I sure hope them riders don't come by today."

"I think the sheriff's keeping them busy." Bud gave him a quick update on the outlaws' activities.

"They must be deserters, don't you think?" Charlie asked.

"Why do you say that?" Rachel eyed him keenly.

"We haven't had any trouble like this since whites started settling this part of the territory," Charlie said. "The Comanche, they bother the miners up in the mountains, and they skirmish now and then with the Arapaho or the Cheyenne, but they haven't come around here. And then, all of a sudden, we get hit by a bunch of white outlaws. Where'd they come from? That's what I'm asking."

"Not from our militia," Bud said.

"Naw, I think not. Our boys are doing their part. They're Rebs, that's what they are."

"What makes you think that?" Bud asked.

Charlie's face screwed up in distaste. "Them two we killed, they had military-issue weapons. Matt Anderson said so."

"Well, yeah," Bud conceded, "but they've been stealing guns everywhere they attack—we know that. They could've picked up their weapons anywhere. And they weren't wearing uniforms."

"I saw one of 'em I thought was wearing a Reb tunic. But then, prob'ly half the Southern army ain't got decent uniforms. I hear tell a lot of 'em are wearin' rags."

"Didn't you see the bearded man's belt buckle?" Bud asked. "It was a U.S. Army belt plate."

Charlie shook his head. "Matt said it warn't right somehow. I'm tellin' ya, those were not Union deserters."

"Take it easy, Charlie." Bud clapped a hand down on his good shoulder. "Right now, we got cattle to think about. The army's going to want beef pretty soon, and we need to be ready."

"I hear ya." Charlie shook his head. "I was thinkin' about joining up, but now I got this bum wing. It ain't fair, gettin' shot when you're a thousand miles from the nearest battlefield."

"Aw, Charlie, you're too old," Bud said.

"Who you callin' old?" Charlie's spine straightened, and he glared up at Bud. "I'm three years shy of forty, which I daresay is younger'n the likes of you." He turned and strode into the bunkhouse.

Rachel couldn't help smiling at Bud. "I guess you've offended him."

Bud shrugged and gathered his reins. "He'll get over it. Come on, let's go see how the men are doing. I put most of them to cutting firewood this morning. We get that done, and we'll start getting timber so we can build you that little cabin you want."

Her hopes rose. "So, you're still going to build it?"

Bud shrugged. "It'll take us a while, but yeah. Maybe by the time we get it raised, the sheriff will have got those yahoos."

Rachel rode along for a few minutes without speaking, but then she nudged Herald up close to Bud's horse. "Do you think I'm doing the right thing?"

"What do you mean?"

"Keeping the ranch and wanting to come live here."

"Well, now, that's not for me to say, Miss Rachel."

"But you'll stay on with me if I do it?"

"Of course."

"Thank you. But what about the men? Will they stay and work for a woman rancher?"

Bud pulled his gelding to a halt and looked over at her. "You want the truth?"

"Of course."

"Mostly, they think you're going to marry Matt Anderson."

"Why do they think that?"

"It's understandable. Your pa talked about it. You two seemed kinda friendly at the funeral, and Matt's been riding over here with you 'most every day."

Rachel was silent for a moment. She wanted to be angry, but she couldn't think of a good reason for that. "I wouldn't marry anyone just because my father thought it was a good idea."

"Course not. So … does this mean you won't?"

"Right now, I'm not thinking about marriage. Some days it seems like it's too hard to take on this job, and I wonder if I should go back East and teach school. But that's not what I want to do. Mostly, I want to work the ranch my father left me, and I think I can do a good job of it." She didn't mention the letter she had sent, exploring the likelihood of landing a job at a school.

Bud nodded. "I'm sure you could if you put your mind to it. Still, I reckon the boys will expect you to get married sometime. Not many women stay single long out here. 'Specially not ones that own land."

"I see."

"Well, I coulda said handsome ones, but I guess that goes without sayin'."

Rachel smiled. "Thank you, Bud."

"Don't mention it. But you know Telly and I will stick with

you, no matter what. The boss brought us up here from Texas, and we're both set on staying until you decide you've had enough."

"That means a lot."

Bud clucked to his horse, and their mounts moved into a jog.

11

St. Louis, Missouri
May 16, 1863

Ryland Atkins left his valise with the stationmaster at the depot in St. Louis. He had plenty of time to stroll around outside and find a place where he could buy lunch. The next train wouldn't roll out for more than two hours.

Now that he'd crossed the Mississippi, the rail service would be spotty. While several companies had short lines running in Missouri, as well as in California and other isolated places, only one major line ran westward from here. War activity had stalled construction.

The rail lines ran to Independence, but if he needed to travel any distance from the Union Pacific's line, it would have to be by stagecoach. That would be a new experience for Ryland. He almost hoped he'd have to go farther west, so he could get a glimpse of the prairies and mountains, not to mention the bison herds and Indian warriors.

He sauntered out of the depot and along the streets, carrying his new cane. In Tarrytown, he'd replaced the ebony one Mr.

Turner gave him with a walnut stick that acted as a sheath for a sword. He hoped he wouldn't need it, but he'd heard stories about the West. Most men out there wore handguns, it seemed, or if not most, at least a good proportion of them.

He wouldn't stoop to buying a pistol—at least not yet. The cane, with its burnished brass handle, gave him confidence, but he still stayed alert and kept away from lonely spots where a thug might attack him. That was an experience he had no desire to repeat.

St. Louis was a large, impressive town. Though still raw, it held several substantial buildings and showed all the signs of a growing, booming city. If only they could find a way to bridge the Mississippi.

His wait on the eastern shore had bored him to tears, but when the time finally came, he'd found himself unprepared for the ferry ride over the rushing, muddy torrent. The water was high, everyone said. They'd seen flooding the previous month, when the snowmelt and runoff had reached its peak. To Ryland, the river's present condition was bad enough. He'd have hated to face it at flood stage.

He found a restaurant inside one of the nearby hotels and ordered the dinner special—fried chicken, baked potato, spring greens, and fresh-baked bread. It sounded and smelled better than anything he'd been able to procure during his last few days riding the rails.

While he waited, he took his small notepad from his inner pocket. He'd read over the facts he gleaned in New York dozens of times, but reviewing them had become a habit. These were the clues that would help him find the missing children Mrs. Rose longed so desperately to see.

The waiter brought Ryland's plate and filled his coffee cup. He put the notebook away, but he didn't need to see the words to remember his mission.

Given a seeming dead end on Jane in Brooklyn, Ryland had

traveled up the Hudson River to Tarrytown. He had set aside the problem of Jane for later consideration. Zephaniah Joseph Cooper was barely eight years old when his bounder of a father had abandoned the children in White Plains. A child old enough to read and write when he was adopted might be easier to find than an infant.

Again Ryland was disappointed. The Anderson family had not lived in Tarrytown for some time. It seemed half of America had pulled up stakes and moved west. It was hard for him to imagine. His own family had lived in Portland, Maine, for more than a hundred years. His parents, siblings, and cousins all lived within an hour of his home.

How could people uproot themselves so thoroughly as the Andersons and the Weavers seemed to have done? Setting out for an unknown territory without ties back home would take a very strong-willed person.

Ryland had set down all the facts in his report to Mr. Turner, but composing his letter to Mrs. Rose had been more difficult. He detailed for her all of the people he'd questioned and the lack of solid information about the children, but he hadn't much hope to offer this time. After two solid days of digging and interviewing people in Tarrytown, he'd gotten one clue. Mrs. Anderson had a sister in Middletown, New York, a short distance to the west. He'd taken a train there.

Two days later, he'd located the sister. From her, he learned the Andersons had headed west twelve years earlier, with their adopted son Matthew in tow.

"The boy would have been around fourteen at the time," Matthew's aunt told him.

"What was he like?" Ryland asked.

She rubbed her arms and gazed off toward the lowering sun. "He was a good boy, intelligent, and willing to work hard. His parents adored him."

"I'm glad to hear it."

"He was always respectful," she added. "They picked a good one when they took him in."

Ryland put her words in his next letter to Mrs. Rose, knowing it would give her satisfaction. The aunt's assessment boded well for his search. If the boy had come to love his adoptive family, chances were, he'd stayed with them into adulthood.

"I had some bad news along about five years ago, though," the aunt told him. "My sister passed on in Missouri."

"I'm so sorry," Ryland said.

She sniffed. "I miss her, though I didn't see her often. Her husband gave up his farm near Independence and moved farther west. I believe he's now in what they call the Colorado Territory."

"And the boy went with him?" Ryland asked.

"Yes, so far as I know, though I haven't heard anything since. He'd be a man now."

"So, you don't have a current address?"

She shook her head. "Sorry. I'd like to know what became of them."

In addition to his letter, Ryland sent a telegram to Mrs. Rose, so she would get the bare facts quickly. It was longer than he liked to make them, at fifty cents a word, but she sent back a message for Ryland in just a few hours.

"Go on to Independence."

She'd advanced him enough money via Mr. Turner for such an eventuality, and Ryland was able to draw from a Middletown bank enough to take him westward by train. The wonders of modern communication! The amount he withdrew for his ticket and other expenses seemed exorbitant, but he reminded himself that Mrs. Rose could afford it, and finding her grandchildren was worth a great deal to her. He only hoped he wouldn't disappoint her.

Mr. Turner, on receiving a copy of his full report, had

telegraphed, "Do as client wishes. More funds to your acct if needed."

Ryland had tried, before leaving the state of New York, to get more information about John Anderson's family. Anderson hadn't kept in touch with his wife's sister for the last five years, but Ryland reasoned that surely he would write to his own kin. His sister-in-law had given Ryland a general idea of where John's parents and siblings lived.

He'd spent more time in rural New York but had turned up nothing further that would help him, and at last he'd decided it was time to head for Missouri. With any luck, he'd learn something more specific in Independence, where John Anderson had farmed for several years.

Ryland would be glad when he could send some real news to the old woman who waited so stoically in the sea captain's rambling house in Maine. He could picture her granddaughter, Abigail, taking his letter from the postman and running eagerly into the parlor. "Grandmother, we've news from Mr. Atkins," she would say, her blue eyes shining.

Ryland took out his pocket watch. He still had plenty of time, so he ordered a piece of pie and more coffee. As he ate, his thoughts roved back to New England, not to the rustic, rowdy West that he faced. Instead of the young man who was now called Matthew Anderson, in his mind's eye he saw the fair face of Abigail Benson. Ryland wasn't homesick exactly, but he wouldn't be sorry when the time came to head back to Maine, and he'd welcome the chance to see that comely face again.

Anderson Ranch

MATT CARRIED his saddle into the barn and slung it over the rail where he always put it at the end of the day. He frowned when he noticed that the rack for Rachel's sidesaddle was empty. He walked outside and stared toward the south and the Box M ranch. Her new cattle had arrived on Wednesday, and for the last three days, she'd spent long hours at her ranch. He could understand that. But the sun was setting, and she ought to be safely home by now.

Confound that woman! It was bad enough that she sneaked into his thoughts a hundred times a day—little memories of the tilt of her head or the sparkle in her deep brown eyes when she talked about her father's ranch. Now he had to worry about her, too.

He turned to get his saddle but stopped. Was that hoofbeats? He held his breath and squinted into the fading light. Sure enough, two horses loped in from the range.

When they got within spitting distance, Herald pulled ahead of the cowboy's horse. She rode into the yard and turned, lifting an arm to wave. The cowboy signaled back with a flourish of his hat and turned his pony homeward.

Matt walked over to help Rachel dismount, but she bounced to the ground before he got there.

"It's late," he said.

She smiled wearily and lifted the stirrup leather. "Yes, it is. The men had a job to finish, and I hated to take one of them away until it was done."

"Here, I'll get that." Matt stepped forward and reached for the cinch strap.

"I can do it." She kept on working the leather.

As soon as the cinch was free, Matt reached to lift the saddle down. "I'll take this inside for you."

"I don't need help."

He paused and tried not to frown at her exasperated tone. "I mean no offense, Rachel."

She stood for a moment, the leather strap still in her hand, then let it fall. "Forgive me. I sounded awfully like Vida just now, didn't I?"

"Has she been rude to you again?"

"No more than usual. I suspect it's just her personality."

"She doesn't take too well to strangers." Matt smiled. "I didn't mean to question your ability. I was thinking you must be tired, is all, and that I could ease that a little."

"It's kind of you. Thank you. It's just that all day long, the men over at the Box M treat me like glass. They try not to curse in front of me, and they've all dusted off their best manners. I can't decide if they're that way with all women, or if they're afraid I'll fire them."

Matt pulled the saddle off Herald's back. "I expect it seems a little odd to them, working for a woman. They'll get used to it." He took the saddle into the barn, and when he came out, Rachel had turned her horse out in the corral and was closing the gate.

He took the bridle from her. "How are you doing?" he asked softly. "It must be hard for you. I've thought a lot about your father this week, and what it must be like for you, losing him in such a senseless way."

"I miss him. But I was always a solitary child, so I've spent a lot of time alone." Rachel looked up at him in the dusk. "After Mama died, I was horribly lonely. Papa and I stuck together like burrs, until I went away to school. He even took me as far as Illinois, so I wouldn't have to ride the stagecoach alone, and only left me when I got on the train."

"That was good of him," Matt said.

"I'm so glad he did. It was the last time we were together. All the time I was away, it was a comfort to me, knowing he was waiting for me. Even though I wouldn't go home to the same house I'd known before, Papa would be here, and we'd make this our new home together."

"I'm very sorry."

"I know. Thank you." A faint smiled twitched the corners of

her mouth. "I guess you know what it's like, most of it. You lost your mother, too, and I guess you're an only child like I am."

"Actually, I'm not an only child." Matt usually let it pass when people mentioned it, but Rachel seemed in a mood to talk about personal things, and besides, he owed her transparency to make up for his initial deception with her.

Her eyes opened wider, reflecting lamplight that flowed from the parlor window. "You're not? Are they older?"

"No. Younger, a brother and a sister."

"Oh." She said no more but eyed him uncertainly.

"They didn't die, if that's what you're thinking," he said quickly. "At least, not that I know of." His voice cracked. He hated that—it made him sound much younger than he was, and weak somehow. But what was wrong with thinking about your family?

"What happened to them?" Her low voice sounded almost fearful.

"I was adopted. Janie, my baby sister, was adopted too. A family took her. I don't know what happened to Elijah." The ache in his heart when he thought about them hurt more than the nagging pain in his leg.

"When did this happen?" Rachel asked.

"After our mother died. My first mother, that is, not Ma Anderson. Our name was Cooper." He chuckled, though it hurt. "My Christian name was Zephaniah. Can you beat that?"

"Zephaniah? Did you have a nickname?"

"I mostly went by my middle name—Joseph. Joey, they called me. I was named after my grandfather."

"Zephaniah Cooper?"

"No." Matt looked up at the sky and automatically searched for the North Star. "His name was Rose. Captain Zephaniah Rose."

"He was a military man?"

Matt shook his head. "A sea captain. I don't remember him—

haven't seen him since I was really small. But my ma used to tell me about him, and how he was sailing off to lots of far places. Once when he got home from a voyage, he sent her a bolt of calico and a pound of the finest tea from India. She made herself a dress from the cloth, and little shirts for me and my brother, Elijah, that matched."

"That's nice."

"Another time, he sent an odd coin for each of us kids. A coin with a hole in it."

The door to the house opened, and his father peered out at them.

"There you are. Are you young folks going to eat supper?"

"Sure, Pa. We're just coming." Matt gestured for Rachel to go before him and followed her to the door.

12

Rachel tried to relax in the little round tub of warm water, but she couldn't, not while she knew Matt and his father were waiting for their turns in the washtub. They'd have to heat their own water on the cookstove downstairs and move the tub when she was done. As awkward as the situation was, she managed to bathe thoroughly and wash her flowing brown hair.

Clad in her robe, she stepped into the hall and called over the railing, "All finished with the tub."

She went back into her room and dipped out two buckets of the cooling, soapy water. The men would have to empty at least half of it before they could carry the tub out. Hearing footsteps in the hall, she ducked behind a fabric screen that would partially shield her.

"Excuse us," Mr. Anderson said. "We'll get right out of your way."

"It's not a problem." She took up her comb and began to work on her hair from the ends up. Having hair that didn't smell like smoke seemed a great luxury. Though the smell had faded at the Box M unless she went close to the ruin, the scent seemed to cling to her clothing and hair every day. Since her train journey, she hadn't felt truly clean, but now the fragrance of lavender hung about her. She felt feminine again.

When the men had removed the tub and the buckets, she hung up her towels and set the room straight, then sat on the edge of the bed to finish working on her hair. This was the one thing she hated about waist-length tresses—they took so long to care for. It would be worth it, though, to appear in church tomorrow as a well-groomed lady, not a rough-and-tumble hobbledehoy.

When all of the snarls were gone, she plaited her hair and tied it at the bottom with a satin ribbon. She opened the wardrobe, where the altered blue dress hung next to her green riding habit. She hadn't worn a hoopskirt since the day she arrived, but surely Sunday was the proper day to resume wearing them.

Would the other women in the community wear hoopskirts to church? She frowned and fingered each one of her dresses. She didn't want to impress them as being rich and snobbish. That would almost be comical, in light of her current homeless state.

It occurred to her that she ought to wear her black dress again, but she gave up the thought. In Texas, people hadn't followed the "rules" of mourning the way they did back East. She doubted the Colorado ranchers did either. Still, she wouldn't want people to think she didn't feel her father's death. She decided on her most sedate dress with the cage crinoline—a gray bombazine with black soutache braid trim. She could add her black lace shawl and forgo any jewelry.

Rachel determined to mingle with the other women tomorrow, and if possible, to make a friend. She needed someone to talk to out here. Vida, the only woman to whom she had ready access, seemed to have taken an intense dislike to her. But there must be some ranch wife or shopkeeper's daughter who would be nice to her. Rachel craved feminine company—

someone with whom she could discuss the ranch and her future, and yes, even the taciturn men she spent her days with.

She'd lived around cowboys most of her life, but somehow she couldn't read Matt Anderson. Perhaps understanding him wasn't necessary—and yet, she wanted to. What did he think of her, really? Had his nerves kicked up the day their conniving fathers had sent him to get her at the stage stop? If so, he'd hidden it well. Maybe he'd assumed she would like him—after all, he was friendly and handsome.

The only thing he seemed self-conscious about was his limp. She hadn't noticed it that first day. But the following morning, when he'd taken her to the ranch to meet with Bud before the funeral, he'd favored his left leg. Was he injured in the scuffle with the outlaws? Now she'd had time to observe him, and it seemed a chronic thing, but not too severe.

She closed the wardrobe, turned back the bedclothes, and blew out the lamp. In the darkness, she climbed into bed and pulled the sheet and quilt up around her neck. Why was she worrying about Matt Anderson? If she stayed here, he'd be her neighbor. Nothing more. And if she went back East ...

Until that moment, she hadn't realized she was seriously considering that course of action. Had her declaration to Bud and Mr. Leigh been a bluff?

Once she had settled down at the ladies' seminary, she'd enjoyed the academic life and the social opportunities she'd had in the city. Even if she had to earn her living there, life in the East would be much easier than here on the frontier. Was that what she wanted?

She could write again to Miss Edgerly and inquire about specific positions. Her mentor might know of a place in a school for girls of means. Rachel thought she'd enjoy teaching and being part of the world of education again. But she'd miss the outdoors, the horses, and the wide open spaces. This was the home her father had chosen, and he'd been certain she would love it. She would, too, if only he were here to share it with her.

Downstairs, a door closed. Had one of the men gone outside or come in? Maybe Matt was out there now, looking up at the sky, or checking on the horses in the corral. Perhaps he was strolling over to the bunkhouse to talk to the hands.

She rolled over and closed her eyes. What was she thinking about him for, anyway?

Monday, May 18

MATT CLOSED the door to his bedroom. The trip into town for Sunday services had gone well, and he and his father had ridden out to their western border after dinner to check on the cattle out there. So far, they'd seen no signs of the outlaws breaching their property. While they were gone, Rachel had stayed at the ranch. He was glad she didn't go to the Box M on Sundays, but he hadn't any idea how she'd spent the afternoon. Reading, maybe, or sewing.

He went to the wardrobe and opened it. He hadn't taken his uniform out in months, but now he removed it and held it up for scrutiny. If he was going to wear it again, it would need some repair. The trousers he'd worn at Glorieta Pass were ruined, and he'd come home in an ill-fitting pair of canvas pants given to him at the supply depot. He'd need a new pair for certain.

He reached up to the shelf and took down his cartridge box, hat, and belt. Those were in better condition. He sat on the bed and studied the belt plate on the cartridge box strap. An eagle was embossed on the round brass fitting. It was the belt buckle that interested him more, though. The oval plate was embossed with *U.S.* in large letters, encircled by a raised edge.

The one Bud took off the fallen outlaw and handed over to the sheriff didn't have the raised outline—he'd been right about that. It wasn't the current army issue. Maybe its owner was a veteran of the Mexican War a few years back. He'd certainly looked old enough.

He realized he'd been rubbing his thigh as he pondered the matter. His leg ached, as it did most evenings. Was he pushing himself too hard? He couldn't march all day in his present condition, and he really wasn't fit to stay in the saddle more than an hour or two at a time. But if he waited until he'd completely recovered, the war would be over.

Heavy footsteps sounded on the stairs, and he jumped up. His father was headed for bed, and he sometimes stopped by Matt's room to say goodnight. If he saw the uniform lying on the bed, he'd be hurt. Not upset, exactly, but sad that Matt was thinking of leaving again.

Quickly he shoved the leather straps and hat up onto the shelf and dropped the tunic and pants on the wardrobe floor. As he closed the doors, a knock came at the door.

"Come in."

His father opened the door and smiled wearily at him. "Just came to say good night, son."

"I'm going to bed, too, Pa."

"Think you'll be able to help drive the herd to the upper range tomorrow?"

"Sure," Matt said, though he knew he'd suffer for it.

His father nodded. "I'll send three others with you. Any preference?"

"Not really. They're all good workers, though Jimmy's a little green."

"Take Royal and Josh, then, and Ruthless, I guess. I need to go into town. Pete and Jimmy can stay here to help Pard with things around the barn."

"All right." Matt hesitated. "Pa?"

"Yeah?" His father's chin came up, and he arched his eyebrows.

"That belt buckle the outlaw had on him ..."

"What about it?"

"I think it's from the last war."

"You mean, Mexico?"

Matt nodded. "Didn't Bob Maxwell fight with Winfield Scott?"

"Yes, I recall him telling about it more than once."

"Funny how things come around," Matt said.

RACHEL COULD TELL Matt's leg hurt him, especially in the evenings. He never mentioned it, but they could all see his limp was worse when he'd spent a long day in the saddle. Mr. Anderson showed his fatigue, too, but then, he was nearly fifty years old. Still, he was out there every day with his men. Watching them gave Rachel a new appreciation for all her father had done to build his ranch.

All week, she went back and forth to the Box M daily. Bud directed the men in branding the new cattle and settling them in on the Maxwell range. She'd learned a great deal from the foreman, and from watching the men go about their work with no wasted motions or nonsense. They all seemed to take their duties seriously, perhaps because of the tragic attack.

They kept a couple of men on guard each night, to make sure no one tried to steal the new stock. But so far, all was quiet. The men had laid sills for her new cabin, and she hoped to be able to move soon.

The next Sunday, she spent the afternoon in her room, though it would have been a pleasant time to sit on the front porch in the warm spring breeze. Matt and his father had installed themselves in comfortable chairs there, and she didn't want to get into conversation with them just now. Matt's father seemed determined to advise her on how to run the ranch. Next he'd be giving her men orders behind her back.

And Matt—what about him? She didn't like to admit it, but the young man was growing on her. She'd said she wouldn't marry him—but then, he hadn't asked. Was she foolish to dismiss him so thoroughly when she didn't know him well?

Before she knew of his deception, when she'd thought he was one of the Box M's ranch hands, she'd liked him. True, she'd thought him a little forward in their conversation in the wagon.

She stood and paced to the window. Attempts to look at that first day rationally always ended in confusion, with the news of her father's death. Matt hadn't actually lied to her, that she could recall. She knew now he'd been following his father's wishes—and her own father had wanted it too. Perhaps Papa had even come up with the plan that forced her to spend an hour alone with Matthew and see what a fine young man he was.

If indeed he was a fine young man. Whenever she thought about the raid on her father's ranch, she wound up in tears, so she'd stopped trying to think it through. But she needed to view the events of that day clearly. Matt had surely gone to aid her father and his men. Bud had told her that he'd helped them win the fracas and drive off the outlaws.

But where had Mr. Anderson been when she arrived at his house? He and most of his outfit hadn't been near the house. Pard Henry had met her in the dooryard and said he knew where the boss was and would fetch him. Was it possible that Mr. Anderson had been among the outlaws until Pard advised him of her arrival? The timing of the attack had put Rachel at the Andersons' mercy. Might the outlaws have been John Anderson's hired hands?

No, she wouldn't believe that. It was too crazy, too sinister. Surely Bud and the others would have recognized some of them if they'd been local men. And they'd killed a couple of the marauders. Her men all agreed—no one recognized them.

She tried to shake off her suspicions, but a faint doubt lingered. Mr. Anderson's desire to combine the ranches permeated almost every conversation they had these days. How could she ever trust the Andersons completely if she didn't know for sure if they were involved? She'd be glad when she was no longer living under their roof.

She wished she had another woman to talk to. The church ladies were kind to her, and she'd enjoyed talking with them on Sunday mornings, but there never seemed to be enough time to really get to know anyone. A few disjointed conversations, and then the Anderson men were ready to head back to the ranch.

Perhaps one of the town women would eventually become a friend and confidante, but she needed guidance now. And could she really share these misgivings with a person who knew and probably liked the Andersons?

With a sigh, she looked down over the barnyard. Most of the men had the day off and were probably amusing themselves in the bunkhouse or in town. Three had ridden into town for church in the morning, tailing the boss's wagon, and they'd not yet returned to the ranch. Maybe they were off visiting their sweethearts—or engaging in less uplifting pursuits at one of the saloons in Fort Lyon. Those establishments never seemed to close their doors.

A phrase from the morning's sermon came to mind. The minister had read from a well-known passage in the book of Philippians. *My God shall supply all your need, according to his riches in glory by Christ Jesus.* Rachel had memorized the verse as a child, under her mother's prompting. But how often had she remembered it in the last few years—and did she really believe it?

She went to the small table she used as a desk and sat down again.

"Lord, I guess I'm lonely. I ought to have a better reason to come to You. I know there's no better friend." She let out a deep breath. God did care about her plight. "Please, Lord," she whispered, "show me what to do."

For a long minute she sat, waiting and hoping, but no answer echoed in the still room. What did she expect, really? A voice from heaven? A disembodied hand, writing on the wall?

She saw three options available to her. She could stay and run the ranch alone, in which case, she wanted to move to her own property as soon as possible. Bud and the other men were building the house for her, but they didn't have a lot of time to spare, and the project would probably take a few more weeks. And when she did move, would she always be afraid and distrustful of her neighbors?

The second option was to stay and marry—whether to Matthew or someone else. She was sure Colorado had no dearth of suitors for a young, healthy woman of property. Or she could sell the ranch and go back East. But that choice wasn't viable unless she had a place to go. What harm would come of exploring the possibility?

She took out writing paper, a pen, and a bottle of ink. This time she didn't hint about eventually going back East. She asked outright what her prospects were. Miss Edgerly would tell her how feasible it would be for her to find a teaching position, and in all probability, offer to give her a reference. Surely by fall, something would open up for Rachel—but only if she let it be known she was looking.

Already she had explained to her mentor about her father's death, but her carefully couched inquiry had remained tentative. She put her pen to the paper. Even now, she confessed, she wasn't certain she wanted to pursue a teaching career, but she was curious as to the likelihood she could find a job.

She read it over twice. Satisfied, she addressed an envelope and placed the letter in it. She didn't have any stamps. She could ask Matt. On second thought, sending it to town with one of the men from the Box M seemed like a better course. She'd told Matt she was staying. No use alerting him or his father that she was corresponding with Miss Edgerly.

WHEN DUSTY TOOK Rachel home Monday evening, she found Pard Henry in the barn. He had a bay horse in crossties and was working on one of its front feet.

Rachel carried her saddle to the harness room and ambled out to watch him.

"Horse lost a shoe?" she asked.

"That's right. Royal took him up into the rocks—like a fool kid would."

Rachel smiled. Royal was past twenty, but still green as far as ranch hands went.

"I hope nobody's hurt."

"No, this fellow will be good as new when I tack this shoe on, and Royal's fine, though no brighter than he ever was. Oughter have his hide blistered." Pard stuck a couple of horseshoe nails between his teeth and bent over his work.

When he put the gelding's hoof down a few minutes later, Rachel said, "Didn't you and Vida ride into town this morning? How did it go?" She'd learned not to ask Vida such things, as she wouldn't get a polite reply, let alone information.

"It went all right." Pard straightened for a moment with his hand at the small of his back and then reached to grab a rasp from his toolbox. "They don't have many pretties in Fort Lyon. I told her maybe I'd take her to Denver this fall, if things go well with the herd this summer."

"Oh?" Rachel said. That would be quite an outing for the couple. "Didn't she find anything at the mercantile?"

"Well, she saw some calico she thought was purty, but when I told her to get a dress length, she said no. Too dear, and too bright, she said."

Rachel smiled. "What color was it?"

"Red, figured all over with brown and gold leaves. I thought she'd look right smart in it of a Sunday."

"Maybe one of the traders coming down the Santa Fe Trail will bring something she likes better," Rachel suggested.

"Aw, she liked it all right. She just didn't like the price. Vida's pretty close with her purse. But her birthday's coming up next month. I gotta get her somethin'." Pard filed the clinches of the nails on the bay's hoof and let the horse stand on his new shoe. "There." He looked over at Rachel and smiled.

"Good job done," she said. "If you don't mind me asking, what day is Vida's birthday?"

13

Portland, Maine
May 27, 1863

Abby Benson let her grandmother hold her arm as they mounted the front steps at Rosemont.

"I must be getting old."

"Why do you say that?" Abby asked, holding up her long skirt with her free hand.

Grandmother grimaced. "Two calls, and I'm worn out. Why, I used to pay a dozen calls in an afternoon." She puffed a little as they drew up before the front door.

Abby opened it and drew her inside. "Those were duty calls, where you left your card and moved on, I'm guessing. We actually stopped to talk with Mrs. Baye and Mrs. Franklin."

"Well, yes, but that means we actually sat still most of the afternoon. I'm still tired."

"There's plenty of time for a nap before dinner." Abby glanced at the hall table. "Oh, look, the post has come."

"I forgot all about it," Grandmother said. "Let's have a look."

Abby scooped up the three envelopes from the silver tray.

Her heart thudded. "There's one from Mr. Atkins. Perhaps he has some news."

"He telegraphed us from that Julesburg place." Grandmother shook her head as she drew off her black gloves. "No doubt this was written before that."

"But still, he'll give us some details." Abby squinted at the postmark. "I think it was canceled in Independence."

"Mr. Turner told us he had to move on from there. Well, let's see what he has to say about it. Bring it into my sitting room, child."

Abby was only too happy to do so. She loved reading Mr. Atkins's reports. He put in such colorful details about the places he went to, and though he had yet to find any of her cousins, he always held out hope the next stop would be more productive.

Once Grandmother was installed in her favorite chair, with her feet on the ottoman Grandfather had brought her from somewhere in the Far East, Abby sat down on the sofa and opened the envelope.

"My dear Mrs. Rose and Miss Benson." For some reason, her cheeks warmed at the fact that Mr. Atkins had included her in his salutation. Abby knew the "my dear" was just a formality, but even so, she liked to think the young man cared about them and truly wanted to bring them happiness by succeeding at his mission.

"I hope the receipt of this letter finds you both in good health and spirits."

"Mm." Grandmother settled further into the cushions of her well-padded chair. "He has such a nice manner."

"Oh, yes," Abby said. "Only a gentleman could write letters like Mr. Atkins does."

The elderly woman didn't give her opinion on that but leaned her head back and closed her eyes. "Go on."

Abby lowered her gaze once more to the letter. Mr. Atkins

had such a strong, masculine script. It was a pleasure just looking at it.

"I made my way to Independence, at your request, making nearly all of the journey by rail. When I reached the Mississippi, of course I had to take a ferry across to St. Louis. I considered riding a boat all the way up the Missouri River to Independence, but I found some arguments against that. While the journey would be less expensive than a train, it would also be slower, and it seems there have been some outbreaks of sickness among passengers on the crowded riverboats, so I deemed it wiser to continue as far as I could by railroad."

Abby turned the page with a sigh. "He writes so beautifully."

Grandmother emitted what sounded like a genteel snort. "He's only explaining why his expenses are so high."

"Do you think so?" Abby frowned. "I wasn't thinking that at all. Besides, in choosing the train, he got there quicker, and I know he wants to find my cousins as soon as possible."

Grandmother made no reply, and Abby quickly found her place at the top of the back page.

"In Independence, I found a rough town, growing quickly but still a bit wild. Here I feel I have truly entered the West—more so than at St. Louis, which had many fine churches, grand business buildings, and a few large and respectable hotels. Independence seems to be a step or two behind, still dealing with growing pains. I must be on guard at all times against ruffians."

"My heavens, I do hope he'll get on with it," Grandmother murmured.

Patsy appeared in the doorway. "Begging your pardon, madam, but I didn't hear you come in. Would you ladies like tea?"

Grandmother waved her away.

"We took tea with Mrs. Baye," Abby explained. "I'm just

reading the mail to Grandmother, and then I think she will lie down until dinner."

"Let me know if you want my assistance," Patsy said.

Abby nodded, and the maid went out.

"Let's see …" Abby skimmed down the page. "Here we go. 'I found a suitable room and asked the clerk about the Anderson family as I checked in. He directed me to the post office. As there were still a couple of hours left before it closed, I went there straightaway. The postmaster informed me that the farm where Mr. John Anderson had sojourned was about six miles outside town. On his advice, I decided to wait until morning to venture there.'"

"I suppose that makes sense," Grandmother said.

Abby looked up. "He wouldn't want to be caught after dark in a strange area, especially one with ruffians hanging about." She went back to the letter. "The next day—that is, yesterday—I hired a horse and trap and drove out to the farm. It took me about an hour to find it. I regret to say the house and outbuildings were in a poor state. Of course, Mr. Anderson left there about five years previous, and so it's likely they were in better condition when he had the place."

"I certainly hope so," Grandmother murmured. "I don't like to think of young Joey living with a shiftless family."

Pursuing that train of thought would be unprofitable, so Abby read on. "The current owner, a Mr. Ogden, told me he bought the farm directly from John Anderson. It was his understanding that Mr. Anderson's wife had recently died when he sold the property. He also remembered that Mr. Anderson had a son of eighteen or twenty, who was planning to travel west with his father. I know this news will hearten you, as it did me."

Grandmother made a small sound of approval.

"While the farmer could not describe the young man to me in detail, I am all but certain this was your grandson, Zephaniah

Joseph Cooper. Unfortunately, Mr. Ogden had no specific direction for me, except that Anderson mentioned to him that they planned to go to the Colorado Territory and raise beef—and Ogden's wife confirmed this."

"Colorado," Grandmother said, eyeing Abby through slits of eyes. "Is that on the other side of Kansas?"

"I believe so." Abby tried to remember the geography lessons she'd had in school, but she'd finished her education more than a year ago, and it had become a bit hazy. "Isn't it what used to be the Jefferson Territory, or part of it?"

"Oh, yes. That's where the mines are. All that talk about silver mines and new gold strikes."

"That's right—in the mountains. But it can't be all mountains, if Mr. Anderson thinks it's a place suitable for raising cattle."

"I'm sure I don't know." Grandmother shook her head. "I'm afraid I know more about Calcutta and Singapore than I do the Colorado Territory, thanks to my husband."

Abby didn't doubt it. Upstairs was a whole room devoted to the captain's logs and maps—charts, he'd called them—and books about the foreign places he'd visited, as well as a small sandalwood box that held his treasured letters to his family.

She looked at the last paragraph of Mr. Atkins's letter. "Listen to this. 'I spent another day here in Independence, talking to neighbors of the Ogdens and some other people in town, trying to discover more about the Anderson family's actions. The only further clue I received was from a man at the feed store. He told me John Anderson had mentioned he planned to take the Oregon Trail until it cut off for Denver and enter the territory from the north."

"Really?" Grandmother said.

Abby nodded and resumed reading. "That was all he could tell me, but it will be my course unless I discover more along the way. Some of the stage routes have been disrupted, but I plan to take a coach tomorrow, through Kansas and Nebraska, and make my way toward Fort Laramie. I shall send you further word as I travel.' And he signed it, 'Your humble servant, Ryland Atkins.'"

"Hmpf," said Grandmother. "He is probably a good way along that trail now."

"Yes. And we know he made it as far as Julesburg from his telegram." Abby folded the letter. "Perhaps I shall go down to Captain Shaw's store at the wharf tomorrow."

"Whatever for?" Grandmother sat up, fully awake now.

"He carries all sorts of maps, and he might let me look at one of the West."

"Nautical charts, child. There are no oceans in the Great American Desert."

"You don't think he'd have something?"

"The free library might. You may go there, but take Patsy. I shan't have my granddaughter going about the city alone—or down to the waterfront, either."

"Yes, Grandmother. Forgive me—it was an impetuous thought."

The old woman nodded and scooted forward in her chair. "Help me up, Abigail. I shall go to my room now."

Abby lent her strength to the old woman, but as she helped Grandmother to her room and assisted in removing her voluminous black mourning dress, she couldn't help thinking about the dashing young man who was out there, braving the West, complete with the Iron Horse and innumerable ruffians, to complete their quest. She wished she was the one venturing into the untamed territory.

Perhaps she'd inherited Captain Rose's wanderlust. She had no explanation, but she felt a powerful desire to be with Ryland Atkins, scouring the plains and the mountain valleys for her vanished cousins.

RACHEL CONTINUED to ride back and forth each day to her own property. Usually, Matt rode with her in the morning, and Bud or one of the Box M cowboys brought her home. She was getting to know Dusty, Sam, and Telly quite well.

On Wednesday evening, when Dusty brought her back to the Andersons' ranch, a letter addressed to her was waiting on her pillow. One of the men must have gone to town for the mail, and Vida had placed her letter in her room.

The envelope was addressed in Miss Edgerly's fine, flowing script. She must have received Rachel's first letter and responded right away. It was too soon for her to have answered the second. Rachel put away her hat and gloves and tore the envelope open.

My dear Rachel, it was so good to hear from you! I have thought of you often since you left, wondering how you fared as you journeyed across this rough land.

Tears sprang into Rachel's eyes as she read the lines. More than ever, she missed her friend.

Your letter gives me hope that you might one day return to Boston, or at least come east again. If you ever decide to do this, please let me know. With your education, knowledge, and communication skills, you could secure a position in nearly any school in the North. Good teachers are sought after, and of course, I would highly recommend your services.

It was more than Rachel hoped for in response to her vague first letter. When Miss Edgerly got her next missive, she would probably go into motion. Was that what Rachel wanted?

She hated wavering on any topic, and this was too important to let it hang undecided for long. She laid the letter down and began to pray in earnest. *Lord, I am of two minds. I would like to stay here—and yet, I expect I'd be much more comfortable back East. I don't want to be a burden on the Andersons or on Bud and the other fellows at the Box M. Show me Your will.*

She sat still for a minute, thinking about her options. It wouldn't be fair to the men she employed to sell the ranch suddenly, without giving them warning enough to secure new jobs if they wanted to. And it wouldn't be fair to Miss Edgerly to vacillate long over whether or not she wanted a teaching position.

Show me what is best, Lord.

"WHAT DO you do all day over there?" Matt asked Rachel on Thursday morning as they crossed the range on horseback. It was the first time he had escorted her all week, and she was glad to have his company.

"Lots of things," she said. "Yesterday, I helped two of the men clear out the last of the burnt mess from the house. We loaded the wagon three times, and the men drove it off to a ravine and dumped it all out." She laughed ruefully. "I about ruined my clothes."

Matt looked at her dark blue skirt. "They look fine to me."

"That's because I spent an hour cleaning this dress last night. I suppose I should take time to sew another riding skirt."

"Are you pretty good at sewing?" Matt asked.

"I'd say so. My mother taught me, and it comes in handy." She hesitated only a moment. She didn't want to tread on Vida's territory, but perhaps this was a small way she could repay the Andersons for giving her room and board. "If you have anything that needs mending, I'd be happy to do it for you."

"That's very kind of you," he said.

"The men work on my cabin whenever they can, but it's going slower than I had hoped. It took a while to get those new cattle settled, and Bud keeps several men out watching the herd and riding the boundary lines all the time."

"You have to, I guess."

"Well, I hope I can move in by the end of June."

Did his frown mean he didn't want to see her leave his home for good?

She guided Herald across the ford in the stream that ran between their ranges. The water was lower than it had been since she'd arrived, but clouds hung over the valley, and she was sure they'd have more rain soon.

If this were a bright, sunny day, she would feel better about the ranch. Gloomy weather always made her doubt her abilities, especially now, when her success as a rancher depended on her working outside for hours each day. Bud had given her a slicker that had belonged to Billy Snow—the poor cowboy who'd died in the raid—but Rachel's wardrobe was still lacking in work clothes. Her next sewing project would definitely be another utilitarian riding skirt.

On the other side of the stream, Matt trotted his dun to catch up to her.

"I'm sorry to keep you or one of your men away from your work every morning," she said. "Don't you think I could ride this far by myself now? It's been over three weeks since the ranch was attacked."

"I don't think that would be wise yet," Matt replied. "The sheriff says the gang is still in the area. Every few days, they hear of another strike. Usually it's just a beef stolen, or a small amount of money, but still, no woman should be out alone in this country. If you truly intend to stay here, you'll have to work something out with Bud to protect you while you're out and about on your ranch."

"I still haven't completely decided what I'll do," she confessed. "I've enjoyed working with Bud and the other men these past few weeks, but I'm not sure all of them are comfortable working with me. Besides the work around the home place, they've been building a new holding pen for roundups."

"Has Bud ordered materials for your new house?"

Rachel shook her head. "They've cut some logs, but I don't want to waste the money on milled lumber if I'm not going to use it."

"But ... what would you do if you left here?"

She didn't really want to reveal her plans, so she shrugged. "I have friends in the East. I suppose I could take a stagecoach anytime I wanted."

"Well ..." Matt frowned. "Those outlaws hit one relay station, you know. Next thing, they'll be holding up stages and robbing them. I'd sure hate to see you travel alone."

"Matt, I traveled here alone all the way from Boston, in case you've forgotten."

"I haven't, and I'm glad you got here safely. But I'd feel terrible putting you on that stage again. At least until the outlaws are caught."

Rachel twisted in the saddle to observe his face. He seemed perfectly serious. "And is the sheriff making any progress on that, other than collecting reports of new thefts?"

"Not that I've heard."

Matt's attitude irked her. She supposed he was just being protective, and she ought to be thankful, but it felt like he was trying to limit her activities, and she hated that. She rode along in silence until they were within sight of the Box M barn.

"I'll be fine from here. Thank you for bringing me."

Matt's mouth twitched.

"What?" she asked.

"After what happened to your father, I'd just like to make sure. When we see Bud or one of your other men, I'll head out."

She gathered the reins. "Suit yourself." Clucking to Herald, she urged him into a lope. Telly and Bud emerged from the barn carrying their saddles. She waved and called to Matt, "See you later." She nudged Herald's side to make him go faster.

They couldn't stop her from going if she wanted to. She could pack her things and ride Herald to the stage depot in town any time she so desired. She wasn't afraid to ride a few miles alone on a sturdy horse. Matt's declaration that taking the stage was too dangerous made her feel hemmed in. She couldn't live on her own property without another woman, they'd told her. She couldn't ride horseback alone or take the stagecoach. The Andersons' ranch was fast becoming a prison.

"Whoa," Bud called, frowning as she barreled into the yard.

She tugged on the reins, and Herald stopped so hard he almost sat down. Rachel recovered her balance. If she had her way, she'd be riding astride by the end of the summer. It only made sense, even though the sidesaddle her father had bought for her was beautifully crafted.

"Morning," she said, avoiding Bud's stern look. She wanted to show Matt Anderson she could very well ride into town alone if she felt like it. But saying so in front of Bud and Telly was probably not a good idea.

14

Matt watched Rachel ride away from him, into the barnyard on the Box M. The paint horse's dark tail soared as he galloped smoothly across the grass. Rachel never looked back. From a distance, he saw Bud and Telly greet her. Matt turned his dun mare homeward. There was plenty to do on his father's ranch this morning.

Though he left Rachel behind, he couldn't rid his thoughts of her. As his horse jogged toward the stream, he reviewed their first meeting. Why had he agreed to the foolish plan? Now she thought he'd lied to her and was generally untrustworthy.

Obviously, she didn't enjoy his company on her morning rides to the Box M. While Matt didn't mind doing it, she was probably happier on the days one of the other men rode with her. Maybe he should permanently assign one of the ranch hands to see her safely across the range.

Once or twice, Rachel had seemed to open up to him a little. The evening they'd talked about their families, Matt thought they'd grown closer. But whenever the subject of her future came up, she avoided it. Had her father suggested other suitors before him? That might have gotten her riled up. Rachel had been thousands of miles away from home for several years. She'd come back to tragedy and an unfamiliar place. Had all the upheaval set her against him? No, she got along fine with some folks. It was just him. She didn't like him and his pa.

The only course he could see was to live in such a way that Rachel would see his true character—and to do his best to make his character worth noting.

Matt had always tried to honor the principles his stepparents had taught him. Before he went to the orphanage and then to the Andersons, his mother had tried to instill in him and his brother a foundation of integrity and faith. As to his father, back in New York, Matt really didn't remember much, except that he was often gone for days at a time.

Mama had always seemed anxious to please him. She would tell Matt and Elijah to be quiet when he was home, and to be careful not to make a mess. His father seemed to get exasperated easily by their childish ways. Sometimes he yelled at the boys, but on other days, he seemed happy-go-lucky and took them on an outing, or he brought home some extravagant gift or expensive food. Mama would protest he shouldn't have done it—not the polite way people said it, but seriously. He *really* shouldn't have.

Over the years since his birth mother's death, Matt had puzzled over his memories, but he never reached a resolution. The most vivid of his recollections were Mama's dying, and his father leaving him and Elijah and Jane with their neighbor a few days after the funeral. He'd be back soon to get them, Pa had promised. Matt remembered sitting on the Pruitts' front stoop, waiting for his father.

Day after day, he sat there. Sometimes Elijah would join him, but the younger boy grew restless after a while and wandered off. Jane would cry inside the house, and Matt would hear Mrs. Pruitt impatiently tell her to hush.

With a start, he realized he'd crossed the range without

seeing it and had reached home. Several hands had been assigned to clean out the barn this morning. They did it every year—got rid of the refuse that had collected and whitewashed the inside. The job was a dirty one and tiring, but he might as well help.

The men respected him and his father when they pitched in and worked alongside them. He turned his horse into the corral and carried the saddle inside. When he'd set it on the rack, he reached into his pocket for a moment.

His fingers stroked the strange coin he always carried on a leather thong. Captain Rose had brought one from China for each of his grandchildren. The coins had come to New York by post at Christmas time, with a few other gifts for them and their parents.

The curious coin was round but had a square hole in the middle. Both faces bore odd squiggles that his mother had said were Chinese writing. Matt carried it with him for almost two decades without losing it. Did Elijah still have his?

Once Elijah had said he wanted to buy candy with his. Matt had told him he couldn't spend Chinese money in America. It was just a remembrance of Grandfather Rose. Elijah hadn't seemed to care about it much after that, but Matt had made sure his little brother had it when their father left them in Mrs. Pruitt's care.

"Our cousins in Maine have them, too," he'd reminded Elijah. "If we ever see Abigail again, we can show her. We all have the same—Mama said so."

"Abigail …" Elijah got a faraway look on his face, and Matt had known at that moment he didn't remember Abigail or Grandfather Rose or their visit to the big, white house in Maine.

"Do you remember Grandmother Rose?" he asked. "She gave us lemon drops."

Elijah nodded.

"Well, you keep remembering," he said fiercely.

Later, when Mrs. Pruitt wasn't looking, Matt had checked once to make sure Janie still had her coin. Grandmother had mailed it after the baby was born, along with an elegant dress for Janie. After Mama died, Matt had tied the pink ribbon with the coin to Janie's ankle. Mama had done that once, saying it wasn't safe for a baby to wear anything around her neck, and Matt had remembered.

He wasn't sure if she'd still had it when she left the orphanage. Probably not. Probably that vile Mr. Cresswick had taken it, or one of the infant nurses. Matt had told himself hundreds of times she still had it, and someday, when he was grown, he'd find Janie, and she'd know he was truly her brother because they both had the Chinese coins their grandfather had brought from across the seas.

Now he knew that was extremely unlikely. If the orphanage employees hadn't taken it, the woman who adopted Janie had probably removed it first thing.

Matt sighed. He had more chance of finding his brother. If he ever did, he'd ask him first thing if he still had his Chinese coin.

"Dear God, keep Jane and Elijah safe, wherever they are." Matt stood for a moment with his hand on the seat of his worn stock saddle. "Thank you for putting me here, but please, Lord …" He didn't know what else to say.

"Hey, Matt!"

He swung around. Pard Henry stood by the divider of the stall space they used as a harness room. "You cleaning up in here? I can help move stuff out so's we can whitewash."

"Sure, why not?" Matt squared his shoulders and stooped to pick up a burlap sack. Whenever he got to thinking too hard about his family—his old family—he found a good, hard day's work helped him keep things in perspective.

Bart Finney and two of his men left their horses under cover of the trees and walked out into the grass. Bart nodded to Toad, and the short, wiry man stationed himself on the hillside, where he could look down toward the ranch. Bart and Jerry walked over to the little graveyard. Three wooden crosses stuck up from the earth, two over recent graves, and the third grown about with grass and weeds.

Bart stood before the nearest one, scowling. "That's him." A small knot of early wildflowers lay on the earth, below the cross with the words "Robert Maxwell" burned into the wooden crossbar.

"Billy Snowe here, and J. T. Aubrey yonder," Jerry said, nodding toward the other two crosses.

"One's a old grave," Bart noted. "Wonder where they put Lew and Hoho." He turned and studied the line of the hillside.

"Likely the sheriff hauled 'em off to town." Jerry spit in the grass.

"I wish you numbskulls hadn't burned Maxwell's house," Bart muttered.

"We searched it real thorough, Bart. There weren't no treasure box in that house, and we got what money he had."

"You can't know that for sure."

"I'm telling you, it wasn't in the house. You know he didn't leave it in Texas."

"Yeah, we made sure of that."

Jerry eyed him anxiously. "Either he didn't have it anymore, or he put it in the bank or some such."

Bart shook his head. "He coulda buried it."

He left Jerry and walked along the crest of the hill, toward an irregularity he'd spotted. He stopped when he came to a spot where two more splotches of turned earth marred the ground, and the grass was just starting to take hold again.

Jerry came and stood beside him. "You reckon that's them?"

"Yup."

"No markers."

Bart shook his head.

"You gonna do anything?" Jerry asked.

"Nope. Don't know who their kin are. Don't even know Hoho's real name, as far as that goes." Bart turned away. "They can stay there. It's a peaceful spot."

Toad walked toward them, hunched over. "That girl's coming, like she always does in the mornin'."

Bart and Jerry hunched down, and Bart studied the ranch below them. The girl on the bright pinto dismounted in the yard before the bunkhouse. A few of the hands gathered around her. Maxwell's daughter, from what he'd heard in town. She seemed pretty popular with the hands.

Different ones worked beside her or rode with her every day, and one of them always took her home in the evening. Seemed they never let her go off by herself, so far as Bart and his men had seen.

"We'd best move along, afore someone looks up here," Jerry said.

"Come on." Bart led the way back to the trees, where they mounted up and headed back to their camp. They should probably leave this area soon, but Bart wasn't ready. He still had unfinished business in the valley. If only they hadn't killed Maxwell.

RYLAND DOZED off and on as the stagecoach headed out of Cheyenne. He didn't like to fall asleep with three other men so close, but the fatigue of the long journey had caught up to him. It would be June in a couple of days. He hadn't expected to be gone so long. He made notes each night in his pocket ledger so that he didn't lose track of the days. Probably he ought to send his mother a few lines to let her know he was all right.

Two of the other passengers wore revolvers strapped to their thighs. That made Ryland a little nervous, but they seemed harmless fellows. One was the foreman of a cattle ranch near Denver, and the other said he was headed for the goldfields.

The third man wore a suit and appeared to be a bit more refined than the others, though he was closemouthed about his background. Ryland tried not to judge him on that—after all, he hadn't been exactly forthcoming about his own business, but had merely said he had come out from New England on a legal matter.

They gained more passengers along the way. Some were tough looking and well armed. Most seemed to have forgotten the finer points of grooming, and the air in the coach soon grew close. They bowled into Denver late Friday afternoon with the stage more than filled to capacity—nine inside, and two riding on the roof.

"Is there a telegraph office here?" he asked as he climbed out of the coach.

The station agent shook his head. "Not yet. They hope to string it this summer, but it only comes as far as Julesburg now."

Ryland resigned himself to being beyond the fringe of civilization. He had sent Mr. Turner a brief telegram from Julesburg to announce his progress, and that would have to do for the present. At least here he had a chance to get a full meal that included a second cup of coffee.

He ate at a rough board building, in which the cook prepared the food in the same room with the diners, and a stout woman ferried it to the long tables. The steak, beans, and bread were tasty, and Ryland filled up on the fare.

The hour stop was longer than any they'd taken so far along the stage route, and he strolled outside after he ate, thankful to stretch his legs.

The rougher passengers appeared to be leaving them here, which was a relief. Several would make their way into the mountains to look for gold. Ryland would go on south in more comfort and leave the city behind.

The sun was setting, and he ambled about, gazing at the crowds, the prevalent construction, and the beautiful setting, with mountains jutting up around the town. He'd been told they were a mile above sea level, and not to do anything strenuous until his lungs acclimated to the altitude. He had discounted this advice at first, but now he was surprised to find himself short of breath after a casual walk down the street.

Denver appeared to be a growing city, and he was surprised that glimpses of wealth and elegance appeared cheek by jowl with primitive crudeness. No doubt, when the war was over, telegraph wires and railroads both would come here.

When he returned to the stage depot, the coach was ready, with a fresh team in harness, and the shotgun messenger and driver were climbing to the box. Ryland got in and found the coach agreeably empty, except for the one cagey passenger he'd ridden with most of the day. The man in the suit was sprawled the length of the back seat, apparently taking the opportunity to catch some sleep.

Ryland stretched out on the front seat. A moment later, the driver called to the team, and the coach began to sway gently. Ryland let himself drift off into slumber. They probably wouldn't stop for a couple of hours.

He slept lightly, awakening often when the coach shifted or the horses changed their pace. Suddenly, he was fully awake. Someone was touching him. Ryland's hand closed around the metal handle of his cane, and he pushed himself upright. The person bending over him pulled back, but Ryland swung with all the leverage he could get in the limited space. The other passenger fell back onto the middle seat with an *oof*. In the semidarkness, Ryland stared at him.

"What were you doing?" he asked as the coach slowed. Their incline told him the horses were pulling up a steep hill.

"N-nothing," the other man said. "Just checking if you were awake. We'll be to the next stop soon."

Ryland clapped a hand to his chest, where he'd felt the other man's touch in his hazy awakening. "My wallet. You took my wallet."

"Wh—No!"

Swiftly, Ryland patted all his pockets. His small notebook was in the side pocket with his handkerchief. He stuck his hand into the inner pocket of his coat, but there was no doubt. His wallet was gone.

Just to be sure, he felt along the seat and studied every square inch of the stage's floor. He supposed it was barely possible it had fallen out of his pocket while he tossed and turned. The other passenger meanwhile scrambled to his original position on the rear seat, where he huddled and rubbed his head.

When he was certain the wallet wasn't on the floor, Ryland moved to the middle seat and lifted his cane. He could whip out the sword it hid in an instant, but he hoped it wouldn't come to that.

"Let's have it."

The man's eyes widened. "I told you, I didn't—"

Ryland shocked himself by bringing the cane down sharply on the man's wrist. He yelped and jumped back into the seat corner as far as he could go, rubbing the injured arm.

"I said give it to me." Ryland put every bit of grit he could muster into his voice, but his heart hammered. What if the man wouldn't give up his loot?"

A shout from the driver and a swaying alerted him that they were driving into the yard of the next way station. Ryland waited until the coach stopped and hopped out.

He yelled to the driver, "The other passenger took my wallet."

"What's that?" the driver said, but the shotgun rider was

already on the ground beside him as the passenger warily poked his head out the doorway.

The shotgun messenger grabbed the thief's shirt front and shoved him against the side of the coach.

"What's up, you? Give this man his wallet."

The passenger tried to gulp in air, but the shotgun rider held him with a merciless grip that choked off his breath. Meanwhile, the driver had climbed down and pulled out a revolver, which he held pointed at the thief.

After several tense seconds, the man held up his hands in surrender.

"All right, then." The shotgun rider quickly searched the man's pockets and came out with four wallets.

"That one's mine," the man protested as the last one came to light.

The shotgun rider handed them all to the stationmaster, who opened the wallets, one by one.

"A Mr. Bonnin," he read off a card in one.

"He got off in Denver," Ryland said.

The second wallet was his, and he reclaimed it, glad to find all his money and papers inside. The third one also belonged to a former passenger.

The driver shook his head. "I'll take those other two back to Denver on our return trip. Meanwhile, let's tie this fellow up. You can send for the marshal to take him off your hands."

The stationmaster scowled. "Oh, and I suppose I have to put him up for free until the law gets out here."

The driver shrugged. "Take what's fair for his food and bed out of his own wallet, but hand the rest of it over to the marshal with the prisoner."

15

Bud offered to go to town on Friday for the payroll money. "Unless you want to get it yourself," he said to Rachel. "Charlie could drive you."

Knowing the drive to town and back, as well as the time spent buying and loading supplies, would take at least half a day, Rachel shook her head. "Thanks, but I'd rather stay here and putter around. I'll be in town Sunday." There were still some things the men had salvaged from the burned house, and she wanted to determine if any would be useful and clean those that were.

"I'll check in with the sheriff about the outlaws," Bud said.

"Oh, and you said the feed store account needs some attention." Rachel frowned. "I suppose I could do all that, but you've been dealing with the feed merchant for two years now."

"You're right. I'll settle it." Bud looked pointedly at Hank, their youngest hired hand, and Ran Crowder, who was just recovering enough from his wounds in the outlaws' attack to ride herd. "You two stay alert and look out for Miss Rachel."

"Sure will," Hank assured him.

Bud looked back to Rachel. "Anything you want from the store, besides what's on the list Dusty gave me?"

"Oh, yes. I'm glad you mentioned it. Pard Henry told me about a bolt of red calico he and Vida saw the other day. It has little brown and gold leaves on it."

"How much you want?"

"Six yards, I'd think."

Bud nodded. "I'll see what I can do."

"Thread to match?"

He fished a piece of paper from his pocket. "Could you write it on Dusty's list, so I don't forget?"

He produced a stubby pencil, and she jotted "red calico and thread" at the bottom of the list. Hank and Ran were fidgeting along with their horses, so she gathered her reins. "Thanks, Bud. And that's a secret. I don't want it getting back to Vida before her birthday."

Bud arched his eyebrows. "All right then."

Rachel smiled. "We'll see you later."

CHARLIE LAGRANDE, one of Rachel's older hands who'd been wounded in the attack on the ranch, rode home with her on Friday evening. The day had passed uneventfully, which was good, Rachel supposed, but it meant a long, boring day in the saddle. As they headed for the Anderson ranch, the wind blew sharply across the prairie, and clouds moved in swiftly over the valley.

"I'll be glad when this cold weather lets go," Charlie said darkly, as they rode down into the bottom, toward the stream.

"Not like Texas," Rachel said.

Charlie grunted. "I worked down there for a year or two. It'd be hotter'n spit on the Brazos today." Charlie looked east and squinted at several large birds soaring over a wooded area. "Wonder what's brought them out."

Rachel stopped Herald beside Charlie's sorrel. Vultures. She grimaced. "Probably something dead."

"Mm-hmm, but ours, or Anderson's?"

"Do you think we should look?" Rachel hoped he would say no, or at least that he'd check after seeing her home, but he glanced around the other direction, to where the sun was lowering toward the mountain peaks.

"Best check now, while there's plenty of light."

They rode off the path they'd made between the two ranches and let the horses pick their way into the trees and through the trackless woods. The dusk deepened, but ahead Rachel glimpsed a patch of sunlight. They came out the far side of the copse into a large open area. They were still on the Box M side of the stream when Charlie spotted three buzzards on the ground, tearing at a fallen heifer's carcass.

"Stay here."

She was glad to wait beneath the overhanging poplar branches as Charlie rode into the clearing and dismounted. The buzzards took wing, and he walked around the carcass for a minute. His horse snorted and pulled back on the reins, and Charlie let him go. The sorrel trotted several yards toward Rachel, then lowered his head and began to graze.

Finally, Charlie ambled back toward her, scooped up the horse's reins, and mounted. A moment later, he was at Rachel's side.

"Well?" she asked.

"It's ours. Someone shot it and took the haunches."

"What, slaughtered it for a little meat and just left it there?"

Charlie lifted his hat, pushed his hair back, and settled the hat again. "Looks like. It's on your land. The brand is mostly gone, but I think it's yours."

"Who would do that? Surely nobody from the Box M."

"Nah. I misdoubt the Andersons would, either."

Rachel eyed him sharply. "Should I tell them tonight?"

"I'd say so. I'll tell Bud about it. He'll likely send one of us to tell the sheriff tomorrow."

"So ... someone's out here butchering my beef." Rachel looked around at the darkening woods.

"They didn't camp there. Might have ridden out here from town for some free meat. Or not." He looked directly into her eyes. "You be careful, Miss Rachel. Don't take no chances, will ya?"

"No, I won't." She shivered, glad she hadn't shaken off the escort and insisted on riding home alone. She'd thought of it, almost every day.

They rode back through the trees and out onto the grassland beside the stream. Charlie led the way across the ford and urged his horse to lope. A few minutes later, they were in the Andersons' barnyard and reined in their horses.

"I'll see you tomorrow," she told Charlie. "Unless it rains hard. If that happens, I'll try to make myself useful here." Whether or not Vida would let her do so was questionable, but Rachel had at least one task the housekeeper could not prevent her from doing.

She'd gathered torn clothing from the men on her ranch. Some of it had been ripped, and a few buttons had been lost during their daily work. She'd insisted they all bring her their derelict clothing and let her take it with her to mend. The bundle was tied securely to the cantle of her sidesaddle.

"Yes, ma'am," Charlie said, "but it ain't gonna rain. Now, you watch yourself, and tell Mr. Anderson about that beef."

"I will. Thanks for bringing me over."

She rubbed Herald down and put her gear away, then went inside to clean up before supper. Mr. Anderson and Matt commiserated with her over the loss of a heifer, but neither seemed ready to jump into action.

"If Bud's going to tell the sheriff, there's nothing for us to do," Mr. Anderson said at the table as he cut into his steak.

Matt nodded soberly. "Except keep our eyes open."

"Yes." Rachel met his gaze. "I'm sorry I've chafed so much about you and the others going with me, back and forth. You were right."

"We only did it keep you safe," Matt said gently. His earnest blue eyes were so intense, Rachel's heart leaped. For the first time, she believed he truly cared about her.

"We'd hate to see anything happen to you, Rachel," his father added.

She eyed Mr. Anderson dispassionately and decided he meant it. While he wasn't a demonstrative man, he did care about those in his charge. And for now, Rachel qualified.

"Thank you both," she said.

After supper, a good hour of daylight was left. She helped clear the table, though Vida threw her baleful glances whenever their paths crossed. When that was done, Rachel went up to her room for her bundle of mending and her sewing kit. She'd be able to sew longer without lighting a lamp if she went outside, so she settled in one of the chairs on the front porch.

The monotonous task soothed her. While her thoughts roved from the ranch work to the friends she'd left in Boston and back to Texas and the home she had shared with her father there, she sewed on buttons, patched blown elbows, and overcast an unraveled seam.

Matt came from the barn with two of his ranch hands, a young man named Jimmy and a dark-haired man in his mid-thirties, whom everyone called "Ruthless." Rachel had learned his real name was Rutherford. Since he was mild-mannered and excessively polite whenever she spoke to him, she assumed the nickname was a joke.

After a brief word from Matt, the ranch hands headed

toward the bunkhouse. Matt turned his steps toward where Rachel sat. As he mounted the steps, he noticed her and smiled.

"Evening."

"Good evening." She clipped the ends of her thread.

"Doing some sewing?" Matt eased down into the chair nearest hers.

"Yes, some of the Box M men were getting a bit ragged."

"I'm sure they appreciate it." Matt stretched out his long legs and leaned back in his chair.

"I suppose Vida does mending for you and your father?"

"Actually, that's a little beyond her province. She says the cooking and the housework are all she can do for us and for her and Pard too. Pa offered to let them live in the house with us, but they prefer the cabin by the stream, and I don't blame them. Privacy's worth something."

"Yes." Rachel set her mouth as she concentrated on threading a needle with white thread. It was the closest match she had for Telly's light blue shirt. "So who does your mending?"

Matt laughed. "Pa and I do when it's urgent. We mostly sew our own buttons and such. If we rip something too bad, we buy new."

She was surprised they'd be so wasteful. "Doesn't Vida sew at all?"

"Not much, I guess."

Rachel was tempted to ask him what Vida did do well, but she restrained herself. The Anderson men probably considered themselves fortunate to have a woman willing to cook for them and do their laundry for wages, even though those services were performed with mediocre quality. She hadn't noticed either of them going around with buttons missing or obvious rips in their clothing.

"Well, I meant what I said earlier. If you or your father have anything that needs attention, I'd be happy to see to it for you. I've found few ways to repay your hospitality."

"You don't need to worry about that, but thank you. Next time I need something stitched, I'll know where to take it."

She nodded and positioned a button carefully. The light was fading, and this would be the last job she could complete out here. A couple of socks that needed darning still waited for her ministrations, but they would have to wait until her next session. Her fatigue was catching up to her, and she didn't feel like sitting close to the lamp to darn this evening.

She finished securing the button and clipped the thread, then laid the shirt down in her lap. "I guess that's it for now."

Matt rose. "Would you like some tea?"

She hesitated only an instant. "All right. Thank you."

In the kitchen, Matt lit a lamp. The full kettle simmered on the back of the cookstove. While she took two cups from the cupboard, Matt lifted down a small crock and opened it.

"It thought you were a coffee man," she said with a smile.

"Not before bed. It keeps me awake. Tea doesn't seem to bother me, though, and I need to sleep."

"Yes, you put in long days."

The lamplight revealed fatigue lines at the corners of his eyes. She supposed she must look weary as well and probably had dark circles rimming her eyes.

"My mother used to drink tea," Matt said as he filled a small wire mesh tea ball. "She never liked coffee."

"Mrs. Anderson?" Rachel asked.

"Yes." A smile flickered over his lips. "My first mother liked tea, too."

"My mother liked it, but she considered it a luxury in Texas. The men always wanted coffee, and she kept a fresh pot going all the time. But on special occasions, or if ladies came to call, she served tea. Tea and ginger cookies." Tears filled her eyes in a rush, and she sniffed. "Sorry."

"Don't apologize. It's all right. I tear up too, sometimes, when I think about Ma ... or my first family."

Rachel plunked down on a chair and let Matt pour out the tea. When everything was to his satisfaction, he sat down opposite her.

"I don't expect Vida left any cookies around here."

Rachel smiled. "I don't mind. It was just a fond memory."

"Memories are good." Matt raised his cup. "To our families."

She lifted hers. "To loved ones lost."

They both sipped the hot beverage. Matt made a face. "That tea has sat in the crock since last year. We should probably get some fresh, but I don't use it up very fast."

"It's not bad," Rachel said. "Matt …"

"What?" His eyebrows arched, and he gazed at her with kindness in his blue eyes.

"It's nice, drinking tea with you, and … and talking. About things that matter."

He nodded and took another sip.

The kitchen door opened, and Mr. Anderson came in. "Oh, there you are, Matt. Wondered where you'd got off to."

"Want some tea?" Matt shifted in his chair.

Mr. Anderson walked to the stove, picked up the coffeepot, and shook it gently. "No, but I'll have some of this."

Matt laughed. "It's probably strong enough to tan a hide, Pa."

"That's how I like it."

Rachel smiled at Matt, and he smiled back. Maybe they were truly becoming friends.

Mr. Anderson got himself an ironstone mug and filled it. He came to the table and pulled out a chair. "We need to drive the young stock up to the east pasture in the morning."

Matt nodded. "Planning on it. I told Ruthless to be ready, him and three others. We'll get to it." He glanced over at Rachel. "Would you mind if one of the boys takes you over tomorrow?"

"No, that's fine," Rachel said, but she felt a pang of disappointment.

Mr. Anderson grinned at her. "I can escort the little lady."

She managed not to cringe. He always seemed to bring up her future plans when no one else was around. "That would be lovely, Mr. Anderson, but I don't mind if you want to send one of the other men. I'm sure you have a lot of work to tend to."

"No bother at all." He blew on the surface of his coffee and took a big gulp.

Rachel gazed across the table at Matt. His eyes held hers, and she realized he wanted her to forgive his father's awkwardness and like them in spite of their many flaws. With a smile, she nodded slightly. Matt's eyes crinkled, and he raised his cup to his lips. For the first time, maybe they truly understood each other.

16

Saturday, May 30, 1863

Matt slowed his horse and slipped his left foot from the stirrup. He rubbed the outside of his knee and kneaded his thigh muscles. All morning he'd ridden up and down hills with four of the ranch hands, driving cattle together and up to a fresh pasture. New grass covered the hills now, and they'd take advantage of that, leaving the lower range for later, to grow hay they could harvest for winter.

His leg suffered from being confined in the stirrup. When his rubbing didn't relieve the cramp, he swung down and walked, leading the scrub bay. Even though his leg ached, straightening it and putting his weight on it felt good.

Josh Brand, one of the cowboys who'd been with his father's outfit since they came to Colorado, noticed him and loped up the hillside toward him. He stopped his horse a few yards away.

"You all right?"

"Yeah, just my leg," Matt said.

"It's close to noon." Josh squinted up at the sun. "We should stop and eat. Rest a while."

Matt hated it when he slowed things down. "It's not much farther."

"No, but it'll take us another hour to get them all up there. And it'll be a couple hours' ride home. We might as well eat now and then finish the job."

Ruthless Small, who cooked for the men, had given them all a cold lunch to carry today, and Matt had taken a portion as well. When he ate with the men out on the range, he preferred to eat the same food they had, to avoid any hard feelings. He'd learned that early, when a cowboy had threatened to quit because the boss's son got twice as much food as the other men.

Today Ruthless had packed biscuits, bacon, cheese, and cookies for each of them, wrapped in a fresh cotton napkin. Thinking about it made Matt's stomach growl.

"I guess we can," he said.

Josh nodded. "I'll tell the others. We'll bunch up the cattle in that ravine and make our stop."

The men laughed and joked while they ate their meal. Nobody mentioned Matt's bum leg or suggested they'd quit early because of him. When they'd polished off their food and were preparing to mount again, Pete led his horse over near Matt's.

"What's the plan after this, Matthew?"

"Thought we'd go over the remuda. I think three or four of the horses need shoeing. And while Pard and Jimmy take care of them, the rest of us can work up Vida's garden."

"She's been jawin' about that."

"Pa mentioned it last night," Matt said. "We really do need to get stuff in the ground if we want a good harvest." Planting a large garden was vital to the ranch. It kept down the cost of feeding the men and provided the fresh vegetables they needed and produce to can for winter. Matt hated it when the men were pressed into helping chop beans or grind mincemeat in the fall, but the men all enjoyed eating the results when the ground was blanketed in snow.

"And I was thinking if we get the planting done tomorrow, the men could have the next day off," Matt added. "We're caught up on most things." In the back of his mind, he'd already planned his own free day. He'd neglected his friends at Fort Lyon too long. It was time he talked to his sergeant and caught up on what the regiment was doing.

His leg hardly twinged when he put his left foot in the stirrup. Surely the post doctor would declare him fit.

He started out with the others and veered off to bring in a small bunch of cattle that had wandered up a ridge. As his pony turned quickly, pain screamed through his knee. Matt kicked off the stirrup and managed to keep his balance as he nudged the bunch toward the herd.

BART TOOK a bundle out of his saddlebag and unwrapped the oilcloth. He kept the ledger he'd nicked from Bob Maxwell's house swathed in it, to keep the rain from getting at the paper. As he had several times before, he turned to the page where Maxwell had ticked off all the men he'd paid wages at the last monthly payday.

"What ya got, Chief?" Jerry ambled to him and looked over his shoulder.

"Maxwell's book."

"Know any more than you did before?"

Bart shook his head. "They's still only one name I recognize, besides Maxwell, and that's Hillman."

"But you're still not sure which one he is?"

"It's been fourteen years." Bart shut the ledger and wrapped the oilcloth around it. "I'll have to get closer. It's about time we finished this and got out of here. Hillman may be the key."

"We could take 'em all," Jerry said.

"That's what I thought the first day." Bart squeezed his eyes almost shut, seeing the flames shoot up from Maxwell's house. He'd really thought it was over for a short while, but when the rest of Maxwell's ranch hands came pounding in from the range, things had gotten dicey, and then even more men came galloping from behind them.

Now he knew they'd come from the neighbor's ranch, but at the time, they'd seemed to swoop down out of nowhere. "Nah, it's too risky. And we don't want to kill the girl."

"I s'pose not. Not unless we have to." Jerry spit in the grass. "You figure out which one's your man, chief, and we'll get him."

"I don't want to kill him," Bart said.

"Oh?" Jerry cocked his head to one side. "Thought you wanted to get back at him and Maxwell for selling you up the river."

"Oh, I do, but not until he's told us whatever he knows about that money. If we can get Telly Hillman alive, he might tell us something useful."

WHEN RACHEL RODE toward the Anderson house at suppertime with Bud at her side, four of the Anderson ranch hands were out in a field behind the house with Mr. Anderson, working up the ground.

"Is that their garden?" Rachel asked Bud.

He nodded. "They've been making it bigger every year. Last fall, Mr. Anderson brought us a whole bunch of squash and a big mess of corn. I heard Vida canned over three hundred quarts of garden stuff, but she said it still wasn't enough."

"That's a lot of vegetables," Rachel said. "But she's right. My mother used to do fifty quarts each of seven different vegetables. She said that gave us enough for one a day all year until the next garden was ready. And with men in the bunkhouse to feed, besides the family, it would take a lot more."

Bud grunted, and she wondered if he hated vegetables. She hadn't seen many in the dinners the cook at the Box M prepared on the bunkhouse stove, but then it was spring. She had assumed supplies were low because it was early in the season.

"Will we have a garden at the Box M?" she asked.

"If you want it, though it's awful late to start planting now. Mr. Maxwell didn't have a plow, but Anderson will probably lend us his, after he's done with it."

"I'll think about it," Rachel said. The cowboys would probably resent it if she added gardening to their workload. That meant she'd have to make it her own project and do the weeding, much as Vida did here.

Bud scratched his bristly chin. "Let me know. It wouldn't take too long to put in a small patch near where the house was. I think you could get a few greens and stuff like that."

"I'll see how it goes here tomorrow and tell you what I think. Thanks for bringing me home." They had reached the dooryard, and she dismounted.

Bud tipped his hat and turned his palomino for home. Rachel untied the bundle she'd carried behind the saddle. At least Vida was busy and wouldn't see her take the yard goods inside. Even though it was wrapped in brown paper, Vida would probably have thoughts about it if she saw it.

Matt Anderson was sitting on the porch, and he struggled to stand. Rachel noted the second chair he'd propped his foot on, with a pillow under his heel to cushion it.

"Don't get up on my account," she called. "I can take care of my own horse."

"The boys are all out working the garden with Pa."

"I saw them. You sit tight. I won't be a minute."

He opened his mouth then closed it. Slowly, he eased back down into his chair and used both hands to lift his left leg and prop it on the cushioned seat opposite. He must have injured it badly to keep him from working with the other men.

Rachel walked Herald over to the corral, stripped off the saddle and bridle, and turned him loose with a dozen other mounts. She lugged the heavy saddle into the barn. The inside of the building was immaculate. She'd heard the men talk about cleaning it a few days ago, and the results were evident. The walls were whitewashed, and all the loose straw and debris had been hauled out. She stowed her gear, picked up her parcel, and then strode across the yard to the house.

"That barn looks beautiful. It's so clean, I could eat off the floor."

Matt laughed. "I don't think I'd try it, but it does look nice. Pa likes to clean it all out once a year and spruce it up."

"What happened to your leg, if you don't mind my asking?" She pulled over another chair and sat down.

"Nothing serious. It's an old injury."

She wondered about that, but he didn't seem willing to give out more. "So, who keeps up the garden?"

"Vida, mostly. If the weeds get ahead of her, she complains, and then we all go out and weed a row or two for her."

"I'm willing to help, if she'll let me."

Matt smiled. "That's kind of you. We'll all be planting Monday. You could help then."

"Great. I've dropped seed many a time. I should have told Bud I wouldn't be over, but I don't think he'll worry too much."

"We can send somebody to tell him if you want."

"No need. If Bud or any of the other Box M men are at church tomorrow, we'll tell them then." Rachel stood. "I should go and change before dinner. I'm grimy as a nightcrawler."

"Working hard all day?" Matt asked.

"Yes, rather."

Matt was eyeing the package in her hands, but he didn't ask what was in it, and Rachel didn't offer any information.

"Have they started building your house yet?"

"No. Just cutting the logs." She eyed him closely. "You know, everyone says I can't live there alone."

Matt shrugged. "You might be able to find someone to stay with you. Some single woman, I mean, or a widow. None of your men is married?"

"No. I asked Bud, and he says to his knowledge, they're all bachelors."

"All too common out here."

"Yes. I suppose it would increase the value of the place if I put up some sort of house—even the cabin will be a help." She watched his face as she said it. "In case I decide to sell."

"That's true." He held her gaze for a long moment. "Is that what you're thinking of now?"

She grimaced and went back to her chair, gathering her dusty blue skirts around her as she resumed her seat. "I must seem awfully fickle to you. First I said I'm staying. And I really meant it at the time. But everyone says I can't. And Bud's been so slow about getting started on the building."

"Do you think he's dragging his feet?"

"Well, I didn't think so, but I suppose he might be. So now I've been thinking about going elsewhere and ... oh, teaching, I suppose. But you told me I couldn't do that either—traveling is too dangerous. So I decided I'll have to stay. But I can't stay here at your place forever, Matt. So, I think about selling ..."

"But then you'd have to go somewhere." He shook his head. "We haven't intended to make things difficult for you, Rachel."

"No? Sometimes it feels that way."

"I do think it's too dangerous for you to travel alone, what with the Indians and the outlaws. There's been more trouble with the tribes lately." He shook his head. "If you can wait until the war is over back East—or at least until that outlaw band is caught—I'd feel easier. Or maybe you could find a family traveling east and go with them."

"That's a thought." She let out a deep sigh. "I'll keep pondering it, and praying, too."

"That's the best course," he said with a smile.

She eyed him for a moment, trying to read his mind, but she couldn't. At last she decided to come right out with it. "Do you want me to go?"

His eyes flared. "Of course not."

"So ... you want me to stay."

He was quiet for several seconds, gazing at her with those unreadable blue eyes. Finally he lifted his shoulders slightly. "You should do what you want to do, Rachel. I'd be sorry to see you go, but if that's what you really want ... I know this is a hard life for a woman. With your pa gone, I could understand it if you didn't want to take this on. Especially ..." He looked away.

Especially by yourself, she finished mentally. Rachel wanted to tell him a woman could run a ranch as well as a man, and she didn't need a husband to make a success of the Box M. But deep down, she couldn't say that. Over the last couple of weeks, she'd worked hard, and she'd seen the effort put in by the men she employed. Without their labor, she certainly couldn't run a cattle ranch, at least on the scale to which her father had built the Box M.

There were some things one person couldn't do alone, and if she were honest, some heavy work a woman couldn't do as well as a man could.

So, did she want to go on hiring men to help her carry out her father's dream? She'd thought the ranch had become her own dream. In her letters home from school, she'd said so. She'd honestly thought she wanted to spend the rest of her life out here. Would she have felt that way if she'd known her father wouldn't be part of the picture?

Vida was placing a platter of beefsteaks on the table when Rachel came down fifteen minutes later.

"Supper's about ready." As always, Vida surveyed her with a sour expression and addressed her in a grave voice.

"Would you like me to ring the dinner bell?" Rachel asked.

"The men have gone to the bunkhouse, and Mr. Anderson just went up to his room. He knows."

"All right. Shall I tell Matt? He was sitting on the front porch last I saw him."

Vida gave her a grudging nod. "That boy should have listened to his daddy."

"What do you mean?" Rachel stared at her. Information coming from Vida was rare, but tonight she delivered it with obvious displeasure.

"When he up and joined the army, that's what I mean."

Rachel took that in. "You mean, that's a war wound he's nursing?"

With a sniff, Vida returned to the kitchen, closing the door behind her.

Rachel hesitated then opened the front door. Matt was right where she'd left him.

"Matt?"

He looked up at her.

"Suppertime," she said.

"Thank you." He slid his foot off the cushion and let it rest on the floor. He gritted his teeth as he pushed up out of the chair.

"Do you need help?"

"No," he said. "It's just stiff."

He limped toward the door.

"I'll fetch the pillow." Rachel ducked past him and snatched the cushion. More things Matt didn't want to talk about—his military service and his wound.

No one mentioned his health during supper. Most of the talk centered on the garden and the little headaches that had slowed the job down.

"We'll do the planting Monday," Mr. Anderson told her when Vida brought in the coffeepot and a plate of spice cake.

"That looks delicious, Vida," Rachel said. Sweets were so unusual, she thought she'd better mention it in Vida's presence, or they might never see more.

"The men worked hard all day," was her terse reply.

Was the housekeeper implying Rachel didn't deserve the cake because she hadn't helped them with the plowing? She turned to her host and smiled. "I thought I'd stay here Monday and help with the planting, if you can use me."

"Surely." Mr. Anderson scooped a generous slice of cake onto his plate. "Is Bud putting in a garden for your outfit?"

"I asked him, and he said they would if I want one. I haven't made up my mind yet. The boys aren't used to it, and I don't want to put them out."

Mr. Anderson nodded. "It would save you money in the long run. Even if you don't do canning, it would help you to grow food during the summer. And you can dry corn and store your root vegetables."

"I'll definitely consider it, but it's so late now, it might be better to wait until next year." She didn't say *if I'm here next year,* but it loomed in her mind.

Mr. Anderson nodded as though that was all he could expect.

Matt remained quiet throughout the meal, speaking only when asked a question. Though he hadn't worked as long as the other men, his face was lined with fatigue.

Furtively, Rachel watched him. How much pain did his leg cause him?

She climbed the stairs slowly a half hour later, knowing she had to work through her mixed feelings about the Andersons and about keeping or selling the ranch. More than ever, she wished for someone to confide in. The disposal of the ranch troubled her far more than the day-to-day decisions like gardening.

Mr. Anderson had his own motives, and she doubted he could give her a neutral opinion on whether she should keep the ranch. While Matt occasionally seemed sympathetic, sometimes, like tonight, he was distant and uncommunicative. Vida—no, Vida would never be one with whom to hash over anything. Bud was her closest friend right now, and her main advisor. But could he be any less biased than Mr. Anderson, when his job was in question?

This was something Rachel had to decide for herself. Colorado was a magnificent land, and her father had chosen well. Could she put her heart into it now, or would she be better off running back to the familiar?

She opened her trunk and took out her small supply of dress patterns, wondering what style would best suit Vida. Nothing too fancy, but surely a bit more tailored than the housedresses the cook wore every day. She paused, looking at the drawing on the envelope that held a pattern she'd used for one of her school dresses.

Yes, with red buttons down the front and full sleeves, that would look very nice. She smiled and untied the twine on her package. She could lay out the pattern pieces tonight and cut them out another day.

17

June 1, 1863

Planting day stretched everyone's nerves thin. The men would much prefer riding off to tend the livestock, Rachel was sure. Working the soil called on seldom-used muscles. Vida seemed to know this, however, and provided a break at mid-morning, and again about three o'clock. She carried a jug of switchel and a bag of biscuits out to the field for the first recess and swapped the biscuits for sugar cookies in the afternoon.

Rachel made good on her offer. She was shorter than the men, and stooping to drop the seeds into the furrows didn't cause her too much distress. Still, after hours on her feet in the loose soil, she was ready to rest.

Corn, potatoes, carrots, squash, turnip, rutabaga, onions, and beans. Just when she wondered if they could possibly come up with more seeds, Mr. Anderson produced packets of pumpkin, Swiss chard, and beets. They would certainly have a good variety of vegetables next winter, if the growing season lasted long enough for all the plants to mature.

The sun was sinking toward the mountains when they had

planted the last of the red beans. As they gathered up the sacks and tools, the ringing of the dinner bell floated over the valley.

The men trudged wearily to the bunkhouse, while Rachel and the Andersons headed for the house. Matt limped badly. He'd kept working all day, though he'd taken more rests than the others. She admired his tenacity.

When they left the table after their midday meal, she eyed him keenly. "No offense, Matt, but do you think you might be better off to find some less strenuous chores this afternoon? I'm sure you could use a rest."

"If the men don't see me out here, they'll think I'm lazy," he said with a smile.

"Surely not."

"Weak, then."

Rachel kept quiet after that. She hadn't been around many men for the last three years, but during her time on the Texas ranch, she'd learned a man's pride was a fragile thing best left intact.

That evening, Mr. Anderson, though he was weary, carried two pails of hot water to her room and two of cold, so she could bathe. Rachel lingered a few minutes in the lukewarm bath to ease her sore muscles, but not too long. The men wouldn't begin their evening meal without her.

They'd barely sat down to supper when a horse's hoofbeats sounded outside. Mr. Anderson got up and went to the door and admitted Bud Lassen.

Rachel and Matt stood.

"Hello, Bud," Rachel said.

"Just making sure you're all right." He nodded to Matt.

"I'm fine," Rachel said. "The Andersons were planting their garden today, and I thought I'd do well to help them, since they've been so kind to me. I guess I should have sent someone over to tell you."

"No need," Bud said. "I wanted to talk to you all anyhow."

"Come have a seat." Mr. Anderson waved toward the table. "Have you eaten supper?"

"We had some beans and cornpone."

"Well, sit down and have some steak."

Bud didn't have to be invited twice. He sat down next to Rachel, and Mr. Anderson went to the kitchen to tell Vida they had a guest. He returned with a plate, knife, fork, and cup for Bud, and he was in business. Rachel and Matt passed him the baked potatoes and biscuits.

A minute later, Vida came in with another steak on a plate in one hand and the coffeepot in the other. She must have had that steak already cooked. Rachel tried to hide her surprise. Maybe it had been earmarked for Vida and Pard's supper. The cook's sour expression supported the thought.

Mr. Anderson treated Bud like an old friend—probably the same way he treated Rachel's father when he was alive. After inquiring about the daily operation at the Box M, he asked, "Did you have some news?"

"Well, the sheriff came out this morning." Bud cut into the steak, and a dreamy smile crossed his face. "Dusty don't make it like this."

Rachel hadn't thought the meat was anything special—in fact, hers was a bit tough. But perhaps Vida had taken special care with that cut.

"You boys will be butchering soon," she prompted Bud.

"Yeah, we need to."

"If you're not getting meat these days, that should be high on your list."

Bud nodded. "I reckon we could butcher tomorrow if you don't mind. We did make a little progress on your cabin today, though."

"That's nice," Rachel said, "but I want you to have a good diet." She'd decided to go ahead with a small garden, but she'd speak to him about that tomorrow. "You said the sheriff called?"

"Yes, ma'am," Bud said between bites.

"I'm sorry I missed him."

"Is there anything new on the outlaws?" Mr. Anderson asked.

"Some. They seem to be staying away from Fort Lyon, but a rancher over near Pueblo said he saw strangers over there yesterday. Could have been them."

"Hmm, I don't like them staying in the area." Mr. Anderson buttered a biscuit and took a bite.

"Well, the sheriff also said he'd been studying the things we took off of 'em." Bud cut a quick glance at Rachel, then back to his host. "Matt put him onto it."

"What?" Mr. Anderson looked at his son.

"The belt buckle," Matt said. "Last time I was in town, I told him. Remember, Pa? I mentioned it to you."

"Hmm." Mr. Anderson frowned. "You said it was an old one."

"That's right," Bud said. "You saw the two men we shot." He glanced at Rachel. "Begging your pardon, ma'am."

"Please go on," she said.

"Well, one of 'em was nigh on fifty years old, by the look of him. The other was younger, but me and the boys agree—some of those outlaws were showing their age. And one of them had that buckle, and buttons too, that were U.S. Army—but not recent."

"So, an old soldier," Matt asked. "That goes along with my thinking."

Bud speared a piece of beef with his fork. "The Mex War. That's what the sheriff thinks."

"My father fought in the Mexican-American War," Rachel said. "I was very young. I remember when he came home, though. I didn't know who he was at first."

Bud smiled at her. "I recall him telling that very story."

"It's odd," she said, "but since you're talking about veterans, and them possibly being deserters, that brings to mind another story Papa told me."

"What was that?" Mr. Anderson asked.

"Several men deserted from his unit after their first engagement. He and his squadron were detailed to bring them back, which they did. Papa said he thought the men would be executed, but they weren't. They were imprisoned, and the leader swore he'd get revenge on my father."

Matt's eyebrows shot up. "That's a little scary."

She shrugged. "Papa always said it was a long time ago, and he didn't seem too worried about it. It was just a story."

"Didn't you worry about it?" Matt asked.

"Yes, when I was younger. I had nightmares."

"He didn't talk much to me about the war," Bud said. "I knew he served. Went clear to Mexico City, didn't he?"

Rachel nodded. "Papa and Telly Hillman both."

"That's right. Telly told me once he'd been with the boss in the war."

"Not his most pleasant memories, I'm sure," Rachel said.

"It didn't come to mind when the sheriff was there, or I'd have told him. Telly was out with the herd then." Bud hesitated. "Sheriff Smith told me something else. I didn't see that it meant anything at the time, but ..."

"What?" Rachel asked.

"There's a sheep farmer on the other side of town who had visitors a few weeks ago. There were five or six men, on horseback, and they asked where your daddy's place was."

Rachel caught her breath.

"They asked for the Box M?" Mr. Anderson seemed as puzzled as Bud.

"No, they asked for Bob Maxwell by name. 'Maxwell's place,' was the way they told it."

Rachel found it hard to draw in a deep breath. "Does the sheriff think they targeted my father?"

"He's not sure. I mean, they've hit other places in the area. But it did seem odd to him. And with the army connection … "

"Lord preserve us." Rachel's mind reeled. The idea that the outlaws didn't choose the Box M at random, but might have come here purposely to attack her father, cast a new and frightening light on things.

"I wouldn't make too much of it." Bud eyed her uneasily, as if he wished he'd kept quiet.

"That's right," Mr. Anderson said. "Don't let it worry you, at least until the sheriff learns more."

Rachel nodded, but she wasn't sure she could follow their advice.

Bud stayed until every serving dish on the table was empty and he'd downed three cups of coffee, the last taken with Mr. Anderson while they discussed beef prices. Rachel excused herself and went to sit on the front porch. She assumed Matt would stay with the men, but a few minutes later, the door opened and he eased out into the shadows.

"Mind if I sit a spell?" he asked.

"Suit yourself." It sounded curt, and she was sorry, but she didn't say so.

Matt limped to one of the rocking chairs and settled into it.

"Do you need your cushion?" she asked after a moment.

"No, thanks."

They rocked in silence, and Rachel let her thoughts rove back to the evenings when they'd sat out under the Texas stars, and her father had spun tales of long ago. Mexico City was one of his most horrible stories, but even so, she suspected he left out the worst parts. She'd preferred his stories of chasing mustangs and rounding up cattle. The war stories made her shiver and look over her shoulder when the shadows lengthened.

After a long time, Matt said, "I do worry about you. Don't

want to smother you, but you'll be careful, won't you? Riding back and forth, I mean?"

"Of course. And thank you."

The door opened, and Bud came out. Mr. Anderson tailed him to the top of the steps.

"Night all," Bud said. "Miss Rachel, I'll look for you in the mornin'."

"I plan to be there," she said.

Bud got his horse and trotted off toward the Box M.

"How you doing, son?" The concern in Mr. Anderson's voice surprised Rachel.

"I'm all right, Pa."

"You've been overdoing it. Nobody expects you to be tip-top yet."

"I'm fine."

"Relax tomorrow."

"Thought I'd ride over to the fort."

"Oh?"

"My outfit's still in camp, I think." Matt shifted in his chair. "Thought I'd get the news."

Mr. Anderson nodded. "I'm turning in. Good night, Miss Rachel."

"Good night."

She and Matt sat still on opposite sides of the entrance. Mr. Anderson went in and closed the door. After a moment, Rachel resumed rocking. She could barely see Matt now. He was a darker spot in the blackness under the porch roof. His chair creaked.

"I'll take you over in the morning."

"No need." He ought to sleep late and let one of the hired hands escort her. No one doubted he'd used his leg too hard, no matter what he said.

"Pa's giving all the men the day off tomorrow."

"Jimmy and Royal have both offered to ride with me anytime I need someone."

Matt chuckled. "I bet they have."

The two young cowboys did seem a bit awestruck around Rachel, but she didn't think it mattered. Both were a bit younger than her, and she didn't suppose they'd been around ladies much. But she treated them impartially, as she did the "boys" at the Box M.

She stood and moved toward the door. "Sleep as long as you can. If you're not up, I'll ask them."

Matt stirred. "If you meant it, about mending something for me ..."

"I did. How can I help you?"

"I'll get it now, if you don't mind." He pushed himself up out of the chair.

"Not at all. Bring it to my room."

She went in and up the stairs. Matt followed more slowly. She didn't look back, knowing he'd be embarrassed if she watched him limp across the parlor. He wasn't happy about her solution for an escort in the morning. But why should he care who rode with her across the range?

She left her bedroom door open a few inches and lit the lamp near the bed. Since she couldn't undress yet, she sat down and pulled the pins from her hair. It cascaded down around her shoulders. She reached for her brush and worked it through the long tresses.

Matt knocked softly on the door panel, and she jumped up and walked over to the door.

"Here it is." He held out a wool shirt.

One pocket was ripped half off, and another tear began at the shoulder seam ran a couple of inches into the shirt front. A uniform tunic. A chill ran through her.

"You're re-enlisting."

"Just finishing out the term I signed up for, if they'll let me."

She took the shirt and examined the tears more closely. "I'll have to patch this one. Is that all right?"

"Have to be, unless they issue me a new one."

She couldn't look him in the eye, but she managed to voice her thoughts. "Are you sure you should go? Your father seems to need you here. And with that outlaw gang still hanging about …"

"I should be with my company, if I'm able. I couldn't foresee these circumstances when I joined."

"No, of course not." She wondered if he was fit enough. Didn't soldiers march all day when they went someplace? Or maybe he was in the Cavalry. She didn't know the uniforms well enough to tell—but she knew he had trouble riding all day as well. "Matt, surely they'd give you a little more time to recover."

"It's been a year. I don't know as my leg will get much better."

"I'm sorry."

He let out a short puff of air. "It's my duty, Rachel."

"I see." She folded the shirt over her arm. "I'll do what I can with this."

"Thanks."

"Goodnight, Matt."

He looked as though he might say something further, but then nodded and said, "'Night."

She shut her door and carried his tunic to the bedside table and turned up the lamp. No working on Vida's dress tonight.

What changes would they face if Matt went off to war again? She didn't want to think about it, or how her decisions about the Box M might be different with Matt away. But what about his father? Matt was his only son. Mr. Anderson had lost his wife. She could only imagine his agony at the thought of losing Matt too.

June 2, 1863
Way Station Near Pueblo

RYLAND BRACED himself and held on. The stagecoach line had ended abruptly in a small town south of Denver. From there on, his stage to the next stop was little more than a farm wagon with a canvas covering. The driver contracted independently to carry mail, a little freight, and a few brave passengers to Pueblo, Bent's Old Fort, and Fort Lyon. Ryland waited three days, renting a bed in a stable loft, until the driver was ready to take his next load south.

As the wagon seat was taken up by the rotund driver and his somewhat slimmer shotgun messenger, Ryland perched on top of a wooden crate under the canvas top with his back against a mail sack.

He was the only passenger for this leg, but Ryland didn't mind. At least this time, he wouldn't have to worry about being robbed if he dozed off.

Sleep was a remote possibility, however. The wagon hit a rut or a rock every few seconds, but not regularly enough for him to anticipate the jarring. Just when he would think they'd hit a smoother stretch of road, *ka-thunk!* Down one wheel would go.

They changed mule teams every couple of hours, and after darkness fell they kept going, with a lantern mounted on the front of the wagon. Ryland nodded off numerous times and hoped he could cobble together, if not a night's sleep, at least enough to take the edge off his fatigue.

Unlike the larger commercial lines, this stage outfit had no relief drivers. After eighteen hours on the road, they pulled in at a way station, and the driver poked his head inside the canvas covering.

"Best get down and get a bite inside. We'll bide here 'til dawn."

Ryland crawled out, stiff and achy, and staggered into the cabin by the road.

"Evenin'," said a stocky man with a full, bushy beard and a bald head. "I'm Mullins. Got some beans and some buffler stew. Four bits for the meal."

Ryland blinked at him in the lantern light. "Uh … buffler? You mean buffalo?"

"That's what I said. Take it er leave it."

Wasting no time, Ryland delved into his pocket for some coins. He had tasted buffalo steak in Cheyenne and found it as delicious as the finest beefsteak. What was more, the little cabin held a savory odor that made his stomach rumble.

"I'll take dinner, and if you have a bed, I'll take that, too."

Mullins grunted and held out his hand. "Got bedrolls in the loft. The bed up there's for Davy, but you're welcome to roll out a blanket on the floor for another two bits."

"Who's Davy?"

"Him what owns the stage."

"Oh." So, the driver had his own bed at the way station, but passengers had to sleep on the floor.

"No other beds?" Ryland asked.

"You can have mine for a dollar. I've even got a clean linen sheet."

A dollar seemed like an outrageous price, but Ryland had slept in stagecoaches for nearly two weeks.

"Private room, over there." Mullins nodded toward a plank door in the corner.

Ryland strode over to it and lifted the latch. The bed chamber was dark, but he could tell it was small and held a rope bed of a decent size.

"Is it comfortable?" he asked.

"Better'n the floor," Mullins said.

"Where will you sleep? In the loft with Davy and the shotgun rider?"

"Nah, I'll curl up in the haymow."

Ryland hesitated. That actually sounded enticing.

"How much for the haymow?"

Mullins laughed. "Two bits, and I'll let you use a blanket."

Ryland dropped three silver quarters into his hand. "There you go, then. Six bits, for dinner and a haymow."

He visited the necessary and returned to the cabin, where Mullins grudgingly gave him a basin with warm water to wash up. By the time Ryland reached the table, the driver and shotgun rider, Gleet, had come in, and Mullins was dishing up supper for them.

The stew was even better than Ryland had expected, and the beans weren't bad either, though they didn't quite have the New England flavor. Mullins's talents apparently ran to baking as well, as a pan of warm cornbread appeared magically on a trivet, and the three men feasted.

After twenty minutes of nonstop eating, Davy pushed his chair back, burped, and pulled out a pipe and tobacco.

"I gotta say, Mullins, your cookin's worth every penny."

"People say I charge too much." Mullins was now filling his dishpan with hot water from the stove.

Gleet shook his head and picked up his coffee cup. "When they say that, you tell 'em it's their loss. Your stew's as good as any housewife's from here to St. Louis."

"And that's the truth," Davy said, tipping his chair back so that he leaned against the log wall.

Ryland stood. "I agree. That was a wonderful meal, and very filling. Now, if you'll show me where to get my blanket, I shall retire."

"They're yonder, by the door." Mullins jerked his head toward the front door.

Ryland spied a pile of blankets on a shelf. "Thank you, then. Gentlemen—" He smiled at Davy and Gleet. "If you'd be so kind as to make sure I'm not left behind in the morning ..."

Davy blinked at him and brought his chair down with a thud. "What, you're sleeping in the barn?"

"Thought I would," Ryland said.

"Not scairt of Injuns?" Gleet sipped his coffee.

Ryland looked from one to the other of them and then at Mullins. "Is there danger from them?"

Mullins shrugged. "They come around now and again and steal mules. Haven't tried it since last fall, though. I reckon they've been concentrating on the gold seekers. Still, I bar the door good and keep the livestock under lock and key in the barn."

Ryland's throat went dry. "So, I'll be locked in?"

"Yessir, you will be. Sure you don't want my bed?"

The prospect of being awakened by an Indian reaching for his scalp made Ryland's skin crawl, but he wasn't about to back down. "I don't think so, thanks."

"Then I'll come out with you and lock the door behind you." Mullins took down the lantern that hung near the stove and then went to the wall by the door and reached for a large key that hung by a string. "Ready?"

"Uh … yes."

With a final nod to the two at the table, Ryland grabbed two blankets and headed out into the starlit night. Mullins walked along beside him with a rolling gait. When they reached the barn door, he lifted a large padlock and put the key in it.

"There you go. Here's the lantern. Be careful of it, and don't burn it all night."

"I won't," Ryland assured him, feeling like a little boy answering to his grandfather.

"Sleep tight," Mullins said with an impish grin.

"Thank you."

Ryland went in and held the lantern high. Behind him, Mullins closed and locked the door. Several mules were hitched in straight stalls, munching their feed. One turned his head around as far as his tether chain would allow and snuffled a greeting at Ryland.

"Same to you," Ryland said.

He spotted a rough ladder leading to the loft overhead. With difficulty, he made his way up without dropping either lantern or blankets. He found a spike in a beam and hung the lantern there while he fluffed up enough hay for a mattress and spread out one of his blankets atop the mound. His shoes slid off easily, but his feet were cold, and he decided against taking off his jacket.

After clearing a bit of floor at the edge of the mow for the lantern, he brought it over and set it down. The woolen blanket warmed him, but it scratched his chin. Ryland lay down and reached for the lantern. He had to crawl half off his makeshift bed to reach it. Once he'd blown out the light, it took him a few minutes to get the blankets the way he wanted and to find a comfortable position in the uneven hay. He wished he had a pillow, but wishing was no use.

Almost at once, he fell asleep. How long he slumbered, he wasn't sure, but several times in the night he awoke to the stamping or whickering of the animals below him. Each time, his heart raced until he assured himself nothing was amiss. If Indians were stealing the mules, the animals would panic and neigh, wouldn't they? And he would hear their hoofbeats and the opening of the barn door.

Each time he rolled over, he whispered a prayer for calmness and slipped off into sleep.

A shout of "Hey, Mister, rise and shine!" awoke him the next time. He sat bolt upright, his heart racing. The light of dawn sneaked in through chinks in the wall, and one of the mules brayed.

"That you, Davy?" Ryland called.

"Yup, it's me. Mullins is cooking bacon and hotcakes. We head out in half an hour."

Glad he'd replenished his cash in Denver, Ryland rolled his blankets, seized the lantern's bail, and cautiously approached the ladder. He'd had no chance to scrawl a report to Mrs. Rose, but he was one day closer—he hoped—to finding her first grandchild. If God was willing, he would soon have good news for her.

18

M att woke when the sun was high above the horizon. He hadn't expected to be able to sleep late, but apparently his mind had taken the message to heart that he needed extra rest.

He dressed and put on his gun belt. The way things were right now, he didn't dare ride far without his revolver. When he opened the door to the hall, there on the floor, neatly folded, was his uniform shirt. He picked it up and opened it. He could scarcely tell where Rachel had stitched the pocket and the seam. The rip below the armhole was neatly patched, with a small strip of cloth sewn in behind.

Today he'd leave the uniform at home. He'd already decided he couldn't rejoin the army without telling his father. If the regiment's surgeon declared him fit, he'd come home tonight for the rest of his things and say good-bye. After tucking the shirt into his wardrobe, he went downstairs and poked his head into the kitchen.

"Oh, you're up," Vida said. "It's about time."

"Anything left from breakfast?" Matt asked.

"I saved you some biscuits and sausage gravy."

"Thank you." He poured himself a mug of coffee while she fixed his plate. "Miss Rachel gone to the Box M?"

"Royal took her an hour ago."

Matt grunted.

"You'd best watch out, if you plan to snag her. That boy's all glassy-eyed when he looks her way."

Her outburst was so unexpected Matt laughed aloud. "What do you care, Vida? You don't like her anyway."

"Who says?"

"Oh, come on!" He set his mug down on the kitchen table. "You hardly give Rachel the time of day. You were so rude to her when she first came, she's quit offering to help with the housework."

"Rude? Me?" Vida plunked his plate down and turned back to her worktable. "I guess she's not so bad. When she first came, I thought she was a hothouse flower and would wilt at the first sign of trouble."

"Well, that didn't happen, did it?"

"I s'pose not, but she didn't make much show of grief when her daddy died."

Matt eyed her curiously, wondering just what Vida considered to be a proper display of mourning. "I think she's been very brave."

"Brave?" Vida snorted. "Headstrong's more like it. Determined to show she can do a man's work. I'm surprised she hasn't started wearing trousers."

Matt cleared his throat and shoved away the image that came to mind unbidden, of Rachel Maxwell in men's trousers, slinging a lariat over her head. "Miss Rachel would never do that, Vida. She's a proper lady, like you said, but she's also a hard worker. You have to admit she's shown that to be true."

"Whatever you say, Matthew." Vida wiped her hands on her apron then untied the strings. "Now, you won't see me again until tomorrow morning. There's ham in the spring house, and

I expect you and your pa can make do for one day. Make sandwiches for lunch. For supper, there's a chicken pie and a dried apple one in the pie safe yonder."

"Why, Vida, thank you kindly. Sounds like a feast. But where are you going?"

"Pard and me's going into town. Your father said we could take the wagon. I'm going to visit with the preacher's wife and Miz Holt at the mercantile and Miz Leigh and any other females whose ears I can bend. And I'm going to do some shopping."

"Well, there," Matt said with a grin. "Have yourself a real nice time."

"I intend to." Vida nodded firmly and went out the back door.

Matt drained his coffee cup. The time had come to ride over to Fort Lyon and inquire about his regiment. He would never have a better chance. For several months, he'd been thinking he should rejoin his unit. Pa had discouraged him because of his injury, but now it was pretty well healed. Still, his father didn't want him to leave again—Rachel was right about that.

He loved life on the ranch, as hard as it was. Army life, when he'd enlisted, had shocked him. It wasn't at all the way he'd imagined it. Weeks of boredom in camp, consisting largely of drilling and fatigue duties, or chores, were followed by a march into New Mexico that seemed endless. Four hundred miles in fourteen days.

When they'd finally gotten there, the heat, combined with a shortage of water and poor rations, had nearly done them in. But the men had rallied when they learned almost at once that a Confederate force was eager for a fight.

Glorieta Pass was a nightmare. Three days of terror in the Sangre de Cristo Mountains. The 1st Colorado Infantry fought alongside the 5th U.S. Infantry, two detachments of mounted cavalrymen, and two artillery batteries. Against them came the Texas Mounted Rifles.

Matt didn't like to remember the final day of battle. Colonel John Slough led his regiment that morning to try to hold back the Confederates as they came down Apache Canyon. One minute Matt had been jogging along between his buddies, his rifle at the ready, and the next his leg had exploded with fiery pain.

His wound was serious, but not immediately life-threatening. His friends tied two bandanas around his thigh and left Matt under a bush to wait while the rest of the 1st Colorado advanced. He was able to staunch the bleeding after a while and lay back exhausted, cringing in the scant shade. All afternoon he lay there, hearing the distant cannon and rifle fire and praying. He had no idea whether his side was gaining or losing ground.

The din grew more distant. As darkness fell, Matt wondered if he'd been totally forgotten. He should have tried to hobble back to the supply line. If he'd set out early, he might have been there already. But now his leg was swollen, too stiff and painful for him to even think about putting weight on it.

The moon was high overhead when Union troops returned and went slowly over the battlefield, searching for survivors. He cried out when he heard them coming, but he was so parched he couldn't make more than a guttural moan. When a mounted trooper came close, he lifted one arm over his head, in hopes the trooper would see him and keep his horse from stepping on him.

"You alive?" the cavalryman called.

"Yessir. Private Anderson, 1st Colorado."

The trooper jumped down and held a canteen to his lips.

After that first heavenly draught, Matt seized the trooper's gloved hand. "Can you get me back? I can make it if you get me to the doctor. It's not that bad. It's just my leg."

"Sure, we can get you to the sawbones."

How often had he thought of that exchange in the last year?

At the camp hospital, Matt learned that the doctor was called "sawbones" for a reason. A heap of shattered limbs lay outside the surgeon's tent. Matt feared he was about to lose his leg. He'd lain on the ground for twelve hours, and the aide who examined him told him it was a miracle he hadn't bled to death.

"It's not that bad," Matt insisted. "It's only because I was out there so long. Please, give me a chance."

The overworked surgeon listened to his pleas, extracted the musket ball, and went on to the next casualty.

"Don't blame him if you die of infection," the aide warned as he bandaged the wound.

It took Matt three months to get back on his feet and feel well enough to travel home. He'd spent another eight weeks mostly in bed with Pa and Vida tending to him. He'd only begun riding and trying to do chores again in the fall.

Almost fourteen months had passed since that terrible day at Glorieta Pass. Now his leg was sound again—for the most part. Sure, it ached if he walked too far or stayed in the saddle too long. But he was able to walk, and that was something. He was thankful he'd regained most of his mobility, if not his entire strength. But that would come. The more he worked, the more stamina he gained.

He finished his solitary breakfast, thinking about Rachel. What was she doing this morning? She'd refused to take the day off, though she'd worked hard all day with the Anderson outfit in the garden the day before. She'd surprised him with her persistence, stopping to rest only when the men did. His leg had given out before she did.

True, last night she'd looked wrung out, but she'd had a soak in the tub and stayed up to mend his uniform. This morning Matt still felt worn to a stub. Was she out riding herd or driving nails at her new cabin?

He arrived at Fort Lyon two hours later and tracked down

his sergeant, who was overseeing a fatigue duty where the men were sawing and splitting firewood.

"Well, now, Anderson! Good to see you," Sergeant Speare said. "How's that leg?"

"Not too bad." Matt was careful not to limp as he approached. "I'm thinking I'll be ready to rejoin soon."

"That right? Whyn't you help the boys with this detail, get 'em finished quicker?"

"Sure." Matt turned his horse into the corral set aside for visitors' mounts and joined his former comrades. Among them was Harry Banks, who had worked two years on the Andersons' ranch. He'd enlisted about the same time Matt did and had come through Glorieta Pass unscathed.

"Hey, look at you," Harry called. "Thought you was all shot to pieces."

"Nearly so," Matt replied. He scooped up an armful of split wood and carried it to the nearby wagon, where the men were stacking it.

"This load's for the kitchen," Speare said. "They need it right away, so get a move on."

Matt exchanged pleasantries with Harry and some of the other men he knew while they worked. Harry wanted all the latest ranch news and pressed Matt for details about the attack on the Box M and Rachel Maxwell's arrival.

After fifteen minutes, Matt could no longer conceal his limp. The heavy burdens he carried put more pressure on his leg, and it ached fiercely, but he worked doggedly until the wagon was filled.

As he wiped his brow with his bandanna and resettled his hat, Sergeant Speare walked over near him.

"Stick around and eat mess with us if you want, but I don't think you'd best rush coming back to active duty."

"I'm ready. Really."

Speare looked him up and down. "We don't have any new

orders yet, but I expect we'll be going after the Cheyenne soon. I'd say you ought to take it easy a while longer."

"I want to do my bit," Matt said.

"Son, you done it. Don't push your luck."

"But—"

Speare shook his head. "That leg tells me otherwise, Anderson. You're better off on that ranch, helping your daddy."

Matt stayed only long enough to eat a hasty dinner and catch up with a few more old friends.

"We're s'posed to be helping the Creek," Harry said. "They've stayed pretty much on the reservation, like they said they would. But the Cheyenne." He shook his head. "They've been out hunting and raiding the Arapaho, and then the Arapaho raids back. Seems they never agree on anything, unless it's to go attack the miners."

"So, you're heading for the goldfields next, to protect the miners?" Matt asked.

"That or ride up to Denver. People up there are getting nervous, afraid the tribes will attack them. No trouble out where you live?"

"Not yet." Matt wondered if he was right to want to leave the ranch. The Box M was shorthanded now. He didn't like to think of leaving his father vulnerable.

When Matt's unit formed up to take on their next chore, he went to the corral and saddled his horse. His thigh muscles had stiffened during the time he sat for dinner. The sergeant was right, but knowing that didn't make him feel any better. Just riding the dun home would keep his leg screeching for the next two hours. It was time to admit he couldn't do a full day's work, either on the ranch or at the fort.

VIDA WAS absent from the kitchen that evening, and Rachel found Mr. Anderson putting a pie in the oven when she returned from the Box M.

"Can I help you?" she asked.

"Vida left a chicken pie ready to heat, so there's not much to do." He smiled at her and lifted one of the lids on the firebox of the stove.

"I can at least set the table," Rachel said.

"Sure, that would be nice."

Between the two of them, they found bread, jelly, and pickles to round out the meal, and Rachel made a pot of coffee. When Matt came in from the barn, his face looked drawn. Rachel kept quiet and waited for his father to ask how his visit to the fort had gone.

"Speare thinks I'm not ready," Matt said in a tight voice.

"Your leg?" his father asked.

Matt nodded and served himself a piece of chicken pie.

Rachel couldn't help the wave of relief that swept over her. He wouldn't be leaving, then. At least not yet.

"They're off to the mountains soon, or so Harry tells me, to settle the Indian trouble."

"Well, I can't say I'm sorry you're not going, son." Mr. Anderson sounded tired, too. How had he spent the "day off"? Both the men looked as though the holiday had worn them out.

Mr. Anderson raised his mug to his lips and took a sip. His eyes widened and he nodded at Rachel. "Now, that's good coffee."

"Thank you." She smiled and took a bite of chicken pie. Salt. It desperately needed salt.

The next morning, Vida was on the scene, and breakfast was as usual—plentiful but flavorless. When she was finished, Jimmy was waiting to ride over to the Box M with Rachel. She was mildly disappointed that she wouldn't have the private time with Matt, but she was glad he was letting the boys take over a chore he must find tedious, and even painful.

"So, Matt went to the fort yesterday," Jimmy said when they had left the barnyard behind.

"That's right," Rachel said.

"He going back to the army soon?"

"I don't think so."

"Huh." Jimmy frowned. "I was thinking of joining. Only I think I'd go to St. Louis if I did. I'd want to fight Rebs, not Injuns."

Rachel eyed him in surprise. "Why is that? The Confederates aren't threatening the ranch, after all."

"No, but they don't take scalps, neither."

They'd had enough of the grim conversation, Rachel decided. She gathered her reins and felt Herald bunch beneath her.

"Race you to the creek." She gave Herald his head, and he lunged forward into a gallop.

19

Rachel spent the morning helping at the cabin site. The men had thoroughly cleared away the debris from the house, salvaging any hardware they could. Dusty had cleaned up the kitchen stove and declared it was fit as a fiddle, anytime she wanted to cook on it. The roughhewn sills were laid for a small, rectangular cabin.

Although she couldn't do the heavier work, Rachel was handy with a hammer. Charlie, whose wound was healing, was in charge of the construction project. He still wore a sling and endured merciless teasing from the other men about how little use he was around the ranch. But he'd built things before—everything, he declared, from outhouses to great barns back in Minnesota, where he hailed from. He soon had Rachel busy driving nails into what would be the main room's floor.

Pard Henry was just leaving the barn when she got home that night.

"How was your trip to town?" Rachel asked.

"It went all right."

"Did Vida buy any cloth yet?" Rachel hoped she wouldn't,

since she was coming along on her secret project, but she didn't want Vida to be unhappy either.

"Nah," Pard said. He looked at Rachel and smiled. "So, our boy's not going off to war again."

"You mean—"

"Matthew."

Rachel returned his smile. It was the friendliest she'd ever seen Pard act, and it made her wonder if he seemed quiet and sober because of Vida's sour personality—but maybe she wasn't like that with Pard.

"I admit, I wasn't sorry when I heard it," she said.

"You and his daddy both. I reckon all of us are glad he's stayin'." Pard took Herald's reins from her hands. "Whyn't you let me put this feller up for ya?"

"I can do it, Pard."

"I know you can."

Rachel hesitated only a moment. Pard was offering her friendship, and she wouldn't deny him that.

"Thanks. I appreciate it."

He nodded and led Herald into the barn.

WHENEVER SHE HAD A CHANCE, Rachel worked on the red dress. She rose early so she'd have a few minutes before breakfast, and she spent evening time in her room while the light was good, stitching by the window. She was tired from working on the cabin, but the dress was coming along nicely. She hoped Vida would be pleased.

On Sunday, she rode in the wagon with Matt and his father to the little church. Matt was still subdued, and he didn't talk much on the way. Rachel sat beside him during the service, quiet and very aware of his nearness.

When they were dismissed after the sermon, she spent a welcome half hour talking to the women of the tiny settlement.

"We're blessed to have a preacher," Mrs. Leigh told her. "Most towns out here don't get one until their population is quite sizable."

"Mr. Bixly's sermons always bless my heart," Rachel said.

"Oh, yes, indeed," Mrs. Leigh told her. "But the man needs a wife. If my Carrie were a year or two older …"

That surprised Rachel. Carrie Leigh was only twelve. "I'm sure some nice single women will move here before long."

Mrs. Dexter, on her other side, laughed. "There be one standing right here."

"Who, me?" Rachel's cheeks warmed. "Oh, please, no. He's a fine man, I'm sure, but …"

She glanced toward where the preacher stood talking with a few of the ranch men. There was nothing wrong with Mr. Bixly, but she'd never once thought of him as eligible.

For one thing, the minister was probably fifteen years her senior, and for another, he probably knew nothing about ranching. She couldn't envision herself marrying a preacher and moving into town. Teaching school and being independent looked far more attractive to her than the option the ladies presented.

"But what?" Mrs. Leigh asked.

Mrs. Dexter chuckled. "But maybe she has someone else in mind."

Rachel's cheeks may as well have been on fire.

Portland, Maine

As Abby Benson and her grandmother descended the church steps, a young man came alongside them.

"Good day, Mrs. Rose. Miss Benson."

"Good day, George." Grandmother's gaze raked him over, from his pomaded hair to his gleaming shoes. "How is your mother?"

"She's better, thank you."

"I'm glad to hear it. Perhaps she will be able to attend services next week."

"That is her hope." The young man turned eager eyes upon Abby. "I wondered, Miss Benson, if I might call upon you tomorrow evening?"

Startled, Abby shot the old lady a glance. "I'm not sure. Do we have plans, Grandmother?"

"None that I am aware of."

Abby swallowed a lump in her throat. Grandmother was no help at all. She didn't wish to entertain George MacLeod, or any other young man in the vicinity, but she could hardly turn him down now without seeming rude. And he waited with high expectation.

"Oh, dear, we're blocking the foot traffic." Abby smiled and swept to one side, adjusting her full skirt so as not to impede the worshipers coming out of the church.

"Well?" George looked like a spaniel, holding his best hat in both hands before him, in almost the same posture as a begging puppy.

"I ... uh ... I suppose so." Abby looked to Grandmother, but she had launched into a conversation about flowerbeds with Mrs. Salley. "Do come early. Grandmother likes to retire by eight."

"Of course." He still waited.

What did he expect? A dinner invitation? Well, Abby wasn't going to give one. She had no desire to encourage him, and she'd have to find a way to let him know that politely during their visit. The only young man she'd gladly allow to court her would be ... but that was silly. That young man was thousands of miles away and probably hadn't thought of her once since he'd left to look for her cousins.

She felt her cheeks flush, just thinking about Mr. Atkins.

"Thank you," George said. "I'll come by around six, shall I?"

"Oh, dear, let's say six-thirty. I expect we can have tea and cake then."

"Fine." He smiled in a manner that made Abby's brow wrinkle without her intending it. Was this how admiration looked on a young man's visage? She didn't think she liked it. He appeared rather silly.

"Good day." She turned and took her grandmother's arm. "Hello, Mrs. Salley. Are you ready to go, Grandmother?"

The older woman was happy to head home but was quieter than usual during dinner. Finally, as tea and brown betty were served, she fixed her gaze on Abby.

"You don't wish to be courted by George MacLeod?

Abby cleared her throat, seeking a suitable reply. "Actually, I don't fancy him, Grandmother."

"I see."

Was she disapproving? Abby certainly didn't want to displease her or cause any tension between them.

"I realize I'm of age and should be looking for a husband," she began.

Grandmother shook her head vigorously. "Who gave you that notion, child? I certainly am not eager to be rid of you."

Abby smiled. "Thank you. I have enjoyed my time here with you immensely. Do you think I should be ... receptive to George's overtures?"

"Not if you don't wish to encourage him."

"He's not ..." Abby hesitated. "Not what I imagine in a husband."

"Oh." Grandmother pressed her lips into a thin line for a moment. "And what do you imagine, Abigail?"

"A man who is eager to meet life. A man who is kind and

courteous, but also one who is curious. One who isn't afraid of adventure."

Grandmother nodded. "One like your grandfather, perhaps?"

Abby smiled. "I should love to meet a man like Grandfather. Like he was when he was young, of course."

"Of course." Grandmother's gaze lost its focus for a moment. "Zephaniah Rose was one in a thousand. No, a million." Her expression soured. "I only wish we'd spent more time together."

"You went on one voyage with him," Abby ventured.

"Yes, and that was enough. I was expecting your Aunt Catherine, and I was ill most of the voyage. Very unpleasant. During my second confinement, with your mother, I stayed on land, and it went much easier, I assure you. You don't want to be cooped up with thirty men in such a situation, trust me."

"I shall remember that if any sea captains come to call." Abby gazed down at her hands and tried to settle her features into a demure expression.

Grandmother laughed. "Look at you. I expect you've more interest in a man like Ryland Atkins."

Abby couldn't keep her eyes from flying wide open. "Mr. Atkins?"

"Yes. He's not Captain Rose, but I expect with a bit of experience—this trip he's on, for instance—he will gain the maturity and wisdom he needs in this life." Grandmother picked up her teacup and sipped from it. "Yes, I suppose he'll make decent husband material after a while. Not yet."

"No, of course not yet." Abby's face felt hot, and she was sure her cheeks were scarlet. "I'm not sure he would even consider me."

"Perhaps not. He may have someone else in mind, after all."

"Yes." That thought had occurred to Abby. Nevertheless, she prayed daily for Mr. Atkins. His letters were quite expressive, and coupled with all the news from the west and travel accounts she could lay hands on, she was able quite easily to imagine herself making the odyssey with him. Why the last letter they'd received—

A knock at the front door shattered her daydream and jerked her back to Grandmother Rose's dining room.

Patsy hurried through the room.

"Put whoever it is in the parlor," Grandmother called after her.

"Yes, ma'am."

Grandmother arched an eyebrow at Abby. "Finish your tea, my dear."

"I'm ready," Abby said.

"Let us wait until the caller is settled."

"Yes, ma'am." Abby lifted her cup of lukewarm tea. It couldn't be George already. He'd said tomorrow evening. She caught a few words the gentleman at the door was saying to Patsy.

"It's no bother, Mr. Turner," Patsy replied quite clearly.

Abby was sure she'd enunciated the name so that she and Grandmother would know who had knocked while she showed the visitor into the front room.

"Mr. Turner," Abby whispered to her grandmother.

"Yes. On a Sunday."

He couldn't have had a letter from Mr. Atkins today. Perhaps he'd received one yesterday and wanted to share its contents. Or maybe a telegram had come through.

"I hope it's good news," Abby said.

Grandmother threaded her linen napkin through the carved teak ring beside her plate. "Shall we find out?"

"My dear Mrs. Rose," Mr. Turner said, standing as the women entered the parlor. "I apologize for arriving while you were at dinner."

Grandmother brushed his comment aside with a wave of her hand. "That is not a problem, Mr. Turner. Would you like some tea?"

"No, thank you. I just wanted to tell you Mr. Atkins is making some progress. I can't promise that he'll be able to locate your eldest grandson, but he seems to be working hard at it. My confidence in him increased with his last communication. He's quite certain the Anderson family bought a ranch near Fort Lyon five years ago, and he is headed there now."

"Yes, we received a letter from him." Grandmother looked at Abby, who had just settled onto the horsehair sofa. "Perhaps you'd like to fetch it, Abigail."

"Of course." Abby jumped up and hurried to her grandmother's desk.

"I should very much like to hear what he says," Mr. Turner was saying as she returned.

"He was nearly robbed in a stagecoach," Abby said breathlessly. At Grandmother's frown, she paused and gulped in a deep breath. "So sorry. It turned out fine, and he was able to retrieve his wallet. Let's see, now." She unfolded the pages of the letter and sneaked a glance at her audience. Mr. Turner sat upright in his chair, his hands resting on top of his walking stick and his eyes focused on her with a sparkle of eagerness.

"By the time you get this," Abby read, "I shall probably be deep in the Colorado Territory …"

MATT WENT to the bunkhouse Monday morning and made a point of telling the men he'd be the one to take Rachel to the Box M.

"I thought it was my turn." Jimmy's voice rose in challenge.

"Easy, bucko," Josh Brand said. "It's always the boss's turn if he wants it."

The comment didn't sit well with Matt. He and Josh usually

got along well, and he figured Jimmy was just a high-spirited young fellow with a crush on the only pretty girl within miles.

"Next time, Jimmy."

"Sure, Matt." Jimmy flushed beneath his tan as he buckled on his holster.

"Got a minute, Josh?" Matt asked.

"Any time." Josh followed him out to the corral.

Matt turned to face him. "Do we have a problem?"

"Not on my account."

"Then what was that remark about the boss? You know I'm not the boss. That's my pa, and Pard's our foreman."

"Oh, is that all?" Josh laughed. "I thought you were marking your territory around Miss Rachel."

"There's nothing between us. We're friends, is all."

"So you wouldn't mind if one of us started courting her?"

Matt eyed him closely. Jimmy, the young whippersnapper, was one thing. Rachel wouldn't look twice at him. But Josh was thirty, and not a bad specimen of a cowboy. He could read and write, too, something not all of the men could claim. He saved his wages and rarely got drunk on payday. He might make a pretty good husband for some woman.

But not Rachel.

"By 'one of us,' do you mean you?"

Josh lifted his hat, pushed his hair back, and settled the hat again. "I'm just sayin'."

"Huh."

They looked at each other for a moment, taking each other's measure.

At last, Matt broke the silence. "I never knew you were interested."

Josh shrugged. "I've worked for your pa for four years, and we've been friends."

"Yeah," Matt said. "So?"

"So, I'd never make a move if I thought you was going to."

Josh looked out over the corral then swung his gaze back to Matt. "Are you going to?"

Matt swallowed hard. He wasn't about to tell Josh that Rachel had turned him down before he even asked.

"Well, I hadn't ruled out the possibility, but I'm ... biding my time."

"How long you going to bide?" Josh asked.

"Not sure."

Josh nodded. "Let me know if you quit?"

"All right. And I appreciate you asking."

The other hands came out of the bunkhouse and headed for the barn.

"I'll get Rachel's horse ready." Matt walked away, feeling Josh's eyes on him. He'd been put on notice, for sure. But this was something that couldn't be hurried.

At least Josh wasn't charging in to begin courting her. If Jimmy thought he had a chance, he probably wouldn't care who stood in the way. Josh was an honorable man. That in itself made him a formidable opponent, and Matt didn't want to become rivals in love. Time to make some progress with Rachel —or give up the pursuit.

20

Rachel reined Herald in halfway to her ranch.

"Oh, look, Matt! Flowers."

Matt swept a glance over the prairie, where the grass was thriving and blossoms poked up to sprinkle it with white, pink, and gold. Weeds, his pa would say.

"It's pretty."

She swung down from the saddle. "Do you mind if I stop to pick a few? I'd love to put some on my father's grave."

"Sure." He dismounted and let his bay's reins drop. "Let me help you."

In just a few minutes, she had a full bouquet.

"Thanks," Rachel said, accepting his final bunch of blossoms. "This is plenty."

"Will you be all right carrying them?" Matt asked.

"Yes, if you'll hold them while I mount."

When they were both in the saddle, she smiled over at him ruefully. "Sorry. I'm making you late."

"That's all right."

They urged the horses into a gentle jog.

"Matthew..."

Her pensive tone caught his attention immediately. "What?"

"I miss my papa something fierce."

He nodded. "To tell the truth, I was thinking of my ma while I picked the flowers. Thinking how Pa and I never get to put anything on her grave, since she died back in Missouri. I'm glad you've at least got him close by."

"I go up there often. It must be really hard for you, losing two mothers."

"It is, but at least I still have my father." He hesitated and then said. "This father, I mean. I don't know about my real father. He could be dead. I'll probably never know what became of him."

"That seems worse, in a way, than knowing how my father died." She nudged Herald closer to his horse. "I wish I could truly understand you, and how you feel, and … all of this. Sometimes I'm baffled. It's like someone punched me in the jaw, and I landed in a heap. I don't know which end is up, or if I'm doing the right thing, following the right dream."

"I guess it's different for me," he said. "I love ranching, and I love Pa. I wouldn't think of going somewhere else or trying to make my living running a store or …"

"Or teaching school?"

He laughed. "No more than I'd want to become a sailor or a lawyer. This is what I know."

"But your family only came here five years ago."

"We farmed in Missouri before that. Pa and I both liked raising livestock better than tilling the ground. We went mostly to raising cattle and hogs there."

"Hogs?" Rachel cocked her head toward her shoulder. "I can't picture you as a hog farmer."

"Me either. We decided we didn't like that end of it, so when the chance came, and we heard about the grasslands out here, we came. Trailed along with some gold seekers and left them when we got to Denver."

"The Pike's Peak bunch?"

"Or bust," he said with a chuckle, but he quickly sobered. "After Ma died, back in Independence, Pa was feeling rootless again. I could tell he didn't want to stay there. Too many bad memories. So, when he started talking about coming farther west, I didn't discourage him."

"My mother's buried in Texas," Rachel said. "I said good-bye before I went to school. At the cemetery, I mean. But still, I wish I could put flowers on her lot today, too."

"You can pretend it's for both of them," Matt said gently.

That was like him. She glanced down at the flowers. "Yes. And you can pretend it's for your Ma. You helped pick them, after all." They neared the Box M buildings, and she looked over at him, feeling a little silly. "Would you like to come up the hill with me, Matt? We can honor both our mothers, along with my papa."

He cleared his throat. "Sure. And thanks."

They rode up to the corral, where Bud was giving orders to the men. Hank, Sam, Telly, Ran, and Dusty called hello to her, mounted their horses, and waved.

"Morning," Bud said. "Howdy, Matt."

Matt nodded. "Thought I'd ride up to the graveside with Miss Rachel."

"Fine." Bud eyed the flowers she held. "When you're finished, I'll be down here, working on your cabin roof. Charlie thought he was up to helping me, and I figured the three of us could make some progress between now and dinner time."

"Sounds good," Rachel said, though she wondered if she wanted to climb up on the roof.

"You can fetch and carry for us," Bud said.

"Even better."

He laughed. "All right, go pay your respects. You know where to find me."

Matt turned his horse toward the graveyard. She rode with

him up the gradual slope. Though much of the ranch consisted of open range, undulations in the land made it far from level.

The burial site was one of the higher points near the ranch buildings. She could look down from there and see anyone who rode in from the road or over the range from the Andersons' spread. She liked to come up here and enjoy the wide view, though Bud had cautioned her not to go without letting them know.

She and Matt dismounted and let the horses graze. She carefully separated the stems of her bouquet and handed him half the flowers.

"Say whatever you want to your Ma," she told him. She walked over to the grave with the wooden cross Charlie had carved and stooped to place her wildflowers at its base. For a moment she stood in silence, trying to calm her thoughts.

"Lord, thank you for letting me have Mama and Papa as long as I did," she said.

Matt bent on the other side of the cross and laid his posy next to hers. "Thank you for letting me know Mr. Maxwell, Lord," he said quietly. "And for giving me my Ma and Pa Anderson in my time of need."

They stood in silence for a minute or more. Rachel couldn't help thinking that a man who honored his mother would also honor a wife. Matt appreciated the people who'd cared for him and sacrificed for him.

"You come from good people," she said.

He gazed at her across the grave, his blue eyes sorrowful. "If you mean the Andersons, yes. Thank you."

"I'm sorry. I didn't mean to bring up bad memories."

"It's all right." He looked up at the sky, where wispy clouds blew over. "But I wonder sometimes about my first parents. Especially Pa. I know my mother was a good woman. She was gentle and kind and ... beautiful." He sucked in a deep breath and looked down at the flowers. "My pa, though ... I don't know. He just left us. That's hard to understand."

Rachel nodded. "I agree. What man would abandon his children when he knew they needed him? Especially children so young."

"Just makes me wonder what sort of people I really come from, you know?"

"I know."

Matt looked down the hill toward the small new cabin, where Bud was climbing to the ridgepole. "I thought once I might try to write to people we knew in White Plains, but I didn't remember enough to direct a letter. There was Mrs. Pruitt, the neighbor Pa left us with. I started to write her once, back when we lived in Tarrytown. But I didn't know what to say or what to ask. And then we moved, and after a while, I couldn't remember the name of the street she lived on." He shook his head.

"Maybe you could write to the orphanage where they took you."

"No. They wouldn't tell me where Janie went. I doubt they'd tell me anything at all."

"But you're grown up now. Maybe they would."

He eyed her doubtfully. "You think they'd know where my real father went?"

"Maybe he came back looking for you," Rachel said. At Matt's grimace, she added, "Or maybe now they'd tell you where the others are—Elijah and Jane."

"Doubt it."

The wind rippled over the knoll, blowing tendrils of Rachel's hair against her cheek.

"Does Mr. Anderson know you wonder about them?"

"We don't speak of it much."

The pain in his eyes was enough for Rachel. His adoptive father didn't like to think about his other family, and he probably wished Matt didn't either. Without Matt's saying so, she knew it was easier for him to keep silent about it. But she felt a bond with him, since they'd both lost so much.

"I have this." He pulled something from his pocket and held it up. A metal disk dangled from a leather thong.

"What is it?"

Matt held it out to her, and she took it.

"It's the Chinese coin I told you about. My grandfather got a bunch of them on one of his voyages and sent one to each of his grandchildren."

"That's wonderful." Rachel examined it closely and handed it back to him. "Your grandfather loved you and gave you a keepsake."

He nodded. "Elijah had one, and Janie. Our cousin in Maine, too. Maybe we have more cousins now that I don't know about. It's odd to think that."

"Wouldn't it be nice to find out someday?"

"My grandparents would be old now, maybe even dead. I don't remember where they lived in Maine. Near the water ..." Matt stood for a moment gazing off toward the trees. He sighed and tucked the coin back into his pocket.

"I'd best go." Matt raised his eyebrows in question.

"Yes, and I'd better go help Bud and Charlie on the cabin. But, Matt..."

"Yeah?"

"Thank you for telling me about your family. If I can help—"

"I don't see how you could."

"Well ... I know people in Boston."

"We weren't in Boston. We were in New York. That's a long ways, isn't it?"

"Not too far. Not with the railroads and telegraphs and everything. Anyway, I'll pray for your brother and sister, if you don't mind."

His eyes glistened. "I don't mind."

They walked to the horses. Before he mounted, Matt reached for her hand and gave it a gentle squeeze. "Thanks."

WHEN MATT WENT to the house for dinner at noon the next day, his father had just returned from town. Matt unsaddled his horse and then went to help unload the wagon.

He picked up a small bundle wrapped in the brown paper they used at the mercantile. "What's this?"

"Some buttons and things Rachel asked for," Pa said. "Just put it up in her room, would you?"

Matt took the package upstairs. He felt odd entering Rachel's room without her permission, and he studiously avoided looking around too much. She was a neat person, however, and he doubted she would leave anything embarrassing lying about. Just the idea that he might glimpse a corset or some of her stockings left him hot under the collar. He dropped the package on the foot of the bed and beat a retreat down the stairs.

His father had enlisted Pete and Royal to finish the unloading, and when Matt reached the main room, Pa was ready to sit down at the table. Vida brought in fried potatoes and side meat, along with cornbread and coffee.

"It'll sure be nice when the garden comes in," Matt said.

Pa looked up at Vida as she filled his coffee cup. "Don't we have any canned vegetables left, Vida?"

She huffed out a breath. "What? You want green beans and carrots every meal? You'll get some tonight with your supper."

"What do we have left?" Matt asked.

"Land sakes, I don't know. Some beets and corn and what-all."

Matt sighed as she went back into the kitchen. "She canned and canned last fall. Where'd it all go?"

"I guess we ate it," Pa said.

They tucked into the food. Matt hadn't realized how hungry he was, but the greasy meat and potatoes didn't satisfy his cravings.

"I heard Harry Banks was killed," Pa said.

It seemed out of the blue, and Matt stared at him. "When?"

"Just recently."

"I saw him a week ago, at Fort Lyon."

"His squad went after some Cherokee, and they had a skirmish up in the mountains. That's all I know."

Matt's lungs squeezed, and he laid down his fork. "It's not right."

"What?" His father eyed him closely. "Now, don't you go feeling guilty because you weren't there."

"This bum leg ..."

"Aw, Matt!" Pa balled up his napkin and threw it on the table. "Would it be any better if you got killed instead of Harry Banks? If you'd been there, maybe you'd both be dead now."

"I just ... I feel like I let them down."

"By getting shot?"

"Maybe. By not being able to go back and pull my weight."

"You're pulling your weight here, wound or no wound."

"You don't understand, Pa."

"No, son. *You* don't understand. If you went away again now, I don't know what we'd do without you. We need you here."

"You've got Pard and the men."

"None of them could replace you, Matthew." Pa shook his head. "If I lose you, what do I have left?"

Matt couldn't answer that, but suddenly his father's life looked very bleak. Before they adopted Matt, the Andersons had been alone. Ma had grieved because she couldn't have children. They'd both sorrowed over that, but then they'd found him. He remembered how he'd been forced to go with them, and how he'd vowed to hate them. He'd sworn to himself he'd run away as soon as he could. He'd go back and find Elijah and Janie.

But an odd thing had happened. Mr. and Mrs. Anderson had shown him so much compassion, he'd stayed. He had come to realize how much better life was in their family than at the orphanage—or even with his birth father, Ben Cooper. As much as he missed his brother, and to some extent Janie, he had stayed.

Guilt had weighed on him for twenty years. He'd mentioned once to Ma Anderson how he'd like to find his siblings, and she'd said after harvest that year she could write a letter to the orphanage. For a few weeks, he'd hoped. But in the fall, Ma took sick and died. He'd tried to tell himself Elijah and Jane had been taken by good families, too, but he didn't feel he could bring it up to Pa Anderson.

Matt took a deep breath. The last thing he wanted now was an argument with his father. "I only went into the army because I wanted to help protect the citizens—"

"Your job is to protect this ranch. Can't you see that? We're citizens, too."

"But the army's doing more than protecting the miners. The government needs the gold, to pay off the soldiers. If the miners can't do their work, the army fighting the rebels can't be paid."

"Yes, war was never cheap." His father sighed. "What do you think would have happened at the Box M if you hadn't come along that day, when they were under fire? You helping them and sending Rachel to get me and the boys—that's what saved their lives. If you'd been off fighting Indians, those men would all have died. Every last one of them."

It made sense, and Matt's altruism was stripped away. He'd been selfish, pure and simple. He'd wanted to feel like he mattered. Why couldn't he feel that way without leaving home?

"I guess you're right. I'm sorry, Pa."

His father picked up his cup and sipped his coffee, grimaced, then set it down. "Don't mention it."

Matt sat in silence for a minute, pondering that. Did Pa mean that literally—don't mention this again? Or did he mean it as a courtesy—"it's nothing"?

At last he said, "You don't have to worry. I'll stay, Pa."

21

The clouds gathered throughout the day, and by evening the wind blew strong across the range. Bud rode home with Rachel. The little cabin was secure from the weather now, and if she stayed in Colorado, someday she and the men would add on to it and make it a proper house once more.

"I'll probably stay here tomorrow," she said as they approached the Andersons' house. "Don't look for me if it's raining."

"That's wise," Bud said. "The boys and I can keep busy inside your cabin, do some finish work, now that the roof is tight."

She smiled. "Thanks, Bud. Now all we have to do is figure out a way for me to move over there without shocking the whole county."

In the morning, rain streaked down the windows. Rachel rose at her usual time and went downstairs.

Matt emerged from the kitchen. "Good morning. Pard just stopped in to tell us Vida's not feeling well. She sent word that there are plenty of leftovers, and … well, she thinks we can get by without too much fuss."

"I don't mind cooking. I told Bud I wouldn't be over today."

Rachel walked past him and put her hand on the kitchen door.

"Oh, uh …"

She paused to look at Matt. "Is anything wrong?"

"No. It's just … Well, I wasn't going to tell you, but apparently Vida said she didn't want … anyone … messing around in her kitchen."

Rachel laughed. "Anyone, meaning me."

"Well …" Matt couldn't meet her gaze. "I started coffee, and there are some biscuits left from last night."

"Matthew Anderson! As if you shouldn't have a decent breakfast." Rachel pushed the door open and surveyed the kitchen. Very few times, she'd been in the room without Vida's oppressive presence. She grabbed a bib apron from a hook by the door and pulled the strap over her head. As she tied the strings behind her, she walked toward the cupboards.

"If that's the way you want it," Matt said from behind her.

"It is. I don't intend to put in a full day's work on a biscuit and coffee." Rachel opened two cupboard doors and eyed the supplies inside, then moved to her left and opened two more. "Do we have any eggs?"

"I can look in the bucket in the well. Vida puts stuff down there to keep it cool."

"Would you please?"

"Sure," Matt said. "I'll check the henhouse, too. I know she's got one hen setting, but there might be a few more fresh eggs."

A few minutes later, he came in the back door. "I found two eggs in the well bucket and four more in the henhouse. That's besides the broody hen's nest." He took them out of his pockets one by one and set them in a dish.

"Perfect." Rachel took one and cracked it into the bowl of batter she was mixing.

"What's that?" Matt asked.

"Pancakes." She stirred vigorously and carried the bowl to the cookstove, where she had a large cast-iron frying pan heating. She hadn't found any butter, but she'd put a chunk of lard in it to melt. Carefully, she poured batter into the hot pan. Matt seemed fascinated, watching her every move. "The coffee's ready," she said. "Could you get the molasses, please, and anything else you and your father like with pancakes?"

Mr. Anderson poked his head in at the doorway. "Smells good in here. Oh! Rachel, what a surprise."

"Vida's sick." Matt handed him three plates and the molasses jug. "Could you put these on the table, please? Rachel's fixing breakfast."

"I see that." Mr. Anderson sounded a bit uncertain, but he took the things and disappeared.

"I saw a dish of applesauce in the pie safe," Rachel said.

Matt went to fetch it. Ten minutes later, she had a platter full of pancakes. She carried them and a bowl of sausage patties to where the Anderson men were sipping their coffee.

"There! Vida was right—it wasn't hard to eke out a meal." She smiled at them.

"This looks wonderful," Mr. Anderson said. "Shall we bless it while it's still hot?"

Rachel bowed her head and calmed her breathing as she listened to her host's prayer.

"… and we thank You for the hands that prepared it. Thank You for bringing Miss Rachel into our lives." As if remembering the cause of this morning's changes, he added, "And we ask that You'd help Vida to feel better real soon, Lord. Amen."

"Vida's birthday's coming up, isn't it?" Matt asked.

His father grunted. "Reckon so. Couple of weeks yet."

Rachel held back a smile. When the day came, she would be ready.

The men ate with gusto, and she had to admit breakfast seemed tastier than it had in weeks, though the applesauce was still rather bland. If Rachel had another chance, she'd add a bit of cinnamon. If Vida had any on hand. She decided to check the cupboard and ask one of her men to pick up some in town if there was none in the house.

"More coffee?" Matt asked.

"No, thank you," Rachel said.

His father held out his cup. "Thanks. And Rachel, thank you. I hope Vida doesn't get too upset."

Rachel waved that aside. "Don't worry. I'll leave her kitchen spotless. After I fix dinner, that is."

"What? You'll cook again?"

She smiled. "It was fun. I've been hammering nails and herding cattle. I actually enjoyed getting into the kitchen this morning."

"Well, the least we can do is help you do up the dishes," Matt said.

"I've got the water heating. You just go about your chores, and I'll be fine." Rachel couldn't help but notice the blown elbow on Mr. Anderson's sleeve shirt. He'd worn it that way for some time, and she hadn't wanted to embarrass him, but now she said, "Oh, and Mr. Anderson, I'd be happy to patch that shirt for you if you'd like."

"What, this?" He pulled the fabric around so he could see the extent of the hole. "I've been meaning to get at it, but either I don't have time, or I forget about it."

"If you have something else you can wear today, just leave that over a chair here, and I'll fix it." Rachel rose and began stacking the dishes.

Matt and his father looked at each other.

"What?" She paused with Matt's plate in her hand. They both looked like guilty little boys caught plaguing the cat. "Did I say something wrong?" She smiled and waited.

"Nothing wrong," Matt said.

"No, no," his father chimed in. "It's just that we're not used to this. You'll spoil us with the good eating and your ... dare I say 'cheerful attitude'?"

She laughed. "I'll take that as a compliment—no, two compliments. I don't mind helping out where I'm needed, and it seems for today it's kitchen work and mending you're needing."

WHEN MATT ENTERED the kitchen the next morning, the coffeepot was already steaming, but Vida's displeasure was obvious. She slammed a drawer shut and plunked a spatula on the worktable with such force that it probably left a dent in the wood.

"Something wrong, Vida?" Matt got down his usual ironstone mug and poured himself a cup of coffee.

"That girl. She cooked in here, didn't she?"

Matt held back his smile. "I assume you mean Rachel."

"Yes, Rachel. Miss Hoity-Toity."

Matt frowned at her. "Why do you say that?"

"She flounces around in fancy dresses and trots off every day to play with her father's men, pretending she's a rancher."

"Rachel is a hard-working woman, and she wants to see her father's ranch succeed."

"She should just sell it to you and go retire on the money."

Matt laughed. "I doubt Pa could come up with the money to buy the Box M."

"Well, then, she probably doesn't need money. At least not from what I see."

"I guess it's true her parents outfitted her well. She went off to school with a lot of clothes."

"A fancy school."

"Maybe. I don't really know. I do know she could be a teacher now if she wanted to, so I guess she got her education there."

"Huh. My mother taught school when she was fifteen. She didn't need any high-falutin' boarding school education."

"That was a long time ago, Vida."

Instead of calming her, that remark seemed to agitate her more. She fixed him with a sour glare. "I'm well aware of my age, young fella. I'm just saying, I don't like to come back and find someone has moved my things around. I can't find anything this morning."

"Oh? What are you missing?" Matt asked.

"The scoop for my coffee canister."

"That was probably me or Pa. We each made a pot yesterday. With all the rain, we spent most of the day in the house, so I guess we drank more than usual." As he talked, Matt opened and closed a couple of drawers. Finally, he found the small wooden scoop in the cupboard, next to the canister of ground coffee. "There you go. I must have left it on the shelf instead of putting it back in the coffee. Sorry."

Vida sniffed.

"You don't really think Rachel's stuck-up, do you?" Matt opened the canister and dropped the scoop inside. It was nearly full, and he smiled, recalling the half hour he and Rachel had spent together during the dreary afternoon, grinding coffee beans.

"The miracle is that you can't see it."

He turned and stared at her. Vida had turned her back and was stirring something in a heavy, yellowware bowl. Her spine was as stiff as a fencepost.

"I guess you're right. I don't see it. Rachel has been nothing but gracious, so far as I know. She's offered to help whenever she could, and if we accept the offer, she does help. And Bud Lassen told me she's done a lot of work over at her place. She's learning some things, but he says she's already a good rider and a fair hand with the cattle. Now she's helping him and the boys get her little house ready, for when she moves over there."

"Can't come a day too soon."

Vida spoke so low, Matt barely heard her comment, but he

did hear it, and the strength of his ire surprised him.

"You're just full of meanness today," he said.

She turned, and the deep hurt etched on her face almost made him regret his words. Almost.

"I've seen what she's been throwin' away."

Matt couldn't make sense of that. Rachel, throwing out something Vida valued? "What are you talking about?"

The kitchen door opened.

"Good morning," Rachel said brightly.

"Morning." Matt smiled at her, but Vida might have taken a slug of lemon juice, if her expression was any indication.

"Can I help with anything?" Rachel asked.

"It'll be ready in twenty minutes," Vida snapped. "Now get outa here, the both of you, and let me work."

"MAY I HELP YOU, VIDA?" Rachel stood in the kitchen doorway without much hope.

Vida paused in her work with her back toward Rachel. Several seconds passed in silence.

Well, I tried. The minister had stopped by the ranch late in the afternoon after calling on a sick parishioner, and Mr. Anderson had blithely invited Mr. Bixly to stay for dinner. Rachel had returned from the Box M to find them leaning on the corral fence, deep in conversation.

"I hear you know how to make biscuits," Vida said without turning around.

Rachel caught her breath. "That's right. My mother taught me."

"Well, if we can stay out of each other's way …"

"I'm sure we can." Rachel stepped forward eagerly. "And after I put a batch in the oven, I can set the table."

"Obliged."

They worked for twenty minutes without exchanging another word. Rachel timed every movement carefully to avoid Vida's proximity and therefore her displeasure. When she needed lard, she checked to see what Vida was doing first, and when she chose a pan, she looked to see which ones Vida had chosen for her chicken and vegetables before taking one from the rack.

When they sat down with Mr. Bixly, Vida brought in the hot dishes. Mr. Anderson smiled at her. "Vida, will you join us?"

"No, thank you." Vida was as sour-faced as ever. "But if you don't mind, I'll take a bit of that chicken and a couple of Miss Rachel's biscuits over to our place for Pard."

"Miss Rachel's biscuits?" John Anderson's eyebrows shot up.

Rachel smiled at him but said nothing.

"You heard me," Vida muttered. She plunked down the bowl of green beans and swept through the kitchen door.

"I must have missed something." Mr. Anderson shot an inquiring look at Rachel. "Well, Pastor, would you ask the blessing?"

"With pleasure," Mr. Bixly said.

After the prayer, Matt picked up the biscuit plate. He took two and held it out to the minister. "Sir, you're about to eat some of the finest biscuits in the territory."

Rachel turned her gaze toward Mr. Anderson, who was offering her the platter of chicken. Their eyes met, and she couldn't hold back a smile at his obvious approval. She almost felt that Mr. Anderson would watch over her as her father would, were he able. And that would include discouraging unwanted suitors.

Not that Mr. Bixly had given any indication of interest in Rachel, beyond what a pastor would normally show. But still, the church ladies' words still tugged at her mind. Rachel accepted the platter and determined to maintain a polite, pleasant, but impersonal demeanor with the minister.

THE NEXT MORNING Rachel hurried to dress, prepared to work several hours on her new little house—"the boss lady's cabin," the men called it. The physical labor tired her out each day, but she was encouraged by their progress. Bud had estimated that with good weather and barring any crises with the herd, they might have the place ready for her to move in by next week. She knew Matt and his father wouldn't approve, but Bud had assured her that he and the other men would look out for her.

"Hey," Matt greeted her in the great room when she went downstairs. "Pard went into town yesterday and fetched the mail. We forgot to give you this last night." He held out a letter.

"Oh, thank you." Rachel took it and saw at a glance it was from Miss Edgerly. She chatted for a moment with Matt, exchanging bits about their planned day's work. Mr. Anderson wasn't down yet, so Rachel retired to her room with the letter.

Miss Edgerly's note was kind, but she had found no definite openings for Rachel. She did, however, include a list of half a dozen quality girls' schools to which Rachel could send inquiries. Her former headmistress promised to write her a good recommendation if she applied for a position.

Rachel put the letter back in its envelope. She'd wait a day or two before replying, but she was pretty sure what she'd tell Miss Edgerly. Her feelings about Colorado and the Box M had changed. She was slowly coming to terms with her father's death and the fact that she was now a ranch owner. Even her smaller grievance—Vida's hostility—had mellowed. She liked to think she and the housekeeper had begun a grudging friendship.

And the last time Mr. Anderson had brought up the subject of her options for her father's property, she no longer felt he was grasping to take her inheritance from her. Instead, it seemed he wanted to offer her his advice as a friend with experience and perhaps more wisdom than she possessed.

He and Matt had both treated her well throughout her extended stay, and she'd always appreciate this time with them. They'd given her a place to heal and allowed her to work and make herself feel useful. Mr. Anderson would still like to add her acreage to his ranch, but he wasn't pressuring her about it or on the subject of marrying Matthew.

Rachel smiled to herself. Oddly enough, while Mr. Anderson seemed to be letting go of that dream, the thought was no longer repugnant to Rachel. She'd make it a matter of extra prayer, and they'd see what time brought.

As she rose to put the letter in her drawer, she noticed someone had emptied her wastebasket. She stood very still. Had Vida been in here? She hadn't noticed the basket was empty last night. Rachel wouldn't ordinarily mind, but she had tossed away some scraps of the cloth she was using to make Vida's dress.

She pulled in a sharp breath. Would Vida think she'd bought the material she particularly wanted? She certainly hoped Vida hadn't seen her sewing project. Rachel had tucked it away in her portmanteau. Surely the housekeeper wouldn't go snooping in a closed bag in the armoire?

Rachel hurried down to the dining area, went to the kitchen door, and peered inside. Vida was filling the milk pitcher from a bucket.

"Is there anything I can help you with?" Rachel asked, putting a pleasant tone in her voice.

Vida grunted and thumped the bucket onto her worktable. She turned away and opened the wood range's top with a clatter, shoved a stick of firewood inside, and slammed the iron cover down.

Rachel gulped. Maybe it was time to reveal her secret. But Vida's birthday was only a few days away. She planned to have the dress done before then.

June 12, 1863
Fort Lyon

RYLAND STEPPED up to the desk in the major's office. He felt as though he ought to salute, facing the trail-worn man in the deep blue uniform with its glittering gold accents on his collar.

"Major Roderick?"

"Yes, sir. How may I help you?"

Ryland took the chair he indicated. "My name is Ryland Atkins. I'm trying to locate the Anderson family. I understand they have a ranch in these parts."

The major studied him for a moment. "May I ask why?"

Ryland blinked. He wasn't used to being questioned, but the man's demeanor and the fact that he was in the midst of a military installation made him feel he should answer. "I've been commissioned by a party in the state of Maine to locate them. It's a legal matter, sir."

"What sort of legal matter?"

Ryland swallowed hard. "I assume this conversation is confidential, sir? I was hired by an attorney to represent a client, and I am not supposed to give out private information unless necessary."

"Understood," the major replied. "And *you* must understand, we've had some unrest in the area of late, and it's my duty to protect our citizens."

"Unrest?" Ryland eyed him closely. "Indians?"

"Some of that," Roderick replied. "But some civilian interference as well. A few of our local ranchers have been attacked by a band of renegades."

"Not the Andersons, I hope?"

Roderick didn't answer but watched him through slits of eyes. "Suppose you tell me the nature of your business for this lawyer. If it's irrelevant to my duties, it will remain between us."

"Yes, sir. A family in Maine wishes to locate their

grandchildren, who were adopted by various families about twenty years ago. I believe the eldest son was adopted by the Anderson family. They moved out here from the Independence, Missouri, area. The boy's legal name would now be Matthew Anderson."

For a moment, Ryland felt as if the major was staring right through him. Abruptly, Roderick opened a desk drawer and pulled out a ledger. He leafed through it and then studied a page intently. Closing the book, he looked up.

"Matthew Anderson was here a couple of weeks ago."

Ryland's chest tightened. He was close. "Then all is well with the family?"

"I can't say for certain. I didn't see Private Anderson personally."

Ryland held up a hand. "Wait. *Private* Anderson?"

"Yes. He's served with the 1st Colorado. He was wounded at Glorieta Pass last year."

Ryland sat very still. He'd read about that battle. It was bloody, to say the least. "But he's all right now?"

Roderick bit his lower lip, then met Ryland's gaze. "Our surgeon did not deem him fit to rejoin his regiment. I expect we'll muster him out, but that's not official yet."

"His wound ..."

"A leg wound, but he has not recovered his full strength. He wanted to return to service, but ..." Roderick shook his head. "I could use him right now, if he was fit. But that's not to be. I trust you won't relay any of what I've told you to Anderson? All he knows is, he was told to go home and give it more time."

"All right, sir. Can you tell me where he lives?"

"I believe his sergeant can serve you best. I'll send my aide to bring him in here. And I recommend you prepare yourself if you continue this journey. I can't guarantee your safety if you travel alone into the area where these outlaws are terrorizing the ranchers."

"Duly noted," Ryland murmured.

"Coffee while you wait, Mr. Atkins?"

"Thank you, sir."

Ryland tried to breathe slowly and evenly. He was nearly done with his first part of the mission. What would he tell Zephaniah Cooper when he met him? Or rather, Matthew Anderson? How badly was the young man injured? Could he leave the territory before his enlistment was ended? And would his wound prevent him from traveling to Maine to see Mrs. Rose? Ryland certainly hoped not.

WHEN RACHEL ARRIVED at the Box M, Bud was assigning tasks for the day to the hands.

"Sam was on night watch, and he found a bunch of steers had wandered off the west end of the range." He looked up at Rachel as she halted Herald nearby. "Morning, Miss Rachel. I'm sending Ran and Hank out to look for the missing cattle."

"Are we sure they wandered and weren't taken?" she asked.

"We've got a length of rail fence on the other side of the spring, at your boundary. They pushed down a sizable length of it. Probably panicked during the thunderstorm. Telly and Charlie will work on the fence, so's we can keep 'em in once we get 'em back. You can either stay here and sand the window frames in the—"

"I'll go with Ran and Hank," Rachel said quickly. Bud needed to stay close to the home base, as he'd hired a new cowboy, who was supposed to arrive this morning. Otherwise, he'd no doubt insist on riding with them. But she was sure the three of them would be all right.

She'd only been to the farthest reaches of the ranch once, and she was eager to get out there again. There were ravines and patches of woods she'd never explored. The rain had let up that morning, and though the ground was soft, she thought a beautiful, sunny day was in store.

Bud frowned. "All right, I guess. Maybe I should go with you."

Rachel shook her head. "You can't."

"I'm sure Dusty could show the new hand where to sling his gear." Bud's face tightened in a scowl. He obviously hated that idea. "No, I think I'd best be here. Only met the fella in town yesterday, and I want to look him over good before I put him to work."

Did he think the new cowboy might be an unsavory type? But if that was so, he wouldn't have told the man to show up at the ranch.

"Go, then." Bud turned away, shaking his head.

Rachel grinned at the two cowboys she'd be working with. Riding the range and, she hoped, herding a few cattle back was better than sanding woodwork all day inside the little house. "You boys ready?"

"You bet, Miss Rachel." Hank, who was only eighteen, grinned at her. He seemed to think they'd have a great adventure.

"Let me get my shootin' iron." Ran, the older cowboy, strode toward the bunkhouse.

A few minutes later, the three rode out together. They jogged back toward the stream first, and then west along the boundary between the Box M and the Anderson ranch.

"I think they may have gone up one of those draws on the end of your property." Ran nodded ahead of them to where the land grew uneven and deep draws cut into the hills. "Could even have gone through onto Bellingham's."

"How many head are we talking about?" Rachel asked.

"Twenty at least. We need to bring them in, closer to home."

"But they're wearing our brand, right?"

"Yes, ma'am. We saw to that when they arrived."

She looked back, but she could no longer see the ranch buildings. They must be at least a mile out.

"My father owned all this?" She didn't like to say, "I own this." It seemed presumptuous.

Ran nodded. "That's right. Paid cash, from what I hear."

"I knew he did well with his herd in Texas—sold most of the beef to the army. He must have made a profit on the ranch, too, when he sold out."

Hank had been scouting a bit ahead of them, and he circled back. "I see their tracks yonder."

"Horse tracks, too," Ran said as he studied the earth.

They trotted along, following the hoofprints, until they came into a ravine, slashed deep between folds of the grassland.

"They're up here all right," Ran said.

A hundred yards farther, and they all stopped their horses and stared ahead.

"They're—they're penned up!" Rachel looked at the two men for confirmation.

"Somebody's driven them up here and corralled them," Hank said.

"I reckon we'd best scout things out before we do anything." Ran looked all around, at the ridges above them, and behind at their back trail.

Rachel shivered. "Should we go back and get Bud and the other men?"

"Maybe."

"Aw, come on, Ran," Hank said. "It'd take us an hour at least to ride to the house and get them and get back here. They were going up to where the fence was down, remember? And it would take them time to load up tools and equipment to fix it. They might not have even left the barnyard yet."

"Yeah." The older man frowned and studied the crude brush fence that held the cattle in the upper end of the ravine. "But we didn't build that pen."

22

June 13, 1863

R yland didn't like the idea of riding so far on his own in country he didn't know, but the sergeant had told him the route and mentioned several landmarks, then assured him he'd be at the Anderson ranch in a couple of hours. Ryland wanted to bring this mission to a close, so he mounted his rented horse when the sun was barely up and rode out of Fort Lyon.

An hour later, the sun beat down mercilessly, and he wished for one of those broad-brimmed hats the troopers wore. Why hadn't he thought to ask for a canteen full of water before setting out on the final leg of his journey? Even the sturdy gray horse carrying him let its head droop, plodding along without enthusiasm.

He'd ridden for well over an hour—the longest Ryland had ever stayed on horseback—when he saw in the distance that the road climbed a long and gradual hill. Surely that was the hill the sergeant had told him about, and the ranch would be on the other side. Still, Ryland had come to believe that westerners thought differently about distances than folks in the East, and the morning's experience had confirmed that. The sergeant had assured him a fork in the road was "just a short ways" from the town, but it had turned out to be more like five miles out.

The horse's steps slowed even more. Ryland sighed and patted the gray's neck. "We're nearly there, old fellow. I'll see that you get a good drink when we get there."

The animal lifted its head and nickered softly. It stopped walking, and Ryland listened intently, every nerve tingling. Then a recognizable sound struck him, and he laughed.

"Yes, I hear it, too, old chum. I'll bet you smell it." He urged the horse forward, and not fifty yards farther along, he saw a path leading down off the trail into the woods, toward the delightful music of running water.

They turned in and were soon on the bank of a swift-flowing stream. Ryland spotted a mishmash of hoofprints near the brink. Many other travelers had stopped here to water their horses. He was pleased with himself for discerning this and dismounted to let the gray have a drink. The horse stepped daintily forward until its forefeet waded in the stream and put its head down to gulp the refreshing water.

Ryland held tightly to the end of the reins. He certainly didn't want to lose his only hold on civilization. He would want to refresh himself after the horse finished drinking—upstream several paces, where the streambed was undisturbed. He looked around for a likely place to tie up the horse while he satisfied his own thirst, then jumped. Two large and scruffy men watched him from the tree line, and one of them held a huge revolver, aimed squarely at Ryland.

CHARLIE HADN'T BEEN able to find any fancy paper in Fort Lyon, but he brought Rachel two yards each of plain brown wrapping paper from the mercantile and bright red grosgrain ribbon. It would have to do. Rachel wrapped the dress carefully.

A last glance in the small mirror told her the blue riding dress looked fine for the day's work she had planned, and her hair was pinned up neatly to keep it out of her way. At least they'd got her cattle back yesterday, so she shouldn't have to ride to the far reaches of the Box M this morning.

Matt and his father were already seated at the dining table sipping coffee, but their plates were still clean, so she guessed Vida was putting the finishing touches on their breakfast.

"What's that?" Matt eyed the package she carried.

Rachel smiled. "It's Vida's birthday present."

"That's right nice of you," Mr. Anderson said.

"Thanks. I just hope she'll accept it."

"Why wouldn't she?" Matt asked.

Rachel started to say something but stopped and gave him a little shrug. Mr. Anderson rose and walked toward his desk.

"I'm ashamed to say I didn't realize today was Vida's birthday, but I'll add a small present from Matthew and me." He reached into a drawer, and coins clinked.

"Now what?" Matt asked. "Should we go into the kitchen?"

"I'm not sure she'd like that," Rachel said.

"I'll ask her for more coffee," Mr. Anderson said.

Before he could move, the kitchen door swung open, and Vida entered, carrying a platter of bacon and fried eggs in one hand and a plate of biscuits in the other.

"Oh, Vida," Mr. Anderson said. "That looks terrific. We have something to say to you."

Her face a stony mask, Vida set down the platter and faced him. "What? You want more coffee?"

He laughed. "Well, that too." He gave Rachel a small nod.

Stepping forward, she held out her package. "Happy birthday, Vida. I hope you have a wonderful day."

Vida grunted, eyeing the parcel.

"And you don't have to wash the dishes," Matt said. "Rachel and I can clean up after we eat."

Rachel wasn't sure that was the best thing to say just then, but Mr. Anderson stepped once more into the breach. He walked over to Vida, took the plate of biscuits from her hand, and set it on the table. Then he held out a closed fist.

"Open your hand, Vida."

She frowned up at him but did as he asked. Mr. Anderson dropped two silver dollars into her palm.

"That's from me and Matthew. Happy birthday."

She looked down at the coins, then back up at him, blinking rapidly.

"Well, I never."

Mr. Anderson laughed. "Now, I suggest you open that package Rachel's holding. We all want to see what's in it."

Matt rose and pulled out a chair at the far end of the table, where the gift wouldn't be near the food. Slowly, Vida walked over and sat down. Rachel put the package on the table in front of her, and Vida tugged on the ribbon, moving with painful slowness. Rachel waited in eager silence, hoping for a pleased reaction, at least a smile.

Turning back the brown paper, Vida frowned. She gazed down at the bright, leaf-strewn dress. "I don't understand." She reached out and fingered the collar of the dress.

"Rachel made it for you," Matt said.

"As a birthday gift," Rachel added quickly. "I hope you like it. And if it needs any alterations, please don't hesitate to say so."

Vida sat as though frozen in her chair.

Rachel's heart sank. Did Vida despise her to the point where she wouldn't accept anything from her hand?

She took a wary step closer. "Vida, if you don't like it, I can get a different pattern and some new cloth."

"No." Vida sniffed.

She was on the verge of tears, Rachel realized. She wasn't

sure what to do, but she certainly didn't want to embarrass Vida.

"Well, we don't want breakfast to get cold. It certainly looks delicious." Rachel went to her usual place at the table and sat down.

Matt caught her eye. "I know I'm hungry." He picked up the platter of eggs and bacon and offered it to Rachel.

As Rachel reached for it with a smile, Vida pushed back her chair and stood.

"Thank you," she said stiffly. "All."

Rachel was sure her other secret was out. "In case you haven't seen it yet, Vida, there's a cake in the cupboard."

"I've seen it," Vida replied.

Rachel smiled. What wrath did that spite inspire this morning?

"I baked it last night. It's meant to be a birthday cake," Rachel said. "I hope you and Pard will join the Andersons for a slice this noontime. I'll be over at the Box M."

Vida's lips twitched. "Thank you kindly, Miss Rachel."

"That's fine, Vida," Mr. Anderson said. "If you'd like to take the day off …"

"No need." Vida sniffed. "I'll be right back with the coffeepot." She strode quickly for the kitchen door, taking the dress and its wrappings with her.

Matt winked at Rachel. "Let's hope it fits."

"Amen to that," Mr. Anderson said quietly.

Matt put a finger to his lips. He got up and tiptoed to the kitchen door and pushed it open a crack. He came back to the table, grinning.

"She's holding it up against her for size. It's very pretty, Rachel."

"I hope she'll wear it," Rachel said.

"Maybe Sunday." Mr. Anderson scooped three eggs and a pile of bacon onto his plate.

Rachel felt warm inside. She didn't tell them how Pard had described the material to her, and Bud had made the purchase. She didn't need credit for the hours she had put in cutting and stitching the dress. It was enough to see Vida's face and have the hope they could work together from now on. Perhaps they could be friends after Rachel moved to her own land.

A brief knock sounded on the front door. It opened, and Joshua Brand entered. He glanced at the three of them, still at the breakfast table much later than usual.

"Sorry, boss, but Telly Hillman's here from the Box M for Miss Rachel. He wants to see you, too."

Telly came in behind Josh and nodded at Rachel. He pushed back his hat. "Reckon you all ought to hear the news."

Rachel's stomach clenched.

"Morning, Telly," Mr. Anderson said. "What's this about?"

"We've looked all around that draw where the cattle were penned up yesterday, and we didn't find anything there, but this morning we found we're missing another fifteen head."

Mr. Anderson's posture stiffened. "What does Bud want to do? We can ride over and help you track them."

"He's gone with four men now," Telly said. "Wouldn't hurt to have a few more come along behind."

"Rachel, you should stay here," Matt said.

"No. I want to support my men."

"You won't help them if they have to watch over you instead of tracking these ne'er-do-wells," Mr. Anderson said.

"Please. I want to go, and I'm ready. If I'm going to live on my own ranch soon and run the outfit, I need to be there when things are happening. I'll ride over with Telly."

Before Mr. Anderson could protest further, she hurried outside. Pard was holding Herald, all saddled, by the corral fence. Rachel swung onto the horse's back and headed him toward her property. When she was halfway to the creek, Telly caught up with her.

"Easy there, boss lady. You don't have to wear out the horses."

"Sorry." She gave him a sheepish smile. "I was afraid Mr. Anderson would hogtie me and make me stay home with Vida."

Telly laughed. "Sounds like a miserable day to me." He sobered and looked off to each side. "Got to keep your wits about you, Miss."

"You're right." It was true she'd been a little cavalier about the men's protective attitude toward her. If those outlaws were still determined to steal her cattle, she should indeed be careful. She kept Herald at a jog and turned to study Telly. He was wiry, with a grizzled beard. She wondered how old he was but didn't want to be rude and ask him outright. "Telly, you've been with my family longer than anyone else on the ranch."

"That's right," he said with a wink. "I recall when you was just a little whippersnapper."

Rachel chuckled. "You used to ride me on your saddle sometimes."

"Yup. Remember that old mare your ma used to ride, down in Texas?"

"You mean Adelaide?"

"That's the one. I used to take you up on that horse, because I knew she was gentle, and we wouldn't have no mishaps."

"Those were good times," Rachel said.

"They sure were."

"Papa used to tell me about when you were with him in the war."

"Yeah, we met in the army."

"Telly, look!" Rachel reined in her horse and pointed far up the hillside. They were close to her ranch, but up the slope, beyond her father's grave, three horsemen were moving on the edge of the woods.

"I see 'em."

"Was that a gun?" Rachel asked as the riders disappeared into the trees.

"Looked like it. That last fella was covering that middle one. Or both the others."

"It seemed like the first rider was leading them."

"Well, all's I know is, there weren't none of our men, or Mr. Anderson's neither."

"You're right." Rachel turned in the saddle. "What should we do? Send for the sheriff?"

"They'd be long gone," Telly said. "We could ride back and meet Mr. Anderson and his men."

"We'd lose them. Come on!"

"I ASSURE YOU—" Ryland swallowed hard and hoped he could keep from stammering. "I am not here to cause any trouble."

The men accompanying him said nothing. One man rode silently before him, in and out between the trees, not following any path Ryland could see. The other horseman followed him. Ryland didn't look back, but he was certain the gun was still pointed at his back.

"I'm on an errand to the Anderson ranch," he said loudly, so that both men could hear him. "Is this by any chance Anderson land?"

"Nope," said the man behind him, "it ain't."

They rode in silence for a few more minutes and came out on the edge of a deep ravine. Off to one side, a ragged canvas formed a dilapidated shelter, and in the ravine below a dozen or so cattle milled about searching for a mouthful of grass here and there. A man knelt by a campfire, feeding sticks into it, and another came from the shelter carrying some sort of iron tool.

"Giddown," the leader told Ryland. The three riders

dismounted, and the other two men came over to stand gawking at Ryland.

"Who's this?" one of them asked.

"Found him watering his horse the other side of the ridge. He says he's here to see the Andersons." The man who held the gun on Ryland took a folded paper from inside his jacket and handed it to another man.

"What's this?"

The gunman shrugged. He had looked at the paper briefly after searching Ryland, but Ryland had his doubts as to whether the man could read. Now he was certain.

The man he'd handed it to unfolded the paper and studied it. Ryland decided this fellow, who looked to be about fifty, was their leader.

"I was sent here on an errand," Ryland said.

"We took this off him too." The other rider held out Ryland's wallet. The leader opened it, looked inside, and smiled.

"Well now, you're prepared to pay your way, aren't you, mister?"

"Please," Ryland said. "You're welcome to keep the money, if you'll just let me go."

The man laughed. "Seems to me we're welcome to keep it no matter what we do with you."

Ryan's face heated. The band of thugs certainly had him at a disadvantage. He'd had no chance to whip out his sword cane when he was captured—not that it would have done much good against a six-gun.

His chest tightened as he realized he didn't have many options.

"Look, I think you should know," he said, nodding toward the man who had carried his wallet. "That fellow took some of the money out of the wallet before he gave it to you."

The gunman hit him hard on the jaw from an angle that sent him flying into the second man's arms. Ryland groaned and tried to stand up, but his legs were wobbly and his jaw shrieked with pain.

"That right?"

The leader was looking at the man he'd accused, not the prisoner, for which Ryland was grateful.

The man gave a nervous chuckle. "Just a little pocket money, boss."

"Hand it over. Every cent. You know I decide who gets what."

The man scowled but pulled several bills from his pocket and placed them in the leader's hand. After shoving the money into the wallet, the older man gazed at Ryland.

"This letter says you have authority to draw money on banks."

"I—" Ryland swallowed hard. Maybe this was a good time to keep quiet.

"Some lawyer wrote this up, saying you can get money for your expenses. That right?"

Ryland couldn't meet his intent gaze. "I told you, I was hired to do an errand."

The leader smiled, his pointy face resembling that of a wolf, or what Ryland imagined a wolf's face would look like when he had just made a delicious kill. "Looks like we need to go to a bank." He looked around at his men. "Let's get us some grub, and then we'll take a little ride."

"They's that little bank in Fort Lyon, Bart," the gunman said.

Bart spit in the grass. "We looked at it. You know the sheriff's watchin' it real close."

"Half a day's ride to the next nearest bank," another man agreed.

"Shut up," Bart, the leader, cried. "You think I don't know that? Tie him up over there."

One of the men led Ryland to a good-sized oak tree.

"Hands behind your back."

"May I sit, please?" Ryland asked.

"Sure thing."

After he was tied securely—too securely, in Ryland's mind—against the bole of the tree, he watched the four men go about fixing their lunch, which seemed to consist of beefsteak and canned peaches. To his dismay, two more men emerged from the woods to join them. Bart ambled to meet them, and Ryland figured he was telling them what was going on. The three men strolled toward the campfire together.

"Are we giving up on Maxwell's stash, Bart?" one of the newcomers asked.

"Not yet, but it won't hurt to go see what this little pigeon can get us from a bank without any gunplay."

Ryland's breathing had eased some, but now his throat went dry, and his lungs squeezed again. He leaned against the tree and tried to breathe slowly, but the lump in his throat and the pain from the blow to his jaw made him gulp in air.

"What about them cattle?" one of the newcomers asked.

Bart scowled. "We'll have to move 'em out of here quick, or we'll lose 'em to Maxwell's men, like that other bunch. Del, you and Toad stay here and move 'em off the property."

"You want us to sell 'em?" The man who spoke had prominent eyes, and Ryland supposed he was the one called Toad.

"Not at Fort Lyon," Bart said. "We don't want to take any more there for a while. They were suspicious the last time."

"We h'ain't even changed the brands on these yet," one of the men said.

Bart frowned. "Yeah. Move 'em into the hills and use that running iron. Then head 'em toward Pueblo."

"That's a long haul, boss, for a few cattle."

"You got any better ideas?" Bart almost yelled. No one spoke, and he turned around toward the man tending the steaks. "Jerry? What do you think?"

Jerry shrugged without looking up from his task. "We could just let 'em go, if you think we'll get more outa the bank." He shot a glance Ryland's way.

Catching a quick breath, Ryland looked away.

Bart's heavy footsteps came close. "How much can you get with that letter?"

Ryland inhaled carefully. "Not that much. Fifty dollars maybe."

"Liar." Bart kicked him hard in the stomach. "You had more than that in your wallet."

"Boss, we can go in the bank at Fort Lyon with him," Jerry said. "Just one or two of us. They won't know who we are."

Bart nodded, eyeing Ryland closely. "If you make one wrong move on this little expedition, you take the first bullet. You understand?"

"Y-yes."

Bart nodded and turned away.

Ryland curled up against the ropes clutching his middle. An odd thought flitted through his mind. Would he ever see Abigail Benson again?

That wasn't what he should be thinking of right now. He tried to ignore the pain and focus on the here and now, not the what might have been.

Was he really going to be forced to take part in a bank robbery? *Lord in Heaven, hear me now. I could use some of those angels they say You have looking out for fools like me.*

23

Telly caught up to Rachel when she'd ridden quickly but quietly through the trees and along a faint trail. His horse snorted behind her, and she threw a glance over her shoulder at him.

"Stop, Rachel," Telly called softly. "Please! Hold on."

Reluctantly she pulled back on the reins, and Herald stood still. Telly edged his mount up beside her.

"We've got to be careful. Come on back. The Andersons aren't far behind us. We should wait for them."

"We'll lose their trail, Telly."

He shook his head. "No, really. It's too dangerous. We know what direction they were headed. Let's make sure we've got plenty of men."

She studied his face for a moment. He was her father's old friend. Surely he wouldn't try to hold her back in order to let the outlaws get away.

"Telly, those could be the men who killed Papa."

"Exactly. And we don't want to lose you, too."

He stared hard at her, and Rachel tried to return every bit of determination in that gaze, but she finally had to look away.

"I just don't want to miss this chance."

"Wait." Telly sniffed. "I smell something. Somebody's cooking."

Rachel lifted her chin and inhaled deeply. "Yeah." They were too far from the bunkhouse or any of the neighbors' ranches to smell meat cooking there. "Smells like beef," she whispered.

Telly nodded. "And woodsmoke. We may be near their camp. We don't want to rush in on top of them."

She looked all around and noted any landmarks she could— a large pine tree, a jagged rock sticking out of the ground. Far away, she heard cattle lowing.

Silently, Telly jerked his head toward their back trail. She nodded and followed as he turned his horse and quietly headed back toward the hill where her father was buried.

MATT WAS RELIEVED when Rachel and Telly loped out of the trees beyond Bob Maxwell's grave. He and his father and four of their ranch hands had paused in the Box M barnyard, where Dusty had told them where Bud Lassen had gone and pointed to where he'd seen Rachel and Telly disappear into the woods.

"Where you been?" Matt called as Rachel and Telly drew near.

Rachel took in the six men in the group. "Good, you're here. We think we've found the outlaws' camp."

"Or a temporary one," Telly said.

"Where?" Mr. Anderson asked.

"It's a ways through the woods and over the hill on Miss Maxwell's back piece. A mile, maybe."

"It smelled like they were cooking dinner," Rachel added.

Matt scanned the horizon for smoke, but with the hills between them, he couldn't see anything that helped.

"We saw three men headed that way and followed them." She

looked back toward the trees. "It looked like one of them was a prisoner. And we think they've also got a dozen or more of my cattle penned up—the ones that were missing this morning."

"We didn't see 'em," Telly said, "but we did hear some steers." He turned his horse. "We'll show you. Bud took four men out this morning to look for those cattle, but we didn't see him. Don't know why he didn't find 'em yet."

"Well, they didn't drive them the way we went," Rachel said. "They must have taken them by a longer way. That, or the cattle we heard weren't the ones Bud was looking for."

"You should stay here, Rachel," Mr. Anderson said.

Rachel just tightened her lips and moved out after Telly.

Matt urged his dun into a lope and caught up with her as they passed the tree line.

"At least keep back, Rachel," he said.

Her gaze rested for a moment on his gun belt and the rifle in the scabbard on his saddle.

"I'll hang back if we get an unfriendly reception."

Matt clenched his teeth. It would have to do. As if she thought the outlaws would welcome them into their camp and offer them refreshments!

They rode in silence but for the horses' hoofbeats and occasional snorts, the creak of leather and the rustle of a breeze through the trees. After ten minutes Telly halted, and the rest drew up behind him. He turned to face them.

"We stopped here, and we smelled their fire."

All the men began sniffing the air.

"I smell wood smoke," Josh said.

Pard only grunted, but it was well known on the Anderson ranch that Pard couldn't smell or taste much. Maybe that was why he put up with Vida's cooking.

"I don't hear anything," Mr. Anderson said.

Jimmy, the youngest among them, said, "I thought I heard some cattle mooing."

They all sat still, listening. Nothing.

After a moment, Matt said, "We'd best move forward. If we keep sitting here, they could get away."

"Or surround us," Telly said.

"Can we surround them?" Matt asked.

Telly shook his head. "Haven't seen the camp, so I don't know. I think it's yonder, over the ridge." He pointed.

"Maybe we should fan out," Matt said.

His father looked pointedly at Rachel. "You stay here."

"I'm not staying alone." She gathered her reins.

Matt's heart sank, but he knew there was no use arguing with her. Maybe he could stick with her and convince her to at least keep her horse behind his.

Gunfire erupted in the distance. They all jerked their heads toward the sound.

"They ain't shootin' at us," Ruthless said.

Rachel's eyes widened. "Bud and his men must have found the cattle."

"Come on." Mr. Anderson urged his horse into the lead. Telly, Rachel, and Matt followed close to him. The other men spread out into the trees, but all headed up the ridge they faced.

A GUN WENT OFF, and Ryland started. The men in the camp jumped up and drew their weapons. Ryland's pulse raced. What was going on? Whatever it was, he couldn't get away. As shots flew between the camp and some unseen assailants in the woods, he tried to shield his head, but the ropes didn't allow him to move his arms. He could draw up his knees, and he did so, burying his face in them.

The shooting continued sporadically, and the men shouted at each other. After a few moments, Ryland dared to lift his head. Bart was crouched behind a log they'd used as a bench near the fireside, and the others were scattered, staying low wherever they could find a bit of cover.

"Jerry," Bart yelled. "Can you see 'em?"

"They're yonder," Jerry replied from behind a stunted oak.

"How many?" Bart shouted.

"I count three, maybe four."

"They want the cattle," the man they called Toad yelled. His face was pale, and his eyes looked fair to pop out of his skull.

Bart stayed calm, seeming to assess the situation. He ducked suddenly, and a bullet ricocheted off one of the rocks encircling the campfire.

Ryland wriggled. He could lean to one side, away from the ravine, and he did so to protect his head. He had to get loose! If the outlaws decided he was holding them back, they'd kill him, and whoever was attacking them probably couldn't tell he was tied up from that distance. They'd shoot him, thinking he was one of the gang.

"Maybe we should let them cattle loose," Jerry called in a lull.

Bart shook his head, reloading his revolver. "Can't get down there without getting' plugged."

Another man ran low to Bart's side. Ryland could barely hear what he said, but they both looked his way.

"What if it's him?" the man said urgently. "Maybe they're friends of his."

Bart shook his head. "He's from back East. He's got no friends here."

The gunfire resumed with new vigor, and Ryland's stomach seemed to plummet down a mine shaft. Would he live to see the sun set?

Dear God, help me!

WHEN THEY TOPPED THE RIDGE, Rachel could make out the camp below them through the trees. She spotted a canvas shelter and a smoldering campfire. Off to one side, several horses milled in a rope corral, whinnying and pawing the earth.

One man was trying to settle the horses, while four more had taken up positions behind logs and trees. They appeared to be shooting over the heads of the cattle in the ravine below them, and Rachel saw a puff of smoke on the other side of the gully.

"Get back," Matt yelled at her. "Bud and his men are over across."

"Look out for them," Mr. Anderson said as he pulled his rifle from its scabbard. "We don't want anyone caught in the crossfire."

"We can pick 'em off from up here," Telly said, drawing a bead with his gun.

Rachel's heart pounded, and she saw the good sense of backing off a few yards. She guided Herald a short way down the hillside and turned to watch Telly and the Anderson men as they began to fire on the outlaws. Herald flinched and sidestepped but didn't try to bolt. She held the reins short and patted his neck.

"It's okay, Herald. We're fine." But she wasn't so sure about her friends.

JERRY SUDDENLY JERKED and fell over on the ground. With horror, Ryland realized the bullet had come from above the camp. He looked up the steep hillside that backed the outlaws' hideout. Men were up there shooting. Enemies were on both sides of them! He pressed himself against the tree trunk, as small as he could make himself, and prayed.

He scrunched his eyes shut and pressed one ear against his

shoulder. *Dear God, if I'm going to die, I want to see You.* He couldn't think of any sins he hadn't confessed already, but just to make sure, he added, *Forgive my sins, Lord, known and unknown.* He hoped it would be quick, not a slow, agonizing death. *God, help me! God, help me!*

More gunfire, shouts, and hoofbeats. The acrid smell of gunpowder irritated his nose. Footsteps, more shouting.

Cautiously, Ryland opened his eyes. Men he'd never seen were riding carefully down the steep hillside. The outlaws seemed to have fled, except Jerry and one other hapless fellow, who lay sprawled near the shelter.

Other men yelled from a distance. He looked over the ravine, where the cattle were still plunging about and bawling. Five men stood on the opposite side, waving and yelling. Ryland shook his head, but his ears still rang from the gunfire. The men on each side appeared to know each other. They shouted and gesticulated, and the men opposite mounted their horses and rode off through the trees.

"Here's your prisoner!"

He heard that all right and looked up, startled, to find a young man standing over him.

"Sir, are you all right?"

Ryland nodded.

The young man took out a knife and sliced the rope that held Ryland to the tree. He toppled over. Before he could try to right himself, he felt the fellow sawing at the line that held his arms behind him.

"Thank you," he croaked as the young man helped him to his feet. "I thought I was bound for heaven."

"No, sir, you appear to be spared."

Half a dozen men had gathered, and wonder of wonders, a beautiful young woman clad in a dark blue riding dress.

"H-hello," Ryland said. "Thank you. My name is Ryland Atkins."

The young man who had released him held out his hand. "Matt Anderson."

Ryland's gaze snapped to his face. Mrs. Rose's grandson! He couldn't see a resemblance, but—yes, there it was. His eyes were like Abigail's.

"Pa," Matt said to an older man, "Bud's going to need more help."

"Go. You and Telly and the rest of our men. Not you, Ruthless. You stay with me. We'll get these men back to the ranch."

Young Anderson and several others sped to their horses.

"Matt!" The girl, for she was not much more than that, stared after them, her hand outstretched, but the men didn't look back. They leaped into the saddle and tore off after the outlaws and their pursuers.

After a moment, when their hoofbeats were fading, the older man touched her shoulder. "Don't worry, Rachel. They'll come back safe."

Ryland certainly hoped so. How cruel it would be to find one of Mrs. Rose's grandchildren and then have him ripped away by violence before he could even tell him about his family.

"I'm John Anderson," the man said, holding out his hand.

Ryland shook it. "Atkins, sir. Ryland Atkins. I'm most grateful to you."

"This is Miss Maxwell," Anderson said, "and one of my ranch hands, Ruthless Small."

"Pleased to meet you," Ryland said. "Very pleased." He eyed the one called Ruthless anxiously, but the man seemed perfectly amiable. "What—If I may ask, what happened?"

"Those outlaws have been plaguing this area for weeks," Mr. Anderson said. "Miss Maxwell and one of her men discovered their camp this morning. We decided it was time to run them out."

"Oh." Ryland peered past him. Jerry and the other outlaw

still lay on the ground. "They've gone after them—and your son with them."

"That's right," Anderson said, "Miss Maxwell's foreman and four of his men, along with several of ours, are chasing them. I figured a couple of us had best stay here and take care of the two that are shot and get you and Miss Maxwell back to the ranch. The men can come back later to drive her stolen cattle home for her."

"Oh. So that's it. Rustlers."

"Partly. We're pretty sure they also burned the Maxwell house and killed Mr. Maxwell and one of his men."

Ryland looked keenly at the young woman. "I see. My condolences, ma'am."

"Thank you," she said. "You were their prisoner? Telly and I saw them bringing you into the woods earlier."

"Yes." Ryland was very happy they hadn't all left him here. He couldn't imagine how it would have felt to see them storm through the camp and ride off after the gang, leaving him helpless and alone.

"Boss, we'd best see to that wounded man, or he'll bleed to death," Ruthless said.

"Yes. We need to take him in. I hope he can give us some information, too."

Mr. Anderson and Miss Maxwell hurried to where the fallen man lay. While Ruthless gathered up the outlaws' guns, Anderson knelt beside the injured man. "You're hurt pretty bad. We'll try to get you into Fort Lyon. There's a surgeon there. Can you ride a horse?"

"It's too far," the man gasped.

Mr. Anderson looked at Rachel. "If we can get him to your cabin, we can take him from there in a wagon."

A rough bandage made of bandannas clung to the man's midsection. It was soaked with blood. Anderson pulled it away.

"Still bleeding."

"Let me give you my linen," Miss Maxwell said. She hurried to the outlaws' shelter.

"What's your name?" Anderson asked the man.

"Jerry Lowe. Mister, if I don't make it, will you send a letter to my brother?"

The rancher nodded. "We will, but I think you'll make it."

Ryland and Ruthless stepped closer.

"Is Hillman here?" Jerry squinted up at the circle of faces.

"He's gone with the others." Anderson frowned. "Why do you ask?"

Jerry swallowed hard and winced. "The boss was after him, but we could never get him alone."

"After Telly?" Anderson said. "What on earth for?"

"Him and Maxwell," Jerry managed. "In the war."

Ryland eyed Anderson curiously.

"You mean the Mex war?" Ruthless said.

"Yeah. They took Bart's stash away from him."

"We don't know anything about that," Anderson said. Right now, we're just worried about getting you some medical attention. You hang on."

"Right." Jerry gritted his teeth.

Miss Maxwell came from the shelter holding a white linen petticoat. Ryland felt his face flush, but she didn't seem embarrassed. She handed the garment to Mr. Anderson.

"Here—you can tear it up if you think it would help. And look what I found in there." She held out a small leather case. When she opened it, Ryland saw that it contained a miniature portrait. "It's my mother." Miss Maxwell's voice caught, and tears glistened in her eyes.

"There now," Mr. Anderson said gruffly. "Ruthless, whyn't you take a look in there and see if there's anything else from the Maxwell house."

"Yes, sir." The hired man walked toward the canvas.

"Well, Mr. Atkins, you may come along with us back to the

ranch," Mr. Anderson said. "From there, we'll see you get to Fort Lyon if you wish. Is there anything we can do for you?"

Ryland hesitated. He didn't want to reveal his mission now. Anderson was ripping strips of cloth off Miss Maxwell's petticoat, and the wounded man lay writhing and moaning. He made a quick decision.

"I came here on an errand, but we need to see this man gets to a doctor. Perhaps when your son returns, I can tell you all my story. I think it will interest you."

24

M att raced after Bud, Ran, and Sam, pushing the dun to its limits. Five more horsemen pounded along behind them. Ahead, the outlaws' mounts were flagging, and Matt thought they might be able to overtake them before they reached the river.

One of the outlaws wheeled his horse, paused, and steadied his rifle at them. A puff of smoke showed he'd fired before the sound reached them. Matt flinched, even though the bullet didn't come near him. Bud and Ran both had their rifles up. They fired, but they rushed it, and Matt couldn't see any effect on the men they were chasing.

"They're taking cover," Bud said.

The band had reached a rocky area, and the men were dismounting and finding spots behind the biggest boulders they could reach. One of them helped a man from his horse and almost dragged him to the rocks. Ran got another shot off.

"What do we do?" asked Josh, who had come up beside Matt.

Bud shook his head. "It'd be hard to get around behind 'em."

"We could shoot their horses," said Hank.

Matt shifted in the saddle, easing his aching leg. "I hate to do that." There were so many reasons not to—he hated harming defenseless animals and wasting good resources, not to mention how hard it would be to get everyone back if they didn't have enough mounts.

"We'd best back off," Telly said.

They all dropped back a few yards, where they felt fairly safe.

"At least one of 'em's wounded," Bud said.

Hank made a face. "Yeah, but there's five of them. Say four of 'em can shoot."

Matt looked around. The ranch men were nine strong. But he didn't want to lose a single man. So far as he knew, he and Telly were the only ones with wartime experience.

"Telly, you and I could get behind them. We could ride back a ways and get to the river. It's the long way around, but we could ride along the bank, down low. They wouldn't see us. Then we could get up behind them." Matt looked at Bud for approval.

"That'd take a while," Bud said.

Telly squinted up at the sky. "Twenty minutes."

Matt nodded. "Can you keep them pinned down that long?"

"We can try." Bud reloaded his rifle. "You all got plenty of ammo?"

"I'm short," Ran said.

While they settled up about the ammunition, Matt nodded to Telly, and the two of them loped down the back trail a hundred yards. Matt turned his horse off the trail. Telly followed him without speaking.

It took longer than they'd estimated to get to the river, and Matt pushed the sturdy dun along the bank. The last thing they needed was for one of the horses to slip and be injured.

In the distance, they heard the gunfire resume. Bud would keep up intermittent shooting to make the outlaws fire back and use up their ammunition. Matt judged nearly half an hour had passed before he and Telly left their horses in a copse by the water and warily made their way to a position where they overlooked the besieged outlaws. Only three of the men were firing toward the ranchers. The other two lay huddled on the ground behind rocks and bushes.

"Two of 'em down," Telly noted. "You ready?"

Matt swallowed hard. He remembered the screeching pain when he was wounded at Glorieta Pass and his crushing ordeal afterward.

"What's the matter?" The older man eyed him closely. "You thinkin' about the war?"

Matt shrugged. "I don't want to go through that again."

"We got to do it right now."

"I know." Matt checked his revolver and then raised his rifle. "I'm all right."

"You take the one on the left," Telly said. "I'll use my six-gun while you reload." Neither of them had the new repeating rifles.

Matt nodded. This is for Rachel, he told himself, and for Bob. And for Elijah and Janie and Grandmother, too. I'll see them again. He and Telly rose and aimed their rifles at the shooters below.

TWO HOURS AFTER LEAVING THE OUTLAWS' camp by the ravine, Rachel helped Vida serve a belated lunch at the Anderson ranch. At last she had a chance to study Mr. Atkins closely. He'd cleaned up, and he looked quite presentable now, in a well-tailored suit and polished shoes, making quite a contrast to the ranch men's worn work clothes and scuffed boots.

Mr. Anderson had sent his young cowhand, Jimmy, to drive Jerry Lowe into the town and report to the sheriff. Jimmy hadn't gone with them that morning but had stayed behind to make sure Vida and the ranch were safe. Ruthless went along with Jimmy to give the sheriff a firsthand account of what had happened. They'd also sent the dead outlaw's body.

"Mr. Atkins seems especially keen on having Matt here when he tells us his mission," Mr. Anderson told Rachel before they sat down to eat.

When all the food was on the table, Rachel sat down with Mr. Anderson and Mr. Atkins. The host kept the conversation general, asking Atkins about his journey. The traveler revealed that he had come all the way from Portland, Maine, by train, stagecoach, and horseback over the last few weeks. Rachel had made a similar journey not so long ago and remembered its discomforts. His errand must be important.

When dessert was served—generous helpings of Vida's birthday cake—Mr. Anderson told their guest, "You might as well plan to stay here tonight, Mr. Atkins. We have plenty of room, and I don't think you want to ride back to Fort Lyon to find a bed tonight."

"Thank you, sir," Atkins replied. "I appreciate that more than I can say."

Rachel spent the afternoon helping Vida in the kitchen, anticipating a large group of men for supper. Vida had started some bread dough, and Rachel helped prepare vegetables and stew and baked cornbread and dried apple pies.

About five o'clock, Mr. Anderson came into the kitchen.

"Mr. Atkins is catching a nap," he said.

"When do you want supper?" Vida asked.

"I'm not sure. Let's try to wait for Matt and the others. If they're not here in a couple of hours, we'll go ahead, I guess."

Vida handed him a plate with a piece of cake on it.

"Thanks," her boss said. "You've got plenty of food for tonight?"

"Stew. Pies, too."

Mr. Anderson nodded and looked at Rachel, who was just

taking the last pie from the oven. "You two seem to make a good team."

Vida snorted, but Rachel gave him a smile.

"We'll set the table," she said. "Let us know when you're ready."

She puzzled over how many places to set, and in the end she put out dishes for four—herself, Matt, his father, and Atkins. But several more men might be included if the informal posse made it back to the ranch soon, so she stacked place settings for half a dozen more on the sideboard. Vida surprised her by producing a coffeepot twice as large as the one they normally used.

"It's the one they take on roundups," she said as she measured coffee. Rachel considered offering to do it but decided Vida would not look kindly on the implied insult to her coffeemaking skills.

When the clock chimed seven, Mr. Anderson gave up and called Atkins to the table. He asked the blessing, and Rachel brought in the hot stew. Vida had long since gone back to the cabin she shared with Pard. Mr. Anderson gazed at Matt's vacant place, and her own heart twisted. Was he thinking what she was, that his son might never share a meal with them again?

They were down to pie and coffee when at last they heard the sound of many hoofbeats in the yard. Mr. Anderson jumped up and hurried to the door. Rachel strained to make out the words as men called back and forth.

"We got 'em, Pa," Matt said.

She slumped back in her chair and gave Mr. Atkins a wobbly smile.

"Sounds as though they were successful," he said.

"Yes." Rachel rose and went to stand by Mr. Anderson.

Matt, Bud, and Telly came in. Outside, the other men were taking care of the horses.

Bud nodded at her. "Miss Rachel, I sent our men on to get

some supper at the Box M. We'll bring in those cattle in the morning."

"Thank you, Bud. Come have something to eat."

The ranch hands would eat in the bunkhouse, and Pard would go home to Vida, but it seemed right for Bud and Telly to be included at the Andersons' table while they told their story. She strode to the sideboard and set two more places, then went to the kitchen for stew and fresh cornbread for Matt, Bud, and Telly.

They were all seated with Mr. Anderson and Ryland Atkins when she returned with the big coffeepot and poured mugs for everyone.

"Let me freshen your coffee," she told Mr. Atkins.

"Thank you very much," he said.

"We met up with Jimmy and Ruthless at the sheriff's office," Bud told Mr. Anderson. "The gang is in the jail. Well, in jail and at the doctor's."

"All of them?" John Anderson asked.

Bud's eyes flickered to Rachel. "We had to shoot a couple of them. And two more were wounded already when we caught up to them."

"Well, tuck into that stew, Bud," Mr. Anderson said. "Rachel, is there any pie left?"

"There sure is. We made extra." She set the coffeepot down beside Matt.

"A good day's work done," Mr. Anderson said.

"Bud, where were you and the men this morning?" Rachel asked. "I thought you were tracking those rustled cattle, but we got to the outlaws' camp before you did."

"We *were* tracking them," Bud said. "We saw horse prints, and we figured the gang was driving them. We went back to the home place to get more men. That's when Dusty told us you and Telly took off with Anderson's outfit. We followed the cattle trail and ended up at the ravine."

Telly sighed. "Well, we were mighty glad to see you on the other side when we got there."

"And we chased down the ones that got away," Bud added. "That's what counts. They won't be raiding ranches hereabouts any longer."

After a quick knock at the door, Ruthless poked his head inside.

"Can I come in, boss?"

"Of course. What is it?" Mr. Anderson asked.

"The sheriff asked me to bring these to Mr. Atkins." Ruthless approached the table and held out a leather wallet and an envelope.

"Thank you so much." Atkins stood and took the items, checking briefly inside. "Good. It's my document and my wallet —with most of my money inside, I am happy to say."

Mr. Anderson rose. "Well, Atkins, are you ready to tell us what errand brought you here? Does it have anything to do with the outlaws?"

"Nothing at all, sir." Atkins resumed his seat. He took a sip of his coffee and put down the cup. "I was hired by a lawyer on a legal quest, and this morning I was merely in the wrong place at the wrong time. Those ruffians took me into custody and discovered I was carrying a legal document they thought might bring them some profit. They were planning to take me to a bank and have me present the paper and ask for funds, which they expected me to turn over to them."

"Goodness," Rachel said. "Totally without scruples, aren't they?"

"I was only with them a short time," Mr. Atkins said, "but I believe that is an accurate statement."

"The sheriff will probably want to talk to you," Mr. Anderson said. "Can you tell us anything about the gang?"

"Their leader was named Bart. He seemed to think a local

rancher had some money hidden away and was trying to find out where."

Telly Hillman cleared his throat. "I recognized Bart Finney after we took 'em down. He was in the same outfit Bob Maxwell and I were in, back in the war. The Mexican War."

"The outlaw leader knew my father?" Rachel sat down and stared across the table at Telly. "Why didn't I know that before?"

I didn't know it was Bart, Miss Rachel." Telly shrugged. "Not until today."

"But ..." She held back a sob. "He killed my father, he and his men. They burned our house. Why?"

"I'm not sure." Telly sighed. "Bart was a bad'un. He and a couple other fellas stole some money they were helping guard. It was supposed to cover the payroll that month. Me and Bob found out about it and stopped 'em. That was nigh on twenty years ago." He shook his head. "If it's the same man, he's had a long time to pile up hate for me and Bob for turning him in."

"He seemed to think the two of you made off with their loot," Atkins said.

"What? No!" Telly scowled at him. "Me and Bob didn't do anything wrong. We turned that money in, every dollar."

Rachel nodded slowly. "I believe you, Telly. Papa would never condone stealing, even from a band of thieves."

"That must be why the gang came here," Mr. Anderson said. "Finney probably got out of prison and figured Bob either still had the money or used it to buy his ranch here."

"Well, he didn't," Telly said. "Bob started out small in Texas after the war with money he'd saved, and I went to work for him. We rounded up wild cattle the Mexicans had left behind when they were driven out. He made a good profit, and I stayed on with Bob. That's how he bought this land."

"Still, that may be what the outlaws were looking for in Maxwell's house before they burned it," Mr. Anderson suggested.

Telly shook his head. "You may be right. But Bob and me, we told the captain what they were doing, and those three were put under guard and taken away. I never heard what happened to them. Guess I figured they were still in jail."

Rachel's mind swirled with questions, but Mr. Anderson seemed more interested in what had happened today.

"So, you didn't know anything about that, Mr. Atkins?"

"No, sir," Atkins replied. "It has nothing to do with my errand. I was hired by an attorney back in Maine, a Mr. Turner. My job here is to locate Matthew Anderson."

"Me?" Matt said.

"That's right."

They all stared at Mr. Atkins. Rachel's stomach tightened. Was Matt in trouble? She wanted to reach out and hold on to him, but she sat still, waiting to hear the rest.

"On a legal matter?" Mr. Anderson frowned at Atkins. "What exactly is this about?"

Atkins turned his attention on the father. "I believe your son is adopted, sir?"

"Well, yes …" Mr. Anderson looked uneasily at Matt.

"Could you tell me, what was his name before you and Mrs. Anderson adopted him?"

"It was Zephaniah Cooper," Matt said. "What do you know about the Cooper family, Mr. Atkins?"

"Your grandmother, Edith Rose, asked me to find you."

Matt clenched his fists on the table, one on either side of his cake plate, but relief washed over Rachel. She reached over and covered his hand with hers. She wanted to tell him it was all right, that this was God's doing. Matt glanced at her, then squeezed her fingers.

"Tell me," Matt said hoarsely.

"My employer, Mr. Turner, sent me to meet with Mrs. Rose." Atkins held Matt's gaze as he spoke. "She told me a very sad tale, of three children whose mother died, and a father who left them with a neighbor."

Matt inhaled sharply.

"I am very pleased that I can now send her a message and tell her that you are found, and you are well. If God wills, I'll find your brother and sister, too. Your grandmother is longing to see you. And your cousin is too."

"My cousin? You mean Abby Benson?"

"Yes. Miss Benson lives with Mrs. Rose now. A lovely young lady."

Atkins's color heightened, and Rachel wondered how well he knew Miss Benson.

"And my grandfather?" Matt asked.

Atkins paused, fingering the handle of his coffee mug. "I'm afraid the captain has passed on."

Matt's eyes took on a pained cast. "When?"

"Last year. But he tried to find you. Mrs. Rose wanted to be sure you knew that."

"He did?" Matt's face crumpled. "When did he try?"

"He was out to sea when your mother passed away," Mr. Atkins said gently. "When Mrs. Rose heard that her daughter had died, she sent letters, but apparently it was too late. Your father had already left the area. She couldn't get word of where Mr. Cooper had gone. It was nearly a year before the captain returned. As soon as his affairs from his voyage were in order, he sailed to New York. As I understand it, he discovered you'd been at the orphanage in White Plains."

A tear escaped Matt's eye and ran down his face. For a moment, Rachel thought he would sob. She stroked his hand, and Matt inhaled deeply.

"He went to the orphanage," Atkins continued, "but you children were all gone by that time. It's my belief that the director refused to help him, although I have no proof of that. The captain may have inquired for you in Tarrytown, or for your sister in Brooklyn. No one seemed to know for certain where your brother Elijah was at the time."

"Grandfather went to New York and didn't find any of us?"

Mr. Atkins sighed and shook his head. "Mrs. Rose said he was assured that good families took you all. I don't think the orphanage director gave him any clues. He probably told the captain the papers were sealed, and he was legally bound not to reveal the families' names or some such rot."

"Why would they do that when a blood relative came for us?"

"I don't know. Perhaps the director was protecting himself, so that his own actions could not be scrutinized too closely."

"You know something," Matt said.

"Only that the orphanage now seems like a pleasant home with a caring staff. The current director only hinted that things were different twenty years ago."

"I'll say so." Matt grimaced. "A pleasant place, huh? They wouldn't let Elijah and me stay together, and we were never allowed to see Janie. It was weeks before we knew she was gone."

Rachel patted his arm, helpless to assuage his pain.

Across the table, Mr. Anderson pulled out his bandanna and swiped at his glistening eyes.

"The last time we visited Maine, my grandfather told me he'd take me to sea one day. He said he'd make me a cabin boy on his ship when I was old enough." Matt shook his head. "After I was adopted, I used to dream he sailed to New York and up the Hudson to Tarrytown and took me away with him. But after we moved to Independence, I gave up that dream. We were so far from the sea."

Silence stretched for a moment. "Mrs. Rose would be delighted to pay your expenses for a trip to Maine to visit her," Mr. Atkins said. "She herself is too fragile to travel such a distance."

Matt let out a shaky breath. "Of course, I'd love to see her." He looked at his father.

"Go, son," Mr. Anderson said.

Matt pressed his lips together for a moment, then met Atkins's gaze. "I'll think it over. There's so much happening here right now."

"I understand." Mr. Atkins reached for his coffee cup.

Rachel let out a long, slow breath. Matt seemed bound to leave the ranch, one way or another.

25

When Bud and Telly had left for the Box M, Matt wandered out to the porch and sat down in a rocker. The house was quiet. Vida had come back after feeding her husband, and she worked with Rachel to wash the dishes and clean up the kitchen. For the first time, they seemed to get along well. Ryland Atkins and Pa had settled down in the sitting area inside, and Pa was pumping the visitor about his life in New England.

Matt rocked slowly back and forth, looking out toward the range and the ridge between his ranch and Rachel's.

His grandmother. She was still alive and wanted to see him. She'd tried to find out where he and 'Lijah and Janie were, and Grandpa had gone to New York looking for them. Tears filled his eyes, and he rubbed his sleeve across them. He'd given up hope of ever hearing more about his first family.

Once or twice he'd thought of going to New York and looking for his brother and sister, but he was sure that would be fruitless. He'd even considered a trip to Maine, but he couldn't afford that. The only time the Andersons had any money was when they sold up in one place to buy land in another. He would never ask them to spend a good part of that money on him.

And now it was here, offered to him free of charge. Dear old Grandmother—she would be quite old now—would pay his expenses. He wanted to go. He *had* to go. But still, Pa needed him here. He'd made that clear when Matt had inquired about rejoining his regiment. In the corral, a horse nickered. Matt buried his head in his hands.

The door creaked open. He needed to oil those hinges.

Rachel came out and sat in the chair beside his. She rocked for a minute without saying anything.

"Quite a day," Matt said at last.

"It sure was." She turned toward him. "Mr. Atkins wants to ride to Fort Lyon in the morning and send Mrs. Rose a message. Your father invited him to come back here and stay a few days, but he says he'll head on from there, back to Maine."

"So soon."

"Yes." She rocked a few times. "Matt?"

"Hmm?"

"Will you go with him?"

"No. I couldn't leave as quick as that. Pa needs me."

"Well, yes, he does, but it's not like you wouldn't come back this time. Not like …"

The light spilling out the window shone on half her beautiful face. She looked wistful, maybe even a little frightened. Unsure, anyway.

"Like when I went to enlist?" he asked.

"That and … this morning. I didn't know if you'd come back today."

He drew in a slow, shaky breath. "There was a minute when I wondered, too."

"I'm sorry."

"We had to do it." He shrugged. "If we hadn't chased them down, they'd have come back. And the sheriff—by the time we got word to him and he got out there, they'd have been lost in the mountains again. But they would've come back. We know now why Finney was so persistent."

"He thought my father had his money," Rachel said.

"Not *his* money. The army's money."

"Right." She resumed her rocking. "I don't know if you heard, but when Ruthless searched their tent, he found my father's ledger."

"His ranch ledger?"

"Yes. I'm not sure why Bart kept it. Looking for proof that Papa had that payroll money, maybe."

Anger and bitterness rose up inside him. What those men had done to Bob Maxwell—and to Rachel—defied logic and justice. "It doesn't make any sense."

"I know, but I don't think Bart Finney was a very sensible man," she said.

Matt remembered the moment when he and Telly reached the men they'd shot from above. He'd rolled over the man he'd aimed at and looked into his sightless eyes, knowing he'd killed him. At the time, he'd felt sick, but Bud and Telly and the others had told him that if he hadn't done it, more good men would be dead. Now he knew this was the man who'd killed Rachel's father.

"I'm so sorry about your pa," he managed.

Rachel leaned toward him, her tears glinting in the dim light. "Oh, Matt, thank you. I know this whole thing has been awful for you. If you'd been shot—" She made a low, guttural sound in her throat. "I've lost my father and mother and my home. What if I lost you and your father, too? When you rode off, I wasn't sure I could stand it."

Matt seized her hand and held on tight. "Rachel."

"I love you, Matt."

He let out a big breath, and the ache in his chest seemed to dissipate with it. "I thought—I mean, you don't want to marry me. You said so."

She laughed. "That was then, Matthew. Things have changed. If you asked me now ..."

He flung himself to his knees in front of her, ignoring the screeching pain in his leg. "I'm asking, Rachel. Will you marry me?"

She was in his arms, her hair wild about his face, and she clung to him as though she would never let go.

"Yes, yes, yes, yes, yes."

"I love you so much." He kissed her, his heart pounding. In that moment, everything changed. He would never be alone again.

ABBY BENSON PLUCKED the envelope from Patsy's hand and ran into the parlor.

"It's a message from Mr. Atkins!"

"Slow down, child," her grandmother said. "Ladies do not run."

"Right." Abby made herself walk the last few steps. She held out the telegram envelope.

"Well, open it," Grandmother said, almost crossly.

Abby tore the flap open and pulled out the sheet of paper.

To MRS. E. ROSE, PORTLAND, MAINE. MATTHEW ANDERSON FOUND FORT LYON COLORADO STOP MORE SOON R. ATKINS.

Slowly, Grandmother's expression transformed from mild irritation to a peaceful smile. "He's found Zephaniah."

Abby flung her arms around her. "Yes! Isn't it wonderful?"

EPILOGUE

One month later

Rachel watched out the window of the train car as they pulled into the station in Portland. Her pulse galloped, and breathing was a chore.

"We're here," Matt said, close to her ear so she could hear him over the train's squealing brakes.

She grabbed his hand. "Are you nervous?"

"A little. Are you?"

"A lot."

He grinned. "Grandmother will love you."

"We don't know that. But it was very generous of her to pay for my ticket, too."

They gathered the belongings they'd had out since leaving Boston that morning and rose.

"Do you think she'll be here to meet us?" Rachel asked.

"I don't know. I suppose she might send Atkins, or even my cousin, if she's all that frail."

"Mr. Atkins didn't seem to think she was beyond getting out to church and things like that."

Matt shrugged. "We'll see, I guess." He kept a hand protectively on her back as they moved down the aisle to the door.

"I smell the sea." Rachel drew in a deep breath.

But Matt was already scanning the platform for familiar faces.

"There!"

Rachel looked where he pointed. Mr. Atkins, with an elderly woman and a lovely girl about Rachel's age, walked eagerly toward them.

"Grandmother?" Matt left her side and strode toward them.

"Dear boy!" The old woman held out her arms, and Matt engulfed her in an embrace.

"Hello, Joey," the young woman said with an engaging smile.

Matt drew back and eyed her keenly. "Abby?"

"Yes, it's me." She laughed. "You're looking well. And very grown-up."

He hugged her, and Rachel stepped forward to greet the man accompanying them.

"Mr. Atkins, so good to see you again."

"Thank you. And you." He clasped her hand warmly.

Matt turned to include her in the family circle. "Grandmother, I'd like to introduce my wife, Rachel."

"So this is the bride." Mrs. Rose smiled at Rachel and drew her in to kiss her cheek. "Thank you for coming. We did *so* want to meet you."

"Thank you for bringing me," Rachel said, her face flushing.

"And this is Abigail, my cousin," Matt said.

"Miss Benson." Rachel extended her hand.

"Oh, none of that. I'm Abby."

Before she realized what was coming, Rachel was pulled into a tight hug.

"You've no idea how we've prayed for this moment," Abby whispered.

"That means a lot." Rachel stepped back.

"We have Mr. Turner's carriage," Mr. Atkins said. "If you'll give me your luggage tickets ..."

A scarce ten minutes later, they were on their way away from the station. The horses climbed a hill, and Rachel gazed out the window at the beautiful old houses.

Matt smiled at her as though reading her thoughts. "There's nothing in Colorado this old. Well, I mean, nothing made by white people."

Abby's eyes widened. "Mr. Atkins mentioned that he passed through a settlement called Pueblo, and I wondered if there were cliff dwellings there."

"I'm afraid not," Matt said. "The word *pueblo* just means *town* in Spanish."

"There's not a lot built where we live," Rachel said. "Ranches, a small town growing around the fort."

"It sounds terribly exciting," Abby said.

Rachel smiled. Abby probably wouldn't enjoy the type of excitement they'd had over the past few months.

The carriage turned in, and the driver opened the door and helped them alight. Rachel looked up at the stately three-story house with brick chimneys and a railed platform on the rooftop.

"Mr. Atkins, you'll stay for tea?" Mrs. Rose asked.

"Thank you, ma'am. I'd like that. But I can't stay late. I'm leaving early in the morning."

Abby smiled and took Matt's arm. "Mr. Atkins is heading out to look for Elijah. Come on inside."

"I should help with the bags," Matt said.

Mrs. Rose and Abby guided Rachel into the house, where a young woman wearing a cotton dress and apron took their cloaks and gloves.

"Come right into the parlor," Mrs. Rose said. "Patsy, we are five for tea."

"Yes, ma'am," the maid said.

"May I help you?" Rachel asked.

"Oh, no, ma'am, you're a guest."

"But I will help," Abby said with a chuckle.

Rachel found herself alone with Mrs. Rose for a few minutes as Matt and Mr. Atkins brought in their luggage. She could hear Abby talking as they went up the stairs with it.

"We were so pleased to hear my grandson was getting married." Mrs. Rose had settled into a wing chair, and Rachel sat at one end of the sofa close to her.

"Thank you. I think Matthew was of two minds—whether to have the wedding first or rush off to visit you."

"Well, I'm glad he set his priorities right," Mrs. Rose said. "I certainly wouldn't have wanted him to dash off and leave his fiancée behind. It's much better this way."

"Thank you. I think so, too. Your home is beautiful."

"It's been in my husband's family three generations. Sea captains, all of them." Mrs. Rose sighed. "I fear that is at an end in this family. We had daughters, and—well, you know what became of our grandsons." She smiled at Rachel. "But ranching is good."

"It's certainly different," Rachel said.

The others joined them, the tea was poured out, and plates of cookies and pound cake passed. Mrs. Rose fixed her gaze on Matt.

"I shall try to call you Matthew from here on, but I'm afraid Zephaniah will be a hard habit to break, since it was my husband's name."

"I don't mind, Grandmother," Matt said. "I'm so happy to be here, I don't care what you call me. Matt, Joey, Zeph—take your pick."

She harrumphed, but her eyes twinkled as she turned her attention to Mr. Atkins.

"Now, sir, lay out your plans, so my grandson can understand what you intend to do next."

"Please do tell us, Mr. Atkins," Rachel said.

Matt nodded. "You mentioned leaving tomorrow to search for my brother. I thought you didn't have enough information."

"Please call me Ryland," Mr. Atkins said. "It's true that while I was in Colorado, I wasn't hopeful about finding Elijah. We knew a man from Pennsylvania, surnamed Miller, had adopted the boy a few months after the Andersons took you. But the transaction took place in Albany, not White Plains, and I wasn't able to unearth anything more while I was in New York. However, Mr. Turner received a letter while I was on my way back here, and we are more hopeful now."

"A letter from who?" Matt asked.

"The director at the orphanage, Mr. Woods. He was quite sympathetic when I went to talk to him, and he told me at the time he would contact us if he learned more about the Cooper children. I really didn't expect to hear from him, but it seems I didn't put enough faith in the man."

Mrs. Rose grinned and nodded. "He found a name," she said with a conspiratorial air. "And a town."

"Wonderful," Matt said.

Ryland nodded. "The man who adopted your brother was named Charles Miller, and he gave his residence at the time as Emmaus, Pennsylvania. The town is not far from Allentown, above Philadelphia."

Matt frowned. "Isn't there fighting in that area? We got a few newspapers along the way, and we heard there had been a large battle in southern Pennsylvania last week. It was all people were talking about in Boston."

"It's true. There was fighting for several days at Gettysburg. Terrible losses." Ryland's expression was grim.

Mrs. Rose looked sad, too, and Abby blinked fast, as though tears threatened her.

"Will you even be able to get through?" Rachel asked. "The

trains were very crowded until we left Boston. The station there was a madhouse."

"If the Lord wills, I'll get through," Ryland said. "With all the upheaval south of New England, I don't want to put it off. Unless rail service has been disrupted, I should be able to go all the way to Emmaus by train."

"So you see," Abby said, more animation in her face, "we hope that we'll hear something soon—while you are still here. Wouldn't it be fabulous if Mr. Atkins could bring your brother to Maine before you leave us?"

Rachel caught her breath. Matt was staring at his cousin. "Do you really think it's possible?" He looked at Ryland.

"Well, I'm not promising anything," Ryland said. "It took me quite a while to run you down. But if the Millers stayed in the same location, I ought to be able to locate them."

"Miller is such a common name," Mrs. Rose said.

Ryland nodded. "It may take a while, but I'm getting quite good at making inquiries, if I do say so."

"I almost wish I could go with you," Matt said.

Rachel rubbed his shoulder. For several reasons, that wouldn't be a good idea, but she didn't want to say so. Matt needed time to get reacquainted with his grandmother and Abby. His leg had also bothered him quite a bit on the trip. They'd had to walk a lot at some of the railway stops, which tired him. When they'd sat all day in the train cars, he got leg cramps and stiff muscles. She hoped they'd stay in Portland for at least a couple of weeks before setting out again.

"You can't leave us so soon," Abby cried.

Matt smiled and reached over for her hand. "No fear, Cousin. I'm here for at least two weeks."

"Do you have to go back then?" Abby asked.

He sighed and glanced at Rachel. "My father needs me on the ranch, but ... well, I told him I would absolutely be back for the fall roundup, but that's another eight or ten weeks from now.

Still, it's our busy season on the ranch, and it may take extra time to get back, depending on whether or not railroad service is further disrupted."

"You have some hired help, I believe?" Mrs. Rose said.

"Well, yes. But ..."

"Mr. Anderson does need him," Rachel said softly.

"Of course." Mrs. Rose sipped her tea.

"Tell us about the ranch," Abby said.

"Actually, there are two ranches," Matt said. "Rachel's father died a couple of months ago, and she inherited his property, which is next to ours."

Rachel sat back and listened to Matt as he described the Anderson and Maxwell ranches and the little house they'd share on the Box M when they returned to Colorado. Although he didn't broach the subject, Matt had no need to claim part of his grandmother's estate. He had come only to reconnect with his family. His first family, as he called it.

But now they were embarking on the start of a new family together. Rachel knew they both needed to return to the land they loved in Colorado, to the ranch family they both loved there.

She was proud of him as he told about their land and the cattle business both their fathers had built, and how they planned to combine both tracts as partners with Matt's father. Coming to Maine and knowing the Rose side of the family would only enrich the heritage they continued to grow. She hoped one day their children and grandchildren would live on the ranchland.

"As much as I've enjoyed this, I should be going," Ryland said. He set aside his cup and saucer and stood. "Mrs. Rose, as always, it's been a pleasure. You'll hear from me soon."

"Thank you," she said.

"You've no idea how much we enjoy your letters and telegrams, Mr. Atkins." Abby stood and extended her hand to him.

"Ryland, please."

Abby's cheeks flushed. "Ryland. We get quite excited when the postman stops here."

"I hope I'll soon have more news for you." He held her hand a moment longer before releasing it and turning. "Mrs. Anderson —Rachel."

"Thank you for everything," Rachel said as she took his hand.

Matt clasped Ryland's hand and clapped his shoulder. "I know you'll do all you can to find my brother and sister."

"I certainly will. Seeing your reunion here today gives me energy to continue the search."

"God bless you and keep you safe," Rachel said.

When Ryland had left the room, they resumed their seats, and Matt caught Rachel's eye. His contented smile thrilled her. Seeing his grandmother and cousin again, in the old house he remembered from childhood, had given him a new confidence and ·steadiness. Learning what became of his siblings, and perhaps seeing them again, would ground him even more.

Matt reached for her hand and squeezed it, his blue eyes glinting with hope and joy. Rachel couldn't imagine a better start to their future together.

THE END

ABOUT THE AUTHOR

Susan Page Davis is the author or more than ninety Christian novels and novellas in the historical romance, mystery, and romantic suspense genres. Her work has won several awards, including the Carol Award, two Will Rogers Medallions, and two Faith, Hope, & Love Reader's Choice Awards. She has also been a finalist in the WILLA Literary Awards and a multi-time finalist in the Carol Awards. Three of her books were named Top Picks in *Romantic Times Book Reviews*. Several have appeared on the ECPA and Christian Book Distributors bestselling fiction lists. Her books have been featured in several book clubs, including the Literary Guild, Crossings Book Club, and Faithpoint Book Club.

A Maine native, Susan has lived in Oregon and now resides

in western Kentucky with her husband Jim, a retired news editor. They are the parents of six and grandparents of eleven. Visit her website at: https://susanpagedavis.com.

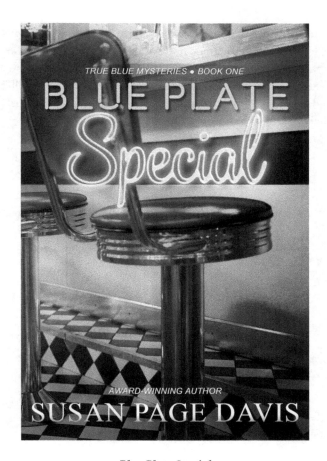

Blue Plate Special

by Susan Page Davis

Book One of the True Blue Mysteries Series

Campbell McBride drives to her father's house in Murray, Kentucky, dreading telling him she's lost her job as an English professor. Her father, private investigator Bill McBride, isn't there or at his office in town. His brash young employee, Nick Emerson, says Bill hasn't come in this morning, but he did call the night before with news that he had a new case.

When her dad doesn't show up by late afternoon, Campbell and Nick decide to follow up on a phone number he'd jotted on a memo sheet. They learn who last spoke to her father, but they also find a dead body. The next day, Campbell files a missing persons report. When Bill's car is found, locked and empty in a secluded spot, she and Nick must get past their differences and work together to find him.

Also, watch for *The Corporal's Codebook*, Homeward Trails Book Two, coming from Susan Page Davis and Scrivenings Press in November 2021.

NEW FICTION FROM SCRIVENINGS PRESS

September Shadows
Justice, Montana Series
Book One

After the sudden death of their parents, Jess Thomas and her sisters, Sly and Maggie, start creating a new life for themselves. But when Sly is accused of a crime she didn't commit, the young sisters are threatened with separation through foster care. Jess is determined to prove Sly's innocence, even at the cost of her own life.

Cole McBride has been Jess's best friend since they were children. Now his feelings are deepening, just as Jess takes risks to protect her family. Can Cole convince Jess to trust him—and God—to help her?

Books Afloat

Columbia River Undercurrents

Book One

Blaming herself for her childhood role in the Oklahoma farm truck accident that cost her grandfather's life, Anne Mettles is determined to make her life count. She wants to do it all–captain her library boat and resist Japanese attacks to keep America safe. But failing her pilot's exam requires her to bring others onboard.

Will she go it alone? Or will she team with the unlikely but (mostly) lovable characters? One is a saboteur, one an unlikely hero, and one, she discovers, is the man of her dreams.

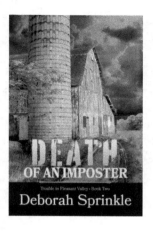

Death of an Imposter

Trouble in Pleasant Valley

Book Two

Rookie detective Bernadette Santos has her first murder case. Will her desire for justice end up breaking her heart? Or worse—get her killed!

Her first week on the job and rookie detective Bernadette Santos has been given the murder of a prominent citizen to solve. But when her victim turns out to be an imposter, her straight forward case takes a nasty turn. One that involves the attractive Dr. Daniel O'Leary, a visitor to Pleasant Valley and a man harboring secrets.

When Dr. O'Leary becomes a target of violence himself, Detective Santos has two mysteries to unravel. Are they related? And how far can she trust the good doctor? Her heart tugs her one way while her mind pulls her another. She must discover the solutions before it's too late!

Stay up-to-date on your favorite books and authors with our free e-newsletters.

ScriveningsPress.com